SNAFU!

The sea erupted, and the beast was alongside us, and was seizing our hull in his huge, dripping crab-legs, while his long, eel-slick body bowed and bowed and bowed at the loins with his fierce, lecherous thrustings. The brute was in rut—the worst kind of glabrous to meet; sure death. Amidships and aft a dozen men were instantly crushed by his legs. His sinewy tail scourged the sea behind him in his lust, driving us forward even as he embraced us. The steep, stony shore of Dolmen loomed towards us at incredible speed.

The impenetrability of our hull timbers quickly drove the ardent giant to a fury. He flung our ship clean out of the water, toppling Barnar and me back onto the deck just as we had mounted the gunwale to abandon ship. The carrack sailed creakily through twenty fathoms of thin air, and crashed down at Dolmen's very shore, and even as it did so, the glabrous surged up behind the vessel—a benthic fetor welling from his mossy, gaping jaws—and swallowed it whole.

The glabrous did this with the blind, uncalculating rage his breed is so well known for. Barnar and I, tumbled to the prow by the bow's impact with the shore, saw the darkness of the brute's maw loom over us, and saw his huge teeth bite off the sky.

Also in this series:

Nifft the Lean

THE MINES OF BEHEMOTH

MICHAEL SHEA

THE MINES OF BEHEMOTH

This is a work of fiction. All the characters and events portrayed in this book are fictional, and any resemblance to real people or incidents is purely coincidental.

A Baen Books Original

Baen Publishing Enterprises
P.O. Box 1403
Riverdale, NY 10471

ISBN: 0-671-87847-6

Cover art by Gary Ruddell

First printing, October 1997

Distributed by Simon & Schuster
1230 Avenue of the Americas
New York, NY 10020

Typeset by Windhaven Press, Auburn, NH
Printed in the United States of America

For Linda, sweet Beloved!
For Della and Jake, so dear to us.

Running Away With the Circus
an introduction to
Michael Shea's *Nifft the Lean*

According to Joan Didion, both Truffaut and Fellini have talked about the "circus aspect" of filmmaking. I take that to mean generating more wildness and color for its own fevered sake than the material actually requires and I've remembered Didion's remark because that's the kind of entertainment that seizes me, and stays with me after it's done. Often the advice one wants to give to a cautious would-be writer is, "From this point on—from this page on—just go crazy."

But of course that's not quite right. If we want extravagant spectacle, then we don't want frenzied stream-of-consciousness from the writer—any more than we want haphazardly splashed paint from a painter, or inept camera work and incomprehensible editing from a movie director. On the contrary, we want the artist to be the proverbial clear pane of unrippled glass, so that we can easily see the gilded towers and the gladiators and the dancing girls and the monsters beyond. That's where we want to see the thundering industry of the grotesque.

And we do want it to be wild. Goya wouldn't have been right for illustrating *Nifft the Lean*—we don't need the subtle expressions, the political commentary, the restraint. For Michael Shea's masterwork, I'd like to see what Dore could have done, or Bosch; vast, deep crowd scenes against stone-carved mountains and Piranesi architecture, with end-of-the-world chiaroscuro.

The handicap that challenges fantasy—especially fantasy prose—is that the events in it are not only impossible today, like the events in hard science fiction, but are just plain impossible ever; the reader must be fooled into forgetting this.

What's required is a suspension of flat-out incredulity. To elicit this foolhardy investment on the reader's part, a writer has to make the fantasy world absolutely tangible. We readers need to be able to vividly—lividly!—see and hear and smell what's going on. *Nifft the Lean* does this at every turn with effortless-seeming power. When Nifft and Barnar are stringing up the corpse of the lurk, in the rafters above the guarded chamber of the doomed Year-King, the dimensions and acoustics are as clear as if we're standing right beside our heroes; when Dalissem appears so hideously out of the desert rock, we see and hear and *feel* the distressing spectacle; when Barnar and Nifft ride their modified ore-wagon down the precipitous mine-shaft into the underworld, we experience what Algis Budrys has in conversation called "The best entry into Hell in all of literature."

Behind and below the spotlit figure on the high wire, a circus is ropes and pegs and grommetted canvas, and in addition to the costumed performers there are drivers and accountants and somebody to sweep up all the peanut shells and elephant manure; and even outside the tent you can smell cotton candy on the night air. That's how you can tell you're in a real event, and not just dreaming.

Now, a circus would probably be just as affecting without these peripheral details, because it's *actually there*. Magic urgently *needs* the weathered scaffolding and worn ropes and scratched bolt-heads, because the reader knows, if given a moment to think, that it isn't really there at all.

And Michael Shea's magic is as unarguable as an overheated car engine. Before going down into the Underworld, Nifft assesses his weapons, and assesses too the physical symptoms of the Wayfarer's Blessing, the Charm of Brisk Blood, and the Life Hook, all as palpable as a hangover or caffeine jitters; the demons he encounters are, though insane and extravagant, zoological specimens on the hoof; and when Lybis leads her mercenary army to find the petrophagic flock, her progress is slowed because her distance from the Goddess is weakening her reception of the telepathic signal. And Shag Margold's prefaces provide us with a fellow member of the audience—a shrewd, erudite, humorous fellow, at that—who obviously believes that the show is real.

Altogether, Shea has snuck in and conquered our credulity before we could muster the forces of our skepticism. And having conquered it, he is a merciless carpetbagger—by the time he has led us to the strangely populated plains and weirdly utilitarian architecture of Anvil Pastures, we can only hang on and gape at the towering wonders around us.

There's nothing wrong with insights into "the human heart in conflict with itself," nor with "holding up a mirror" to a community, nor with having valuable things to say about the ills of humanity—

But sometimes we just want a big, loud damn circus.

Tim Powers
Santa Ana, CA
1994

Shag Margolds's Introduction to *The Mines of Behemoth*

MY OLD FRIEND, NIFFT, with a perhaps unintentional candor, has displayed a personal flaw or two in this narrative. I honor his memory none the less for it. The good of Nifft always overbalanced the ill, and just so here where, whatever slight moral shortcomings may appear in our narrator, he gives us in his tale the most vivid and enlightening natural history of the Behemoth's life-cycle yet put on record.

Hadaska Broode, a Minusk historian, has penned the following tetrameters in homage to Behemoth. While I cannot pretend the lines are accomplished poetry, they are at least heartfelt:

> *What dread Being dares to farm*
> *where every breed of demon swarms?*
> *Who dares till there? Who shall go*
> *and scythe the harvest row on row?*
> *Who in that sunless gulf of harms*
> *could drive the plow? Would dare to sow?*

1

Behemoth's jaws alone the share
to carve the flinty furrow there.
Behemoth's strength the reaper's blade,
her bowels the barn where harvest's laid.
To hers, what husbandry compares,
that has half demonkind unmade?

Broode's ardor for Behemoth is understandable in one of his nation. His native Minuskulons, though the smallest of the major island chains, loom large in the Behemoth sap trade, for they are the only landfall the Sea of Agon affords between southern Kairnheim, where sap is mined, and the sap's two greatest overseas markets: the Ephesion Chain to the south, and the Great Shallows to the east. The sap in its cake form is of course excellent fodder for kine and draybeasts the world over. In the Ephesions—on my native Pardash, for example—it is also used in its fluid state; a dilution is sprayed on our fields to enrich our somewhat lean soils. Meanwhile the Great Shallows' many sea-dwelling races use sap cake to mulch their mariculture and nourish their polyp patches, whelk beds, crab pastures, bivalve grottoes, and every kind of raft garden. The Minusk mariners who have flourished in this sap trade all know Broode's little poem by heart.

Given Behemoth's incredible utility to men—both in the havoc she wreaks on the demon race, and in the boon of her stolen sap—it is not surprising she inspires such paeans. The work of Kairnish scholars (theirs another race especially in her debt) abounds with similar encomiums. Both these schools of Behemoth's most ardent admirers share a further accord. On the question of Behemoth's origins, Minusk and Kairnish authorities alike aver that the Mountain Mother was born of some now forgotten human sorcery.

I will perhaps be forgiven a smile at this. If Behemoth be the scion of some thaumaturgic science man once wielded, then how much less at fault we must feel to play the vampire in her nests, even as she scours the subworld of our demon foes? For if the Mountain Mother be the fruit of philanthropic wizardry, where's the flaw in getting double good of her? Is it denied a man to use his own wagon or draybeast to his profit?

Kairnish folk might have the most need of this balm to guilt; in the northern reaches of their continent (as I have noted in my preface to *The Fishing of the Demon Sea*) the subworld preys upon the overworld all too vigorously, and men there fall in great numbers to demonic predation. Meanwhile in southern Kairnheim, where Behemoth nests under the Broken Axle Mountains, the demon nation still reels under a millenial defeat at the jaws of the Mountain Mother's legions, even while the southern Kairns most vigorously steal her sap from her nests.

Yet those of the opposing mind, who argue that Behemoth was born naturally of the Earth, point to her form which, in all but the scale of it, is so common through the natural world. Many scholars of unimpeachable erudition take this side of the controversy. Etiolatus the Praiseworthy notes, "How can those who go open minded on the earth, feeling the heart of the planet murmuring against their footsoles, ever think that Queen Earth in her Robe of Stars could fail to breed of herself the cure for any ill that blights her? Demons infested her; she gave birth to Behemoth."

For my part, though I have profound respect for the Earth's powers of invention, I think the answer is unknowable. My awe and love for the beasts, in any case, is great. I find cause for rejoicing in the fact that the sinking of a new sap-mine is the difficult and costly task that it is. The lithivorous ferrecks used to dowse for larval chambers, and then used to sink the first shafts down to those larval chambers, are creatures akin to certain brood parasites within Behemoth nests, and are both fierce and highly dangerous to manage. In consequence, these ferrecks have been almost entirely preempted by the sorcerous sisterhoods of the Astrygals, who have the means to command the beasts' angry energies. The ferrecks then being hard and costly to procure from the witches, the proliferation of new sap-mines throughout the Broken Axle Mountains has slowed almost to the rate of replacement for old mines fallen defunct through the phenomenon of "nest wander." Perhaps the sorcerers of the Astrygals intentionally sustain this equilibrium. In any case, our rapacity is shackled, and we plunder Behemoth less gravely than we might.

All that lives is flux, and a question Nifft raises disturbs me: might Demonkind grow to engulf Behemoth? The black yeast of demon vitality cooks unsleeping in its planetary cloaca; its vapors of infection float up fine as finest soot, soundlessly, steadily blackening, blackening what they blanket. Its patient twisting tendrils imperceptibly find purchase. . . . The reader will perhaps—when the fate of Heliomphalodon Incarnadine is learned, and Nifft's fears thereat—share my own unease.

Having touched on the question of human rapacity, I cannot close without confessing that it is with some misgiving I make public Nifft's account of the so-called "giants' pap" produced by Behemoth Queens, and of its apparent powers. Two considerations have persuaded me it is safe to expose this powerful substance to the greedy attention of entrepreneurs. In the first place, Nifft's narrative must tend to discourage exploitation. In the second, who but Nifft and Barnar, endowed as they were with rarest luck, could contrive to milk a Queen?

While I naturally shrink from burdening my dear friend's narrative (and the present manuscript is unmistakably of Nifft's own composition) with an excess of commentary or exegesis, I cannot leave certain lacunae unglossed. But since a prefatory voice must fade from memory as the history unfolds, the best procedure seems to be to deploy a brief Interjection or two within the narrative. Thus commentary can lie nearer what it touches.

I

We were still wet from Mayhem's maw
When first those golden glades we saw

MY FIRST STEPS along the path that led me to the greatest fortune I have ever won, or could sanely hope to equal in the future, were inauspicious enough. That twisted and darkling journey commenced, for Barnar Hammer-Hand and me, with an indignity, and then led straight to a disaster.

The indignity was that we were contracted to a stint of hard, dirty toil in a sap mine. The disaster fell when we were two weeks at sea en route to this uncouth endeavor. For just as we hove almost in sight of our inglorious goal, our vessel was swallowed by a bull glabrous.

One often hears this sort of thing about "inauspicious beginnings" from people relating strokes of great good fortune. It is my belief that Luck schools those she is about to bless by dealing them a preliminary box or two about the ears. Thus, with a draught of bile, she reminds their palates of the taste of woe, that Fortune's sweetness might ravish them the more.

Barnar's nephew Costard owned the sap mine we were bound for. Our dreary underground labor there would be in the way of a family favor, for young Costard had written that the mine was in difficulties. Our route lay northwards along the Angalheim Island chain, and the northerlies that scour these isles all summer long had set our sails a-spanking, and chased us smartly along. Now the Isle of Hadron dropped astern, and we were drawing close to Dolmen, the northernmost isle. Beyond Dolmen, we already had in view the rim of the Kairnish continent. There, in the Broken Axle Mountains, our destination lay.

Our vessel was the carrack of a Minusk cloth-and-oils merchant. She was a yare but smallish craft, scarcely six rods from stem to stern. She skipped from crest to crest, outrunning the swell, frolicsome as a shimfin when it runs breaching from sheer exuberance. The vessel's surge, the sunstruck sea around us and the gem-blue sky, were almost enough to cheer us out of the gloom that our coming toils had sunk us in.

Then someone shouted from the mizzen-mast lookout, and we turned and saw a long black-and-tan slick strung out in the milky jade of our wake. Every man-jack of us went cold at the sight. That slick was the length of our vessel, and we knew it was only part of a glabrous' dorsal ridge, breaching as the brute came sinuously up to attack our stern.

We had no sooner seen it than the sea erupted, and the beast was alongside us, and was seizing our hull in his huge, dripping crab-legs, while his long, eel-slick body bowed and bowed and bowed at the loins with his fierce, lecherous thrustings. He had clusters of stalked eyes on his great blunt head, and these writhed and rotated in his ecstasy. The brute was in rut—the worst kind of glabrous to meet; sure death. Amidships and aft a dozen men were instantly crushed by his legs. His sinewy tail scourged the sea behind him in his lust, driving us forward even as he embraced us. The steep, stony shore of Dolmen loomed towards us at incredible speed.

The impenetrability of our hull timbers quickly drove the ardent giant to a fury. He flung our ship clean out of the water, toppling Barnar and me back onto the deck just as we had mounted the gunwale to abandon ship. The carrack sailed creakily through twenty fathoms of thin air, and crashed down at Dolmen's very shore, and even as it did so, the glabrous surged up behind the vessel—a benthic fetor welling from his mossy, gaping jaws—and swallowed it whole.

The glabrous did this with the blind, uncalculating rage his breed is so well known for. Barnar and I, tumbled to the prow by the bow's impact with the shore, saw the darkness of the brute's maw loom over us, and saw his huge teeth bite off the sky. Only the carrack's stout bowsprit extruded beyond the reach of the monster's bite. This bowsprit doomed the beast.

For even as it engulfed us, the glabrous' onrush drove us hard aground; the bowsprit lodged against a boulder, and the whole craft was rammed a fatal two fathoms deeper into the monster's throat. The glabrous at once began to choke to death.

His jaws gnawed frantically at the sky, trying to gobble down air, and in the intermittent floods of sunlight we saw our craft crumpling in the black velvet fist of his convulsing throat, the timbers cracking with a noise like fire, as the purple blood welled out of the huge, spar-torn tongue and drenched us to the knees.

The glabrous—desperately climbing toward the air he could not have—heaved himself half ashore, and as his struggles slowed toward extinction, hammered himself against the steep, rocky slope of the island. We were so tumbled about by these great concussions we could not leap out of his jaws when he opened them. Then his jaws fell slack, and crashed shut in death.

In the utter darkness, we could hear the beast's mouth still bleeding from a dozen wounds. Back in the utterly crushed stern of the vessel, muffled human death-moans briefly droned, and were snuffed out. Still the hot velvet blood inched up around our legs, with a trickling noise in the perfect blackness.

Not quite perfect. A feeble star of light grew slowly visible. We slogged groping through the sticky, inching rise of blood. Already the air felt hot and dead and hard to breathe. We groped our way out along the bowsprit—foul, slippery work—as good as blind. Our hands encountered the huge mossy teeth of the glabrous, clamped not quite shut on the bowsprit's stump. "I think we might just worm through," I said. "Then we might just hack our way out through one of the lips."

The cusps of the teeth were like oiled boulders reeking of carrion. We bruised our ribs wriggling between them. Had the splintered bowsprit slipped out, the simple weight of the teeth falling shut would have crushed us flat.

Our emergence from between the teeth was a head-first drop into the blood pooled within the glabrous' lips, whose rubbery meat was teetery footing for us once we stood up, calf-deep in the blood. It would have taken a titanoplod and a block-and-tackle to hoist those lips apart. The bowsprit's tip had been pinched between them and a faint ray of light leaked in along the spar. "At least it gives us an aiming point," Barnar muttered. "I'll go first. Stay clear."

And I heard him go to work with Old Biter, his broad-axe, on the lip-meat. "Ugh!" he grunted, hewing. "Loathsome! Slimy! Here's a gobbet free. *Huh!* . . . *Huh!* . . ."

"How he bleeds! I'm thigh-deep in blood! Here, give me a turn now—you sound winded. Set my hand to the spar . . . got it! Now Biter's haft . . . got it! Stand clear. *Huh!* . . . *Huh!* . . ."

I couldn't match stroke to stroke in the dark. I had to hew blindly, then grapple the wet meat for what chunks I could pull free. Barnar mused moodily as I worked.

"You know, Nifft, dying would be bad enough, of course. But by the Crack it would gall me, after all we've done, all we've seen, to die on this . . . demeaning, pedestrian errand of ours!"

"I have to . . . agree. . . . To think of them . . . talking . . . back in the Tankard and Titbit . . . ."

"Or over mulled tartle at the Thirsty Knave. 'Did you hear about poor Barnar and Nifft, then? Dead and done for at last, it seems! What were they about, you ask? Well, it appears the poor lackwits were northbound to Kairnheim to work in a sap mine!' 'What? Work in a *sap mine* you say? Well then, their best years were already past, it would seem!'"

"Peace, Barnar . . . .you're using up . . . air . . ."

"Here, give me old Biter back—I'll do a turn."

The hot blood was up to our waists, and the unbreathable darkness choked out all conversation quick enough. We hewed the invisible meat, groping the sticky wedges from the wound. Toward the end we were gasping stertorously, and it seemed we dug ourselves a bottomless grave of flesh. Then I struck that blessed stroke that bit out a little wedge of sunlight, which bled a delicious trickle of salt sea air into our nostrils.

With light and air, our butchery progressed apace, and at length we had a carnal tunnel we could wriggle through. Reborn beneath the sky, we lay exulting, and roared with laughter to look on one another, both of us slick and sticky as fresh turds.

But as we bathed and washed our gear in the sea, and reclothed ourselves, we came to feel sobered, reduced. We had emerged from that monstrous sepulchre with our arms, the slender contents of our moneybelts, and nothing else. The joy of escape soon yielded to a

sense of ill-luck, and a nagging conviction that we were
entirely too impoverished for men of our years and
expertise. A dozen men lay dead in the glabrous' throat,
yet somehow our destitution loomed larger to us than
our miraculous evasion of their tomb. There is a tide in
men's spirits, and ours had perhaps been at ebb for some
time now, even before our half-hearted undertaking to
rescue nephew Costard's mine.

Glumly we trekked along the shore, and reached
Dolmen Harbor by mid-afternoon. This was like most
Angalheim ports, less an actual bay than a smallish cleft
in a steep shoreline. Most observers agree that the whole
Angalheim chain is just a slowly drowning mountain range,
and its harbors thus merely embayments in the flanks of
the sinking peaks. Above the docks, most of the harbor's
buildings and houses climbed on stilts up the slopes.

We found a mead house and bespoke an ample jar
of the fiery-sweet potation that the Angalheims are famed
for over half the world. Still, our hearts remained gloomy
as we drank. The mead house itself was somber—a
former clan hall from the islands' piratical days, long since
converted to its present commercial use, but proud of
its smoke-blackened roofbeam and the crude traditional
weaponry racked on its wall; the battered bucklers and
unwieldy falchions of a privateering era. Throughout the
Angalheims folk hold a similar reverence for a squalid
and villainous past.

Mead has of course long replaced piracy as these
islands' livelihood, and from the windows we could view
the colorful bustle of a vigorous economy. Men bearing
panniers of bright seaweed, and plod-trains laden with
the same briny cargo, streamed upland. This seaweed was
mulch for the flower-pastures on the island's heights,
where the sonorous blizzards of bees hummed in the
pursuit of their golden harvest. The harbor thronged with
island trade; Kairnish vessels laden with hides, salt meat
and sap waited at anchor for dock-space, while Angalheim

scows scudded outbound riding low with the weight of
mead casks. Out in the open channel beyond the harbor,
the wind curdled the jade water with veins of foam. There,
where the big shoals of 'silvers ran, rode the fishing ketches
all at their stern anchors, and we could see tiny men on
them toiling at windlasses, and gaffing aboard nets bulging
with glittery catch.

But this loveliness and liveliness of sea and sky failed
to cheer us. We felt the dejection of men who are imper-
fectly employed, whose work-in-hand is mediocre and
indifferently paid. In point of fact we had only a general
notion of the specific duties of a tapper in a sap mine.
But it was paid labor, drudgery, and that was enough to
put this touch of autumn in our hearts, to make us brood
on the long years behind us, and make us ask ourselves
where our lives were drifting to.

Barnar downed a third jack of mead, and sighed. His
melodious baritone broke a long silence. "It's not so much
the toil of it," he mused. "It's the . . . ignominy."

"Why mince words? Mining is wage-work, and from
this your soul recoils instinctively, of course! All we can
do is try to fix our minds on the charity of it. Your
nephew's in a pickle, and his mother would never forgive
you for failing to help him."

"Do I rightly infer that you two gentlemen are discussing tapping?"

A sleek-fed man, wearing a green velvet fez, had
turned on the bench and, leaning near us, presented us
with this query, wearing a smile of prying amity.

"I will be frank," I told him, straining for civility. "My
friend and I are far from keen that you should infer
anything, rightly or wrongly, from what we are discussing."

"Oh!" He gaped his concern. "Do I intrude? Forgive
me!" And he turned back on the bench.

"Anhyldia would break my neck," Barnar resumed,
answering my previous remark, "if I didn't help Costard.
That's the long and short of it."

I nodded. "And you are wise to remember that she is quite strong enough to do so." Barnar's formidable elder sister had, about two years before this, settled her sap mine on her son and gone off a-pirating.

"But what I keep sticking on," Barnar said, "is that poor Costard is such a dolt! I say it utterly without bias against the boy! He has a sweet, affectionate vein towards his kin, but he is such a petulant young jackass!"

"Yes," I sighed. "At least he'll be topside while we're underground. And mark you that after all, the wage is not stingy. You could do worse a-thieving, half the time."

Barnar dismissed this feeble solace with the snort it merited. "Of course! The pay is more than many a prize I've worked twice as hard to steal, but at least I was thieving, not grubbing!"

"Would it be overbold of me"—again the green velvet fez bobbed just starboard of my shoulder—"to suggest that, if it's a tapper's wage you speak of, I know a way to *quintuple* even that handsome sum, and at cost to yourselves of no more effort than a brief detour taken through the tunnels of the nest."

Barnar held up one hand in a gesture of polite prevention. Swordwelts veined my old friend's knuckles, rather in the way that veins of smooth quartz sometimes run through rough granite. "You have so lavished your attention on us, sir, that I cannot tamely bear any further generosity. Please. Attend to something other than ourselves!"

The stranger's fezzed brow crumpled with apology. "I have, in my elan to serve, offended you! Accept my most abject apologies!" He turned away again.

"This minework is not just undignified, it's clownish!" Barnar at length resumed. "To be stripped and painted! Orange! And then tapping itself is . . . grotesque! Inherently ludicrous! And we'll be novices, prone to all the humiliating missteps that entails."

"There's more to it of course, eh?" I nudged him

gently. "I know at least that I for one just plain don't like being deep underground in Kairnheim—in any part of it."[1]

Barnar gave that a bit of a sigh. "Sure enough. The flesh of me recoils, right to the bone. At least on this venture, we may count on coming nowhere near the subworld; the only demons we meet will be those the Behemoths bring into the Nest as food."

"Forgive me a thousand times, but I cannot contain an impulse of hospitality toward yourselves!" Here was green fez yet again bobbing near us. "Let me show you my hives!"

We gaped at him for a heartbeat, aghast. "My *bee*-hives!" he added. He had a chinlet of black beard—it was barbered close and neat as a tatoo. His plump face crinkled with hostly fervor.

"Sir," I told him, "you bring me to the point of speaking bluntly. We must know why you focus your regard with such tenacity upon ourselves in particular."

"The fairest of questions! Apart from what I could not help but overhear—that you seem to be bound to work in a sap mine—I am motivated by a certain look of competence you have about you. You yourself, Sir, for one, so long and limber yet with a lizardly muscularity (if I may say so), and you Sir, of bulky sinew, with the mass to exert prodigious leverage. The two of you have, as well—how shall I put it? . . . an air of enterprise. You strike me as thoughtful, original spirits, men who can see the world from many points of view. Please, gentlemen. May I have the honor of showing you my flower pastures? And of giving you to sample the comb of my Centennial Hive?"

It seemed an acquaintance with the man was not to be avoided. He introduced himself as Ha'Awley Bunt, a mead magnate with his own hiveries, cooperage and

---

1. Nifft's and Barnar's sojourn in the Demon Sea, related elsewhere, commenced in the Bone Axe Mountains in northern Kairnheim, where the subworld portal Darkvent lies.

casking plants, and trading fleet; owner also of seven hundred hectares of Scarlet Croppies, Devils-garters and Umber Dandinnias right here on Dolmen. Owner too of the almost ten thousand hives these flower pastures sustained. We decided that, at the least, the man would divert and inform us, whether or not his proposal proved profitable.

His open carriage, hitched to three matched skinnies, stood outside the mead house. We all got in, he flicked the reins, and we sped up the switchbacks of the upland highway toward the flower pastures on the island's crest.

Bunt had an amiable and tactful way about him, explaining that when he made his proposition to us, he must in the same breath disclose a lucrative secret. To satisfy himself that this chancy disclosure was warranted, Bunt begged us to indicate, at least, our destination and projected doings. Accordingly, we conceded that we might indeed be going into the Broken Axle Mountains, and there taking work as tappers in a sap mine. The Broken Axles had in fact just then become visible as we climbed the island's heights in the wind-scoured afternoon: beyond a blue reach of sea to our north, on the coast of the Kairnish continent's southern rim, the Broken Axles were a pale pimpling of low peaks.

"You should know one thing more, Hive-Master Bunt," Barnar told him, "before disclosing your business to us. It is our policy, Nifft's and mine, never to undertake ventures proposed by strangers without a substantial surety in raw gold or specie, on account of services to be rendered."

"This is highly sensible, and acceptable!" Bunt enthused. Then he dropped the business for the moment, and fell to suavely annotating the windswept, scalp-tingling beauty of the prospect that our ascent was opening out below us. The northerlies polished the sky like glass, and its blue was an infinite flame. South of us the other

Angalheims rode formationed on the blazing sea, their surf-collared crests like a great docking fleet, cruising in to moor in the mothering underbelly of the Kairnish continent. The windlicked channels, tufted with blown spray, were molten silver rouged with copper fire. Barnar and I traded looks. We were feeling some zest for life return to us. Raw gold (or specie), in substantial excess of the stipend we had but lately, forlornly contemplated, now glowed before us, above a changed horizon.

Dolmen's uplands are all gorgeously crested and pelted by flower pastures. How they ravished the eyes in the slant gold light, those meadowed acres of silken wildfire! Bunt drew a gauzy curtain round our carriage now. The bees thronged every inch of air, hanging stubborn in the wind's sweep, dropping to the blossoms like a steady rain, a rain that hovered, fell, rose, and fell again.

As we toured the pastures, the last of our gloom fell from us like a moulting. Smooth paths brought us to breathtaking vistas, or sank us deep in meadows where we spun along, walled in by choirs of living rainbow, all the colors uniting with the scents, and with the bees' sweet, sonorous hymn, to ravish our senses. Many other tourists were likewise being carriaged through the aromatic maze in similar vehicles bearing the crest of the Bunt Hivery, but the pathways were so cunningly designed and artfully laid out that we glimpsed these fellow travellers but rarely, and felt we had the flower-fields for our own.

"My Centennial Hive is unrivalled here on Dolmen," Bunt told us. "It is equalled only by five or six others throughout the Astrygals. My Centennial Hive shelters seven dynasties of queens, the youngest of them a hundred generations long."

Younger hives, we had seen, were housed in poly-hedral wooden cabins, their panels of dark, oiled harmony wood all gorgeously carved with bas-relief motifs of comb and bee and blossom. These structures could be walked through, and were labyrinthed inside with carpentered frames all solid with comb and densely furred with working bees.

The Centennial Hive was thrice the size of any of these others. Inside, we found that skylights of stained glass admitted a murky amber light, allowing maintenance and cultivation. Gossamer netting formed diaphanous tunnels for us to move through in the sweet-scented gloom and deafening primeval song of sleeplessly vibrating wings.

"Hadra-Archonia the Sixteenth," quavered Bunt, drawing us to a deeply grottoed vault. We stood beholding her. This queen was a titan of her race; her restless, gravid abdomen alone was larger than my hand. Her gaster, ever-probing, ceaselessly planted the seeds of workers in new-made cells. Her attendants were not a tenth her size. They flanked her like busy sycophants, seeming to kiss her flanks, speaking to her with touches of jaw and antenna, ceaselessly coming and going, always replaced, worshipping at her side in clusters constantly renewed.

If Bunt had meant some disclosure to accompany this portentous viewing, he changed his mind. He wore an air of inward debate as we drove back to the Hivery. There we retired to the comfortable armchairs of his private office, and he served us some very impressive mead. He drank with us, and sighed.

"Gentlemen. There is much I might explain, but I feel a reticence I cannot overcome. Will you forgive a vagueness that might be mistaken for distrust? Merely specifying what I seek puts my purpose within the reach of inference to any thoughtful hearer.

"Well. Here, then, is my proposition. Your work as tappers will put you in the larval nurseries of a Behemoth nest. In your work's normal course you would find no cause to venture from that nursery chamber.

"But it is my hope that you will agree, with the inducement of three hundredweight apiece of gold specie, to venture at large through the nest till you have found the Royal Brood Chamber, where the Queen lies a-laying her eggs, and there to retrieve some twenty gills or so of a certain ichor which the Queen exudes from her body, and bring it up to me when your tapping tour is done."

Barnar and I exchanged a look. We both did an almost superhuman job of concealing our astonishment and delight at the enormous sum that Bunt had just named. "Let us banish ambiguity completely," I said. "You are telling us you will pay us three hundredweight of gold *before* we leave here, a hundred and fifty apiece, in exchange for our undertaking to attempt your task? That this three hundred will be inalienably ours for the attempt alone, and that a like sum will be paid us if we succeed?"

Bunt's hesitation was quickly overcome; we saw only the briefest quiver of a merchant's haggling reflex. "Just so!"

With some further struggle, Barnar and I hid our elation. That very morning we had been but a single swallow from an agonizing metamorphosis into glabrine fecal matter. And this afternoon, we were already rich.

II

Oh let us bathe, and put away dissension—
Let's with lissom ladies of the Bath
Explore what joys the golden Present hath,
For Now is Having's only real dimension.
Let not Phantasmic Future wake our wrath!

OUR DEPARTURE was set for the tide's turn, not long past nightfall, and Ha'Awley Bunt would be going with us. Barnar and I would have liked to knock around on our own before setting out, asking questions here and there, gathering our own judgment of the strange work we'd agreed to. But Bunt proved adhesive, loath to leave our sides. Perhaps he feared precisely such inquiries as we might make, and what these inquiries might suggest to those who heard them. He took us with him to see to the outfitting of a ferry he owned, which would convey us to the Kairnheim coast. He involved us in the choosing and bringing aboard of the carriage and team that would whisk us from KairnGate Harbor up to Costard's Superior Sap Mine in the Broken Axle Mountains. Then, as the sun westered, he took us to his imposing harborside residence.

Here, safe within his guarded doors, his sturdy retainers stood ready to transfer to our possession two compact but weighty pairs of leathern saddlebags. Bunt then, before repairing upstairs to see to our further entertainment, put his opulent baths at our disposal. He was perhaps not surprised—though he arched a brow—when we told him we would take our pay with us into the baths.

A lissome bath attendant—a gauzily clad woman wearing a tantalizing citron scent—conducted us to a sweat-room, and at our request left us there with an amphora of water to splash on the embers glowing in the huge brazier. At last we had some blessed privacy. We un-shouldered the saddlebags, and stripped down to sweat the last traces of glabrous slime from our pores. I flipped open one of my bags, as Barnar did one of his.

"Oh my," I murmured. I chuckled as my fingers plunged into the coins, and the rattly coins seemed to chuckle with me. The ruddy light of the coals warmed them, and made them glow rich as butter. "Look Barnar," I burbled. "Kolodrian lictors! Such a wonderful mintage!" Admittedly this was the fatuous utterance of mindless glee, but the hefty octagonal coin is indeed a handsome one, bearing the profile of Jarkel VII, conqueror of the Laddga Tundras. The monarch was an indifferent soldier who triumphed through his generals, but his plump, prosperous cheeks look wonderfully apt on a coin, as does, on the verso, the imprint of the fatted sacrifice, a kaurok (ancestral, most agree, to the Kairnish hornbow), its horns wreathed in garlands.

"Mine too!" Barnar chortled, "With Kairnish quadroons mixed in!" I had to laugh to see my friend looking so like a child with his basket of sweets at an Ephesion harvest-fest (although so, I daresay, did I). Barnar's eyes are the dense, smoky grey of the always-rainy skies of his native Chilia, and the glow of our gold brought out the flecks of green in them too, like the forest green that clothes that same great isle of his nativity. His broad, flat, not unbattered nose seemed like a bull's who snuffs excitement in the morning air. Barnar is a man with great laughter in him, though his stolid face is seldom seen to brim with it, as it did now. "Do you know, old waybrother," I told him, "in this fine, ruddy heat, I feel that the gold and we ourselves could melt together, refashioning us into utterly new, shining beings, lustrous and immortal."

"The words," Barnar beamed, "of a perfect lunatic. I too am quite mad, you know, to find myself so rich. So very rich, in fact, Nifft, that . . . ." His look turned graver; he was about to broach some serious matter, but I cut him off, such excitement did my own sudden thought bring me.

"Do you realize, Barnar, that now we can do that great deed we have been sworn to these five years past and more?" The look he gave me was so blank, I faltered. "Can you fail to understand me? The Buskins and Gantlets and Cowl of Pelfer the Peerless! To be had by storming his tomb and subduing its deathless guardians.[2] Surely you see that now, once we have the remaining three hundredweight, we can actually hire six good ships and a hundred first-class mercenaries. We could be fighting our way across the steppes before autumn was half out, if we're done in your nephew's mine in a fortnight or so."

Barnar's brow, to my bafflement, had taken on an injured look. "You may be right to reproach my memory, Nifft, for forgetting your ardor to have the great Pelfer's accoutrements of power. But I think I have even better reason to reproach your memory in turn. For did we not, two years ago, at the Pickpockets' Ball in Karkmahn-Ra, most solemnly vow that if ever we could afford the Witches' Seed to do it, we would infallibly go forth to

2. See Interjection

Chilia and there reforest the Ham-Hadryan Vale, so long in the holding of my family's line, and so cruelly despoiled during its long captivity?"

I all but snapped at him, *What, will you hold me to drunken promises?* For I remembered the occasion the instant he reminded me of it; a bit too much wine had made me vow with sentimental fervor that I would regard the reforestation of Barnar's native valley as my solemn duty, as soon as circumstances warranted the exploit. And of course I was indeed bound to help my friend in an enterprise so near to him as the rejuvenation of his homeland and his clan, and I had every intention of doing so, at a more convenient time. "Old friend," I urged him, "when Gildmirth's path crossed ours a second time, and when that great mage put in our possession the whereabouts of Pelfer's fabled tomb—was this not five years and more ago? Did not the vow we swore to one another to seek his tomb as soon as we had wealth enough to mount the effort—well, did not this vow antedate our vow to re-forest your family's valley? And look you! With Pelfer's Gantlets, Cowl, and Buskins in our possession, we would shortly be the richest thieves on earth! The reforesting of the Ham-Hadryan Vale with Witches' Seed would be childsplay to us then!"

For answer Barnar gave me a steady, mournful look. He felt himself ill treated—there was no getting around it. On my part, I felt a keen resentment of my friend which it was hopeless to conceal from myself. How could Barnar allow this golden moment of ours to run aground on this shoal of his stubbornness?

"Look you," he sighed at length. "The other three hundredweight is not yet ours, is it? Indeed, can this ichor of Bunt's be so easy in the taking that we can be wholly sure of managing it? Would he have offered such a huge sum outright for something that was lightly had? Let's go bathe, and put away dissension. Let's enjoy what we have, and the moment we have it in."

"Fairly spoken!"

As soon as we emerged from the sweat room, our bags once again on our shoulders, three bath attendants materialized—the slender one who had first ushered us in, and two others as gauzily clad and shapely as herself. These second two swiftly persuaded Barnar to undergo a massage which began with the pair of them walking up and down on him, treading the length of his recumbent bulk with their bare, scented feet. The first, a sloe-eyed woman with a wise, wicked smile, conducted me to a pool a bit apart. "Oh sinewy traveller," she teased (her voice was slow, gritty honey), "you seem to be entirely made of tendon and tight, snaky muscles! You will need a thorough soaping, and a most meticulous scrubbing, to get all the creases and ridges of you clean. . . ."

I replied, my voice cracking only slightly, that I would be deeply grateful for any such hygienic assistance as she would be pleased to lend me.

A rapturous interval ensued.

Her name was Higaia. We were chortling like children when at length we rinsed each other off. She told me she had freelanced in bath houses and dancing troupes three decades now on both sides of the Sea of Agon, and clearly she had seen the world and drawn sweet wisdom from it. Knowing we could not meet again before our setting out tonight, I asked if she meant to stay on Dolmen a while. "Well," she said, "the wanderlust is coming on me again, and I'm thinking of seeing the Minuskulons. I suppose I might stay here another fortnight or so."

"Then I have good hope of finding you here again. Perhaps we might travel together for a time."

So little did I forsee how our present venture would detain us under the earth.

Bunt's balconied dining room, four floors up, opened onto an unobstructed view of the harbor and the channel beyond. We viewed the windlicked waters all purple in the dusk, and dined sumptuously. Bunt proposed that we present him to Costard as a chance-met traveller, a man in the market for sap whom we'd brought along so Costard could sell him some. Bunt needn't hide he was a Hive-Master. Hiveries used plods, skinnies, and other draybeasts for mulching and transporting mead and the like, and were always buying sap as bulk fodder. Meanwhile Costard's financial straits might make him open to partnership. Bunt, by investment, might secure a stable source of the ichor he sought—the substance, that is, we were to obtain for him from a Queen, and which he also referred to as "giants' pap."

I listened patiently, toeing my gold beneath the table, feeling the shifty coin within its leather swaddling. This morning, I was waist-deep in blood in the stenchful glabrous' maw; this afternoon, I was in a dazzling world of breeze-licked flowers; this evening, there was Higaia in the baths, this rich food, and wealth. I had to be on guard at moments, to stop myself from breaking out into a stupid grin of delight and disbelief.

But then my glance kept meeting Barnar's, as if by some odd synchrony in our inner musings. And each time our eyes met, I felt pass between us that little chill of mutual disappointment that had first struck us in the sweat-room's warmth. Our difference would not leave us, but was an icy spark our eyes struck off each time they met. I knew that Barnar's will still clasped as stubbornly his pet ambition, as mine clung to my own.

"The opulence of your entertainment," Barnar told Bunt jocularly, "somewhat troubles me as I reflect on it. We must affirm that your stipend is princely. Yet I find myself asking key questions too late. How dangerous must it be to penetrate the Royal Brood Chamber of a Behemoth nest? Let alone to gather some sort of exudate from the Queen's own body? I have never heard such an exploit even conceived of, much less undertaken. Nifft and I naturally regard ourselves as bound," (I bowed here

my assent) "but for all we know of what we've undertaken, even six hundredweight might be too little payment."

Just at this juncture, a tall, robust young woman
marched into the room, caped against the dusk winds
outside, her back-swept pompadour of brazen hair still
charmingly mussed by those same winds.

"Sha'Urley! Dearest!" cried Bunt. "My sister, Sha'Urley,
gentlemen! Please dine with us, my dear!" There was a
grit of irritation in his voice that all his attempt at honey
could not quite candy over. Bunt presented us to her
as a pair of wayfaring fellows who had agreed to guide
him on a ramble into Kairnheim. For he was feeling stale
with work, he told her, and we were to be his breath
of fresh air. Sha'Urley did not uncloak, but she sat to
take a brief, amiable chalice of wine with us.

"You look quite fit and . . . trail-wise, gentlemen," she
told us. Her pale eyes smiled at us with a frosty little
light of irony in them. "My brother is well met with you.
And how richly he deserves a stroll abroad! He is too
much at business. It is a business which our mother left
to our joint direction, but which Ha'Awley dreads to
burden me withal, and so he strives to manage it almost
single-handed. Dear brother! You fret to spare me
burdens, yet you treat your own health villainously. Look
how fat you have grown! But nothing I say makes the
least bit of difference to you, does it?" Already she was
rising, and kissing her brother good-bye, at which Bunt
wore a look both nettled and relieved.

She paused at the door before stepping out. "I am
lucky at least," she said, "that Ha'Awley would not dream
of making any major investment without my prior and
full involvement in the decision. With this certainty I rest
content. It was a pleasure to meet you, gentlemen. Good
night, all!"

III

If we are still to manage deeds that shine,
We must be up and doing them. First, mine!

WE TOOK SHIP not long after dark. There was the bustle of boarding, and getting under way, and then Bunt retired at once to his hammock, and lay snoring within moments of our casting off. It was true he had partaken liberally of mead and viands at table, but his haste to bed down smacked of evasion too, for we had discreetly urged on him our wish to know more of our errand to the Royal Chamber in the Behemoth's nest.

Barnar and I stood at the rail of the creaky craft, an old pirates' caravel re-decked to ferry beasts and carriages like our own to and from the Kairnish coast. The half moon, zenithed in the early dark, made spectral statuary of the bare-masted vessels in the harbor. These fell astern of us, and the bright-windowed houses of the harbor dwindled to a little crescent-shaped constellation on the moon-silvered sea, as the wind took us out in the open channel. We leaned at the rail, enjoying the rickety dance of the old tub on the smoothly rolling waters.

"Well," Barnar ventured. "'giants' pap'. . . . Have you ever heard of it before?"

"I've heard Behemoth workers nurse or feed in some way at the flanks of the Queen, but I have also heard that same notion mocked as myth."

"It smacks of myth to me," Barnar said. "Who's ever been in a Royal Brood Chamber and seen a Queen? If it's been done, I've not heard of it."

"Well, we'll get what else we can out of Bunt. The rest, I suppose, we'll learn first hand in the attempt. . . ."

We stood at the rail through a long silence, our separate dreams wide awake in us, roaming through our minds. The night wind chased us, and set our scow creaking and lumbering through the easy swells. Above the shadow of the Kairnish coast ahead were thick-strewn stars only a little dimmed by the high half moon, and blazing as if they were coals that the wind blew to life.

"Barnar," I said, "I'm feeling lucky. I'm getting a feeling that luck is gathering itself under us like a great wave. Like a rising tide. I should have known it this morning, even before we came by this gold, for are not men who are swallowed by a glabrous, and emerge alive, among the world's luckiest imaginable?

"Let me tell you a story, old friend," I went on, "about a man we both know, a man who is dear as a brother to my heart. This man has nine living uncles and seven living aunts, and cousins uncountable, and thirteen brothers and sisters of his own"—Barnar made to interrupt me but I thrust up my palm—"and all four of his grandparents living and great aunts and great uncles at least half a score, and no less than four of his great grandparents still stepping most lively on the skorse-scented, needle-carpeted mountain slopes of his native valley, Ham-Hadryan Vale, the immemorial holding of the Ham-Hadryan clan. Can any doubt remain that the man I speak of is Barnar Ham-Hadryan, called, only half

facetiously, Barnar Hammer-Hand, and Barnar Ox-Back?
Don't answer! Hear me.

"This Barnar, whose beloved kin thrive near as thick
on his natal slopes as does the timber that is their
livelihood, is an earth-loving man, who wielded an axe
from his earliest youth, who winched the howling blades
of his family's sawmill since he was a stripling, and who,
long before he came a man, had by his own sweat and
skill done his part to set many a straight-keeled ship
afloat, many a stout-walled home a-standing, many a
strong-axled wagon a-rolling.

"And, when the Kragfasst clan of the Lulumean
Highlands began its depredations in the Great Shallows,
and thrust its blade of conquest down half the length
of Ham-Hadryan Vale, who exchanged a tree-jack's axe
for a battle-axe with half the furious will that this our
Barnar did? Nine years of war transformed him from a
fresh youth to a seasoned veteran, tough as an axe-haft
of ironwood, but still with the same tender heart for his
kin and his homeland beating in his formidable body.

"But when the invaders were repulsed at last, they
left a clear-cut waste, and these shorn slopes were a
torment to the eye of this same Barnar Hammer-Hand
who, having fought for his valley till its deliverance,
turned away from it when he had helped to win it back.
He went abroad a-thieving over the earth, too grieved
by his hearth-land's despoliation to long abide in it.

"In the decades since, he has lavished the better part
of all his takings on his kin, refurbishing their faltering
saws, replenishing their teams of plods, and generally
nourishing along their laborious husbandry of the trees
remaining to them.

"How can we not think, then—we who love and
honor this same Barnar Ham-Hadryan—that his eyes may
have grown . . . too fixed upon the earth? Of course it
will most infallibly come to pass, that Barnar Hammer-
Hand will drive home the Witches' Seed in the flanks

of his native hills. Most surely he will do this, and call up his homeland's vanished hosts of skorse to stand tall again out of the soil! This will come to pass! But if, beforehand, an incalculable enrichment may be had—if, first, this Barnar—"

"Enough, Nifft! Stop it. Do you not realize, my friend, that you and I are at that point in years where, if a great thing lie in hand, then we must do it, then and there? We are not made of immortal stuff, old waybrother. If we are still to manage deeds that shine, then we must be straight about them when they offer. And this dream of the Witches' Seed I have held so long, it is not a thing I will set by for any other venture, now that it has come at last within my reach . . . or almost in my reach."

"Use reason, Barnar! If we possessed the Gantlets, Cowl and Buskins of Pelfer the Peerless, then we could shortly make ourselves so rich we could reforest all of Chilia, make even her stoniest ridges green with skorse, have the great trees growing thick as grass even in the high barrens of Magnass-Dryan."

That last shaft made him startle just a bit, for in the high barrens still dwelt Marnya-Dryan, whom Barnar had loved since boyhood; Marnya was the daughter of a proud but tree-poor clan. How might she not be wooed with Witches' Seed, and the forestation of her natal highlands? He repossessed himself, however, and smiled wanly. "Look at us, jarring over the spending of phantom gold!" He hauled his bags of gold up onto his shoulder and, before trudging off to his hammock, he thwacked my shoulder in his old friendly manner. But I knew him; though he was carefully concealing it in his well-bred way, he was hurt and resentful.

I lingered at the rail, bitterly resenting my friend's stubbornness. I was so vexed it ended by surprising me. I struggled for composure.

And I could admit, after a while, to feeling this same sad, mortal urgency Barnar had confessed to. While I'd trudged around Dolmen's shore this morning, shivering from the briny bath that left us still smelling of glabrous blood, this same bony finger of Time had indeed touched my own heart, and the Specter had murmured with lean lips at my ear that I was a vagabond who had achieved nothing, and now, never would.

But by the Crack, Key and Cauldron, under it all, I did indeed feel . . . lucky. Strange fortune had come to us, and was still coming. I looked north, to our future's unfolding. There, unveiled by the moon's decline, the blaze of stars brightened above the dark line of the Kairnish mainland. Those stars swarmed as thickly as I imagined Behemoths might swarm, down the subworld walls, and across the subworld plain, a-hunting the fleeing hosts of demons. . . .

IV

With beverage that giants sip
Fill up my beaker to the lip
But how to tap that brew Below
I cannot tell. I do not know.

WE DOCKED at KairnGate Harbor in the first light, and by the time of the sun's rising, our barouche had already whirled a league out of town up a north-trending highway. The highway was a fine, smooth-flagged thoroughfare that thrived with commerce.

Across the river-knit southern plains of Latter Kairnlaw, Bunt cracked the whip above his thoroughbred skinnies and set us racing through the honeyed spill of morning light. He kept the wheels rattling, and the wind ruckusing in our ears, perhaps to forestall the questions he sensed in us.

But I insisted on a sit-down at an ale house we glimpsed in a riverside hamlet, one that Bunt would have galloped past had we let him. The establishment had a pleasant garden fenced with proom trees and rumkin vines. We chose our table in a nook amidst these fragrant growths, and decanted a delicious honey-wine, a drink as golden as the grassy prairies that unrolled across the river from us.

"I believe this is our own vintage," Bunt murmured, tonguing a sup of the wine judiciously.

"May we speak of other beverages?" Barnar prompted. "This giants' pap for instance. Must we, as it were, milk a Queen Behemoth for it? Kindly share with us now what you know of this thing you send us after."

"I may not share my sources," Bunt gravely answered. "This would—forgive me—give away too much to those who might wish to emulate my venture. But the gist of it I will give you, though it is admittedly slight. Adult Behemoth workers, all castes of them, nurse in an unspecified manner at the flanks of the Queen. They do it occasionally, you understand, but they all do it. They drink from Her.

"From a documentary source unknown even to the erudite, I have learned that, in all likelihood, each Behemoth by this nursing imbibes an ichor specific to her caste and form of body. The exudate, it seems, prompts and sustains the several shapes and orders of the Queen's progeny. The specific ichor I would have you obtain is that particular pap consumed by the Forager caste, far and away the giants of all workers, and the scourges of demonkind. The precise How of the obtaining, I'm afraid, is completely unknown to me."

"Would it be fair to infer," I ventured after a silence, "that this giants' pap is believed specifically to promote the Foragers' hugeness? And might I further guess that it is specifically this giantizing property of the sap which you crave it for?"

"This much I will admit, if you will be so kind as not to press for any further particulars."

"Well and good, Bunt. Still, assuming this pap to be what you think it is, what virtue would it necessarily have outside the Nest?"

"Well," smiled Bunt cooly. "That would be the question, wouldn't it?"

The highway, swinging northwestward, cut a course to intersect the north-trending line of the Broken Axle Mountains. This was a low, pale mountain range, the peaks blunt and knuckly, a bony old range rounded down by a million winters.

Yet I seemed to sense a movement, an unrest in their eroded eminences. These old mountains were alive within, were the swarming wombs of uncounted Behemoth Nests, each Nest itself uncountably aswarm. As we drew towards our night's rest in the city of Dry Hole, which lies half in the plain and half in the foothills of the Broken Axle Range itself, it seemed I could almost feel the faint vibration of this activity. We lodged in a hostel in the city's upland half, and here, perched on the mountain's very flanks, I fancied I felt the faintest tremoring through the floor underfoot, and almost heard the sleepless giants rivering through the mountain-bone.

Dry Hole (named for a sap mine that went bust in the days before the place thrived as a cattle town and crossroads of commerce) is a comely city, especially when viewed from the heights. From our hostel we could enjoy the sweep of Dry Hole's rooftops down to the plain, where the Broken Axle River, issuing from the mountains just to the north, stitches its silver thread through the city's outskirts. Most of the feedlots, corrals, tanning yards and slaughterhouses lie along the river, and thus up in the hills we were spared the smell of dung and stale blood, and the flies, that haunt all cattle towns. Not that even up in the hills a certain carnal perfume was lacking, for I nosed a waft of raw hides, of salt meat and new barrels at the picklers' yards, of hay, and the dry scent of dust raised by ten thousand hooves.

We watched the sun sink past the vast, straight prairie horizon, watched the plain's sea of golden grasses blaze fiery copper, then turn amber, then silver, while the window lamps freckled alight all down the slopes, and the lamps on the bridges over the Broken Axle River sparked white above the sword-steel thread of the water.

Then I went to my bed with a will. On the boat last night my brain so blazed with golden ambition I had but a fitful sleep of it, what with the sea, too, restless under me. I lay listening for a while. No sense is more doubtful than the hearing, wherein the thought so imperceptibly becomes the sensation, but I could have sworn the mountain under me faintly hummed. Then I slipped snug into oblivion, like a sheathed sword.

V

High in the peaks She hides the treasure troves
That nest Her newborn spawn as rife as stars,
As numberless as shingles on earth's shores.
Down in the deeps Her warlike daughters rove
Where demons flee them in their bleeding
* droves,*
But high in the peaks, Her sleeping young ones
* are. . . .*

WE SET OUT into the mountains at first light. A viaduct plunged up into the range not far from our hostel; it ran, where needed, on piers or arched bridges, and made a smooth, safe climb of it for our carriage. We rolled amid slopes thinly wooded with black skorse and dwarf-cone: the arid, thin-soiled old mountains were balding, as it were, the peaks and ridgelines bare, polished by steady winds.

Sap-mines were nestled everywhere on the flanks of the heights. They were rather plain, sprawly installations of bleached wood, and conformed to a basic pattern. Typically, they comprised a large central building—which housed the drill site, the pumps, and the barrelling operation—and an array of smaller structures that housed the offices and the miners' dormitories.

They were, on the whole, shabby structures, but their numbers testified to Behemoth's multitudes at work within the peaks. At nightfall, we withdrew from the highway into a ravine to take our rest. I lay in my blanket on the soft sand listening for the thrum of Behemoth's vast business deep in the mountain-bone.

Next day at midmorning we reached Barrelful Heights. This was a nexus of ridgelines and saddles, in whose canyoned and arroyoed flanks half a dozen sap mines flourished. No one knew how many separate Nests sustained these mines. Though more than a mile separated even the closest mines, it was still quite possible that at least some of them fed off a single Nest; any one Nest has dozens of the larval nurseries that are sap's source.

The Superior Sap Mine did not flourish. It stood utterly silent. We walked our team into the main building, and the click of their hooves and the rattle of their harness echoed from the lofty rafters. The building's rear wall was the bare flank of the living mountain, and inset into it were huge brass petcocks, designed to pour the pumped sap into three brazen vats, big as houses. Regiments of casks stood ranked below the vats.

But no one was barrelling. No one was here. The whole plant was void of humanity. In its echoey silence we could hear a faint, drumlike rumor, and after a moment, we were able to identify it: it was the noise of the barrel chutes over in the nearest neighboring mine, a thriving place clear on the other side of the ridge from us.

"Difficulties with his crew," Barnar rumbled bitterly. This was how Costard's letter had described his dilemma to his mother, Barnar's formidable elder sister. She, Anhyldia, with doting faith in her sole issue's every word, had enjoined her brother to supply that youthful paragon with the "fortnight's help or so" that was plainly all

Costard needed to have things "running right as rain again." "Difficulties with his crew," Barnar repeated, his exasperation mounting.

"Dear old Uncle Barnar! Oh, this is a joy!" And in ran the young man in question, hurling himself against my huge friend and hugging him. I had to smile at seeing, in the grizzled granite of Barnar's weathered cheekbones, the crinkling of a smile despite his vexation. Perhaps he was remembering Costard as a loud little boy coaxing him for presents, or demanding a shoulder-ride. Indeed, Costard looked small enough hugging his uncle. He was a trim young man just a handsbreadth less than tall, and just a ten-weight or so more than slight. His hair was short, and shaved in a spiral pattern that was locally modish. Crossing his forehead diagonally was the recent scar of a sizeable laceration. The injury was garish rather than severe, pebbly now with old scab about to flake away. He made his courtesies to me, and we introduced Bunt as a trail-met merchant out shopping for sap.

"Knowing your difficulties," Barnar added, "we told good Bunt here that you might perhaps give him a slightly discounted rate if he would tarry here to be your first customer, once we've gone down and started tapping."

"Absolutely not!" Costard's refusal had startling resonance in the vaulted emptiness. "It's plainly and simply unthinkable that the yield of a mine like the Superior should sell for less that ninety lictors to the ghyll!" Costard uttered this with a level stare, his brows raised, as at a suggested outrage. One sensed that the young man had rehearsed this response for use in any discussion of price. Apparently, Costard favored a very strict Manner and Method when doing business.

The embarrassed Bunt sought only a pretext to abide here until Barnar and I had been underground long enough to execute his secret errand. With five other mines at hand to fill Bunt's sap order without delay, his patience in waiting around here would not seem plausible without some slight bargain on the price. But now the hive-master bleated hastily, "Of course! I have certainly heard the high quality of the Superior's sap most feelingly reported, and will gladly wait for it at your stated price!"

Costard nodded, baffled—even piqued—by this prompt and unconditional compliance. Apparently he yearned to employ some more Manner and Method on this lone petitioner for the product of his paralyzed mine.

"Well," he said, re-collecting himself after a moment. "Let's go to my quarters now for some refreshment!"

The main building of the mine had been thin-walled and drafty, and the deserted barracks which had housed the miners looked still more weathered and ramshackle, but Costard's residence was lavishly carpeted, tapestried, and furnished with very cushiony divans and lounges. He served us delicacies from a gilded salver, describing his labor troubles with rising fervor.

"How did Mama *handle* this crew? I've asked myself a hundred times. They were all such greedy idiots! I tried to make them understand that a wage reduction was an absolute necessity! The current sag in sap prices *demanded* austerities—Another pickled quiffle, Uncle? They're quite delicious, imported from Kolodria!—*demanded* that we suck in our stomachs and tighten our belts, so to speak."

"So the crew decamped in a body, all of them, just like that?" Barnar asked. "Where did they *go*?"

"They actually had the gall to threaten me! To say they'd go work for my competitors!"

"And that's what they did? They are all now employed at other mines?" Barnar's voice was fainter; the extent of his nephew's folly was beginning at last to dawn on all of us.

"And how long will their jobs there last?" Costard snorted with contempt. "I alone have understood long-range trends in the sap market; I alone have seen the need for mine owners to amass large cushions of surplus capital against the harder times ahead! When the Superior is the only operating mine in the region, my workers will return in humble pilgrimage, upon their knees!"

"I see," murmured Barnar. "When you are the only operating mine in the region. . . ." In the following silence, once again we faintly heard the drumlike jostle of barrels being filled in the operation across the ridge.

Had we not come with the lucrative secret enterprise of the giants' pap already in hand, we would have left the doomed Superior Sap Mine then and there, Anhyldia's wrath be damned. This formidable woman was not to be lightly crossed, of course, but she was quite unlikely to cross paths with us. Anhyldia had been touched by a restlessness of middle life, a haunting sense of paths not taken, and two years ago she'd gone a-pirating. Since then she'd sent Barnar several enthusiastic epistles recounting the peace and joy she'd found in hewing heads and plundering merchantmen on the high seas.

But her attention to sap-mining had been wavering even before her setting-forth, and she'd bequeathed to her son a mine that drew from only one larval nursery chamber. Behemoth Nests are subject to what miners call "nest wander;" nursery chambers in use through four or five human generations will, in the mysterious tidal ebbs and fluxes of the Nest's life, be abruptly abandoned. A new nursery chamber is invariably established near the abandoned one, and usually still in range of the mine's "drilling field," its legally owned piece of mountain.

But sinking new gangways and pipelines to the new larval chamber required hard work at great expense, which Anhyldia had not cared to muster, and which her son had been unable to. And now that his own greed and folly had lost him his labor force, and pinched off the flow of his remaining profit, Costard's whole enterprise looked as good as dead.

Barnar and I, with our covert motives, must now do

what we could to prolong the foundering mine's death throes. Through that long afternoon we lounged, gathering strength for the morrow, and suffering Costard to entertain us with his theories on global trade, his views on effective business management, with his opinions on every conceivable subject, in fact. Even the pleasant view of the mountains we enjoyed from his office balcony, and the abundant food and wine he served, could only partly palliate the torment of his monologue.

The urbane Bunt tried now and then to deflect the youth's pontifications into the more adult channels of congenial conversational exchange. At some reference to Behemoth, Bunt ventured, "One can't help but wonder, can one, about the giants' origins? Are they our natural allies, or our offspring? Are they our earth-born benefactors, evolved over time, or are they a living weapon wrought by our ancestors through a thaumaturgy that is now long lost to us? It's a question, I suppose, as old—"

"As all informed people agree," Costard announced, "Behemoths were fashioned by a wizard, of whose name not even an echo now survives." For Costard, the contrived perplexities and feigned bafflements by which polished folk set conversation going were plain and simple entreaties for instruction. Having made this pronouncement, he studied Bunt for any failure to agree; the young man seemed still vaguely nettled by Bunt's earlier acquiescence in the matter of the sap's price.

"Surely, esteemed Costard," Bunt answered, irked in spite of himself, "if it is to the sorcerous hypothesis that you incline, then its proponents generally agree that the great Hermaphrod was Behemoth's creator. His legendary words are often cited: *'Behold my Behemoths, my Watchdogs, Diners on Demonry.'*"

"Impossible." Costard shook his scabbed brow serenely from side to side. The helix of his cropped hair seemed, at this moment, to bring his head towards a point. "I have never heard this name anywhere."[3]

I burst out laughing here, and had to struggle for self-command. I soothed the youth, "Perhaps, good Costard, this is because you have not yet learned all there is to know of the subject."

While scowling Costard struggled to digest this preposterous suggestion, Bunt regained his poise, and resumed the work of self-ingratiation. "Well, whatever those titans' provenance," he offered, searching for a distraction, "your place here in the very heartland of their domain is enviable, good Costard!" He waved an enthusiastic hand at the peaks around us, whose wrinkled barrenness the

---

3. Nifft can be forgiven for the laughter with which he greets this pronouncement of Costard's. A person of any reading at all knows Hermaphrod's name, and he figures in many popular ballads. The following, *Hermaphrod's Vow*, is widely current through both the Lulumean and Kolodrian continents:

A Mage of days forgotten
By subworld spawn assailed,
His left arm sundered, eaten,
Escaped with sore travail.
Then he knelt and swore a vengeance
On the subworld's savage legions:
"Dire jaws that my art fashions
Shall make of ye their meal!

"At this endless feast of titans
Your flesh shall be the meat.
Your bones shall hellfloor whiten—
Still my giants ye shall eat!
They shall your limbs dissever,
And imbibe your blood forever.
Naught can ye from them deliver,
Nor shall their jaws abate!"
——Shag Margold

sun's decline had accentuated with shadows. "These very peaks seem to bulge and buckle with Behemoth's busy energies! Their—"

"We are far from the heartland of their domain," snapped the captious young man. "The great bulk of their Nests lie far below us. Only their highest and most protected chambers lie in reach of the peaks here."

Who is not aware that Behemoth Nests back their way up into the mountains? That their Nest-mouths open in the stony walls of the subworld, where the giants descend to forage and to feed on demonkind, and that their brood chambers and larval nurseries are recessed high into the peaks at the greatest possible remove from the demon realms they ravage? Costard's petulant pedantry at last conquered our efforts at adult discourse. We gave our attention to the wine and viands, and let the youth resume his monologue until we could decently retire.

VI

I met a Titan in the earth
Where Mountain Queen gives endless birth,
And though so terribly She glowered,
Her helpless babe I half-devoured.
And then (I am afraid you'll laugh!)
I met what ate the other half.

WE ROSE well before the sun to make our elaborate
and irksome preparations for our descent into the mine.
While thus engaged, we questioned Costard closely for all
he could tell us about working in the Nest. The young man
had himself done a brief stint of tapping, back at the beginning of his "labor troubles," when he still had a few employees
left to help him topside working the pumps. Naturally we
were eager for the most circumstantial details he could give
us about surviving down in the larval chamber.

But Costard proved evasive; specifically, he avoided
direct answers about the abrasion on his head, which we
felt almost certain he had suffered while he was tapping,
and thus concerned us very closely. At last Barnar lost
his temper.

"Out with it, Costard, at once! Tell us the circumstances, or we abandon you on the instant!" Costard stood blinking and gaping at his uncle's anger. At this point we were all standing at the very mouth of the gangway, which was the narrow, steeply inclined shaft down which we were to ride a wheeled bucket-car to the larval chamber.

Barnar and I were now fully outfitted for tapping, and were both feeling most keenly mortified by the personal indignities this outfitting had inflicted on us. We were near naked, clad only in stout buskins, leathern short-kilts, and bandoliers that bore our gear and weapons. And we were dyed. Our hair, skin, clothing, weapons—every square inch of us—was dyed a screaming-bright orange. We'd had to step into a tub of the tint, like plods into a tick-dip. We had known—who does not?—of this practice. It is only this strange "hole in the eyes" of Behemoth, the giants' perfect blindness to orange (or to the color that orange becomes in the bluish light of the Nest) that makes tapping possible in the first place, and potentiates the whole sap industry. This defect in Behemoth's vision has, time out of mind, profited humankind and their livestock the world over.

But knowing of the dyeing was nothing like suffering it—nothing like standing there at the gangway half naked and pumpkin-hued, gaudy as carnival clowns in the morning light that streamed through the rafters of the mine's main building. To stand thus chagrined and discomfitted, on the very point of being bucketed down a dark shaft to the mountain's bowel—to stand thus on the brink of our peril and still be denied by Costard the information we sought, was too infuriating.

"You will tell us," Barnar boomed, "precisely how you received those abrasions to your head, or we will now and forever leave your mine to its fate! You were picked up, were you not? Though dyed, you were seen, and seized by a Behemoth? Why did this occur?"

"I slipped," said the young man with frigid dignity, "in some larval excrement."

We shortly had the gist of it from the testy young man. Costard, after his little fall in some excreta, had neglected to wash his boots, whose movements then grew visible where the fecal stains obscured their dye. One of the ever-vigilant Nurses who feed and tend the larvae had rushed to devour him as a brood parasite, and Costard had burst his flask of brood scent (a precautionary measure every tapper goes equipped for) at the last possible instant. Doused with this aroma, an unlucky tapper is instantly perceived by a Behemoth as an infant of its own kind, and is tenderly reinstalled among the larval shoals. That Costard had received only such minor lacerations as he suffered was testament to the finesse of a Behemoth's giant jaws in the handling of so relatively minute a morsel as a man.

We found it most vexing that Costard would have allowed his personal vanity to deny us the useful lesson to be drawn from this incident: we must be alert to the danger of casual befoulments of our persons, for such besmirchings had power to make us fragmentarily visible to the titans we robbed.

Too soon arrived the moment when we must step down into the bucket-car, and divest ourselves of sky and sunlight, of winds and rains and stars. But before Barnar slid the hatch-cover over us, he could not forbear a final scolding of his nephew. "Look that you take full advantage of Bunt's generously offered help," he admonished. "We'll have our hands full getting the knack of it below—things must go smoothly up here." Costard's frigid nod was not reassuring. He still regarded Bunt with a look of unappeased distrust, as if the young ass sensed some dissembled opponency in the hive-master's unfailing affability and compliance.

"Look here, Costard," I put in. "Accept the help Bunt offers. You *need* help. Doesn't the failure of this once-great concern—" (and here I thrust an arm up from the

bucket, and swept it at the empty building around us)
"—suggest to you that perhaps you have shown some
ineptness in your management of this mine?"

Costard stood apalled, thunderstruck, his wildest
imaginings outdone by this grotesque suggestion.

"Enough!" boomed Barnar. "Let's be down and have
done. Two weeks, no more, Nephew! Ready, Nifft?"

"I am," I sighed. Barnar pulled shut the gangway door.
The pulleys fed us rattling down into the dark.

The stony sinus that swallowed us breathed a faint
organic stench, a lair-smell that grew stronger the deeper
we sank. Some years before, and some hundreds of
leagues away, Barnar and I had made another trip
together under Kairnish mountains (as recounted in *The
Fishing of the Demon Sea*) and it was an experience we
were both remembering as we stood sinking into that
creaking, rattling darkness.

But now it was decidedly not a demon aura we sank
into. The Nest smell was a more vital fetor that breathed
of fecundity and relentless energies. Our descent felt not
like an infernal entombment, but rather like entering the
domain of deities, where an elemental vitality surged and
swarmed.

When we clanked to a stop we had long expected it, as
the Nest-aura hummed ever more strongly around us, yet
the actual jolt of arrival sent a pulse of fear through me.

There before us was a rectangle delicately outlined
in faint blue light: the hatchway to the larval chamber.
I groped, and found the latch, and thrust the hatchway
open.

Only when I felt the pang of anticlimax did I learn
the pitch of my expectancy. Here were no giants, but
only an equipment-filled nook, a deep natural recess in
what must be the wall of the nursery chamber. Here,
in our operations center, were racks of tools, supply
lockers, bales and boxes of provisions, a pair of ham-

mocks. All were orange like ourselves—or rather, in the pale blue light of this place, were of a smoky, smouldery hue that matched our own.

"Come on then!" I blurted. We all but ran out into the chamber, in haste to front our fears, and have them faced.

Human constructions, even the greatest of wizard-raised manses, are utterly dwarfed by even one chamber of Behemoth's fashioning. A luminescent fungus marbled the walls and limned the chamber's vastness with its cyanic sheen.

Even empty, that great void of chewn-out stone would have stunned us by its scope alone. But filled with that larval trove. . . ? By Crack, Key, and Cauldron! Our hair stood up upon our bodies! Each pale grub was as big as a trading sloop, and shoals of them shimmered in that great lagoon of blue light, their obesities heaped in glossy hillocks, like seadogs sunning on rocks. In the rich gloom, barrel-ribbed and oily-bright, the numberless larvae looked to be exactly what they were: bulging casks of purest nutriment.

"An adult! A Nurse!" Barnar seized my arm and turned me. The Nurse's hugeness swam nearer through the larval sea. She was bigger than an ocean-crossing galleon, and yet so eerily swift and nimble! Her complex jaws—black, antler-like mandibles—were delicately scissoring, mincing some fleshy mass they held. She tenderfooted through the nurslings to a point not distant from us, and thrust the masticated mass down into the supplicant jaws of a grub. The meal would be demon-flesh, of course.

The grub fed greedily. Only the tapering head and tail ends of the grub were capable of moving very much; this one's tail wriggled in sympathy with her busy little black jaws at the other end.

We stood long, and again long, gazing at the Nurses coming and going, and at the Lickers, almost as large, that patrolled the chamber walls, and fed the luminous

Michael Shea

fungus with their saliva. There was an ebb and flux to the ministrations of these adults, who were at times few and far, while at other times scores of them swarmed at once in view, each feeding grubs by the dozens.

The torn demon fragments that these Nurses bore were received, we knew, out in the tunnels from the mighty Foragers who harvested the subworld far below. These piecemealed prey were sometimes still conscious, and gave voice, cackling and jabbering as they were borne to their doom in a larval gut. But, their infernal utterances apart, all this huge life moved in relative silence, with a whispery friction of chitinous abdomens, and a muffled click of tarsal claws on stone.

We gazed and gazed, aghast. The brutal, plundering work we had come here to do seemed to us in those first moments to be the most arrant lunacy imaginable. How dared we slay the babes of such awesome brutes even while they came and went in plainest view? We stood frozen.

When we essayed some movement, we were timorous and tentative in the extreme. We grew bolder by only the tiniest degrees. At length, though, when we had grown confident enough to dance and jig and wave our arms at a Nurse who stood not four rods distant from us, we saw in her eyes' black, faceted globes her utter nescience of our existence.

We could no longer doubt our freedom to begin the awful work we'd come to do for Costard. Only after we had provided him with some sap could we absent ourselves on Bunt's far more lucrative errand. With fear and loathing, then, we turned to the task.

The tap lines, or "suck lines" as they are also called (all eight of them of course dyed orange), radiated like spiderlegs from the drill-hole's port in the chamber ceiling. The lines, at regular intervals along their lengths, were attached to ceiling bolts by tough, elastic tethers. Using a long, hooked pole known as a crook, a tapper could snag and pull down a given line over his chosen larva; when he was done with it and released it, or if it slipped from his control by any accident, the tethers snatched the line safely back up against the ceiling and out of harm's way, for though these hoses were invisible to them, Nurses blundering against them would quickly tear them down in a natural litter-clearing reflex.

Our task, in brief, was to mount a grub with the help of steel climbing spurs, hook a line down from the ceiling, drive home the line's Spike (or "suck-nozzle") into the larval dorsum, and then use the signal cord in our operations nook to tell our partners topside to start pumping.

We disburdened ourselves of our bandoliers of gear, and bore only our weapons strapped to our backs. We awkwardly lashed the climbing spurs to our insteps and calves, and hefted our crooks. "Well. . . ." My voice sounded hopeless, hesitant. "What about that smallish one there? It looks quieter too, less twitchy than the others."

"Good idea," rumbled Barnar. "Start small and easy."

Though by now we already felt deeply submerged in this inhuman realm, we did not truly enter Behemoth's world until that moment when we touched her flesh. The grub's hide was finegrained, translucent, and supple, like oiled parchment to our palms. We slipped and floundered till we learned to drive our spurs home fiercely. I was slow to believe in the young giant's indifference to my steel's negligible bite. Climbing her, I felt her slow, seismic heartbeat, and withal, something else: a gurgly unrest, as of troubled digestion, within her.

At length, we stood unsteady on the grub's dorsal hump; the blubberous footing made us falter, and our first efforts with the Crooks were awkward. But at length we pulled down the nearest suck-line, with the suction spike on its tip. I gripped the line at mid-length to give Barnar a slack end. Two-handed, he raised the Spike high. "All right then," he grunted, and drove it home in the grub's blubbery hide.

Our terrified suspense as to the outcome of this stroke may be imagined, as may the depth of our relief when we felt scarcely a tremor of response in the larva under our feet. Its heart thrummed steadily away; its guts gurgled perhaps a shade more vigorously, but that was the grub's sole reaction to the setting of the spike.

One heartbeat . . . two . . . three thrummed away. We heaved a sigh and grinned at one another—and then I saw Barnar's jaw drop. I turned, squawked with terror, and hauled out Ready Jack from his scabbard between my shoulders.

Almost too late, as a brambly black bug-shape, twice the size of the biggest 'lurk, loomed down on me, fangs high. I swung Jack with not an eyelash of space to spare, and clipped a fang and foreleg from the fearsome larval parasite—for such it was, a Sucking Star, the brood-bag on its abdomen swollen fat with eggs. It retreated scarce one step, rearing high, full of fight, its thorny palps darting for me. The 'Star was not about to quit this host; we had found the parasite with its bag full, just on the point of burrowing inside the luckless larva, there to hatch its eggs hidden from Nurses. With its clutch of eggs ripe and its habitat secured, the monster was not about to retreat. Barnar, freeing the spike and flinging the line ceilingward, swept out his mace, Jolly Breaker, and crippled two more of the Star's left legs. Then, seeing something I did not, he bellowed, "Nifft! Jump!"

I have more than once dodged death by instantly heeding that tone of voice in my friend. I vaulted backwards and trod thin air. We plunged down into the shadows between two neighboring larvae. High overhead, a Nurse's globed eyes peered down. Her jaws plunged and reared aloft again, the Sucking Star between them, a writhing meal that dwindled as those jaws scissored.

But this was the least of the Nurse's sanitary labors. She bent as if to sniff the flaccid grub, her antennae making dainty-quick inquiries. Then with jaws and forelegs she seized up her infested grub and began to devour her outright. The larva hung in that terrible grip, its slack meat like a moon above us that dwindled as we watched, while its rich larval sap drizzled and spattered down to the stone before us.

Such was the remorseless, perfect economy of the Nest, the failed spawn consumed, regathered to the tribal body, not one pulse of energy wasted. The Nurse even lowered her jaws and grazed up the debris from the chamber floor. One of her eyeglobes hovered not five strides away from us. Her eyesight touched us, and possessed us not. When she was done, she rose and sped away.

VII

Where Aim and Act do inadvertent battle,
Unsteady is the hand that robs the cradle!

WE MADE a glum meal in our operations nook: execrable jerky, chalky hardtack, and sour wine. Apparently, the Superior Sap Mine, when it came to its workers' provisions, spared every expense. After this repast Barnar and I took a second stroll along the margins of the larval shoals. Our eyes were now alerted, and we began to discern significant details.

To our more searching gaze, larval parasites proved not uncommon, once we learned their trick of attaching themselves to the shadowed under-surfaces of the grubs. And, as often as not, the parasitized grubs displayed clear symptoms of their affliction: flaccidity, dulled color, deficient size. A further discovery, once we had watched a while longer and strolled a little farther, was that the Nurses not infrequently seized and devoured parasitized larvae which showed these symptoms to a marked degree. This gave us double reason to identify and avoid infested grubs.

After spotting another loathsome Sucking Star, its

brood-bag swollen with eggs, in the very act of eating
its way into its host's flank, I was moved to shudder, and
remark, "Our competitor-parasites are an ugly lot."

"Yet their work has exactly the same result as ours:
an empty bag of larval skin."

"Be as philosophical as you like," I rejoined, "but our
vampirism is in every way more elegant than what these
spiny horrors do. Ugh!"

"Yes. Or at least, our way would be more elegant if
we got around to doing it."

But still we delayed, wandering through the larval
trove, watching. We learned it was well to avoid areas
where the natural nest-litter (larval droppings, and the
feeding debris of such tougher demon parts as horns,
barbs, hooves, spikes, and jaws) had not recently been
cleared up. Nurses were likely to visit these untidy areas
to devour the mess. Similarly, those parts of the chamber's walls where the patches of luminous fungi had most
recently been nourished with the Lickers' spittle gave
off a more robust light; these more visible areas seemed
also likelier to draw Nurses.

Having made these useful observations, we could no
longer delay making our next attempt at tapping. Our
second choice was a large, healthy-looking grub lying in
a litter-free area that was not over-well illuminated, and
was neighbored by equally healthy-looking grubs exhi-
biting no visible parasites.

We spurred our way up her flank with creditable
address, and trod pretty steadily across her dorsal hump.
Determining the exact midline, I marked the spot with
a spur-sliced "X" in her hide. Again our crooks plucked
down the nearest suck-line. Again Barnar lofted the spike,
and drove it home. The larva didn't even twitch. I dogged
down the suck-valve with four little hooked pitons
hammered into the hide.

Tapping protocol now required me to stay on the grub,
standing by the spike-valve and maintaining its security,

while Barnar went back to our operations nook and used the signal cord to call for the pumps to start. I watched him go. I was uneasy standing alone atop the larva, and I kept a restless eye about me. I recalled certain most unsettling descriptions of the Crab Rat, the Sucking Star's chief parasitic competitor for Behemoth broodmeat.

Barnar emerged from the nook, and waved to indicate that it was done, that the pattern of pulls on the signal cord, calling for suction on line three, had been performed, and acknowledged by the appropriate pattern of clicks from Costard.

Long moments passed without event. It was a pause protracted enough to reawaken in me gloomy fears of Costard's incompetence in the above-ground part of the operation. I was about to signal Barnar to repeat his sending, when the suck-line surged powerfully, and the larva shuddered under me.

The pump was geared far too high; it drank with such fierce greed that it deeply dented the grub's dorsum, and threatened my footing—the more so because the galvanized infant began wriggling powerfully. Dropping to all fours to keep from toppling, I bellowed, "Half power! Half power! The grub's throwing fits!"

The instant I'd howled this out, I shrank in fear of what my outcry might draw down on me, coupled with the Nurse-beckoning effect of the grub's convulsions. For half an eternity I clung to that heaving hill of oily flesh.

Then the pump cut off—in time, apparently, since none of the Nurses moving in the distance seemed to be heading my way. Now our victim lay far slacker than she had, almost a quarter diminished in her mass. She still twitched, but far more feebly than before. We waited, Barnar and I, our suspense uniting us across the chamber.

Again the line jerked—recoilingly this time. I stood uncertain for a moment, a sickening suspicion growing swiftly in me. A moment more, and there was no mistaking. The grub was swelling back up—swelling up rapidly, my meaty floor rising underfoot. "The idiot's on blow!" I bellowed. "Reverse pump! Reverse pump! He's got it on blow!"

Again Barnar dove into the operations nook. I scanned the chamber. Had one of those distant Nurses twitched her antennae in my direction? Perhaps not. The larva still swelled alarmingly, lifting me. I knew that the pump's plod-driven bellows were gated to blow out the lines when declogging was wanted. Now the air, at cruel pressure, was a swelling bubble in the larva's innards that crushed out what might remain of her vitality. Her tapered head and tail tremored, and were still. Up, up, up bulged her oily, pliant integument. Already she was half again the size of her largest neighbor.

"Still on blow!" I howled.

"No acknowledgement!" Barnar boomed back to me. "I've signaled four times! *Look* at it, Nifft! Jump, by the Crack! Jump!"

And jump I did, right on the instant. Afterwards, my incompetence was glaringly, comically plain to me. A single swordstroke would have saved the grub, and still left suck-lines a-plenty to work with.

But flustered as I was, I jumped—and at the last possible moment. Before I'd even reached the ground the larva exploded, her dorsum erupting in jagged tatters and a spew of cloudy oils and fatty tissue that sprayed almost ceiling-high, and then came smacking down in loathsome abundance. A great rag of fat fell on me and pinned me to the ground.

I fought up through the weight of my greasy mantle. I had scarcely cleared my face to see about me, when two Nurses filled my little sky, their eyeglobes glinting, their jaws and antennae probing.

Their decision was swift. They instantly fell to devouring every tatter of the burst grub. I lurched to rise, and very plainly I saw that one Nurse *noticed* me. I froze at once, understanding: smeared with tissue, I was a visible piece of moving larva-meat. Moreover, moving or not, I was something to be eaten systematically as soon as the Nurse got to me.

Fixed where I lay, I dared to start scraping—carefully, carefully!—the fat from my face and hair, and then off my neck, and, inchingly, down my chest . . . From the head down I stealthily became orange again, cautiously sculpting off my adventitious larval luster.

All the while the great jaws whickered and clicked and flensed. Seizing, sectioning, sucking in, the Nurse's jaws were the frugal hands of the Nest, gathering in the waste life to stoke the still-living. The impersonal grandeur of it moved me, even in the terror of my predicament. I felt Behemoth and her inscrutable providence all around me, felt the Nest-life like a single spirit filling every tunnel, glinting from every worker's eye, feeding with a million-million jaws.

I had not stripped the last betraying slime from my legs and boots until the Nurses were scouring the very stone beside me for larval tatters, their jaws rattling like weaponry on the rock. Then, a last scrape, and I was up, and diving into the shadows of the larval shoals.

"One more grub," Barnar vowed, back in the nook, as I sluiced myself down with a waterskin. "If that idiot subjects us to the slightest further mishap, we leave forthwith on Bunt's mission." I touched up my coat of dye from one of the flasks with which we were plentifully supplied, and we went forth and made our third pick.

Well versed as I already was in this trade's catastrophes, I felt like a seasoned tapper as we clambered up our next larva's flank, and I marked her midpoint with my spur. We rammed the spike valve home, and dogged it down, then both of us dismounted. "I'm damned," I grumbled, "if I'll 'man the valve' until I see that they can work the pump!" I accompanied Barnar back to the nook and he signalled for half suction on line five.

Comfortably removed from the point of impact of any further mishap, I enjoyed a pleasant, detached curiosity about what the suck-line might do next.

It gave a twitch, a shudder, and went stiff. A little dimple of suction surrounded the spike. The larva shuddered a little, and settled. Her drainage was in progress at the proper, painless rate.

Barnar sighed. "This means, I suppose, that we must set other lines now. Why delay?"

VIII

Begged a demon with many a radiant eye,
"Plant my poor head, and I'll teach you to fly!"

AS A LARVA'S DRAINAGE progresses, and she sags flatter and flatter, she grows more likely to be noted as debris, and consumed by a Nurse. A tapper might set one grub draining, then go spike a second, even a third, but by then he had to go unhook his first set before it got perilously flat-looking. We were constantly climbing up and down the huge babes, and the work was extremely tiring. When we took our first sleep we'd drained only seven.

Though dead weary, I hung sleepless a while in my hammock. When a man lacks that glimpse of stars or moon that makes him feel it is truly night, then sleep seems to him an airless, casketed state, and his soul slips less willingly into it. Now and henceforth, of course, "night" would be merely a synonym for exhaustion, and "day" would mean the longest stretch of time we could work before dropping.

Unspeaking we hung there. At any other such time, pausing together on the brink of sleep, Barnar and I would have talked, lazily tossing our thoughts back and forth till one of us fell off oblivion's edge. Our silence now I understood too well. The terrors of the Nest were met and managed. Today's first fruitful labors proved we could work down here and win what we sought from Behemoth. The giants' pap now seemed far more obtainable, and we hung silent, remembering that in the matter of our coming wealth, our ambitions had utterly parted ways.

Six hundredweight of gold, our combined shares, could just suffice for Barnar's great vision. It would buy the Witches' Seed, and the little fleet to ship it from Strega (darkest of the Astrygals in lore and sorcerous resource). What was left would pay the same witches for the loan of a gryph-gryph, for this monster must micturate on each and every Witches' Seed as soon as it has been sledge-hammered into the earth; lacking these effusions, the virtue of the seed remains immured, and the tree will not leap forth. The six hundredweight would also just cover the cost of hiring a troop of bog Ghuuns (from Strega's nightmarish swamps) to control the gryph-gryph, to bring the monster constant drink, and to hold it shackled to its work.

On my side it was the same. However obscenely rich we shortly grew by means of the great Pelfer's Buskins, Cowl and Gantlets, our outlay in the first instance must be huge. We could not hope to cross the Cidril Steppes without three hundred men-at-arms, with enough engineers among them for deploying heavy weaponry on the march, and for doing siege work when the Tomb was reached. Men of the quality we must use, and for the time we must have them, would cost no less than four hundredweight to keep them loyal. Added to this must be the cost of the ships to carry them; then there was the cost of shipping them, from the Great Shallows (where the best recruiting was), thence through the Taarg Straits, and thence eight hundred leagues north, across the Sea of Cidril.

We must act together to fulfil either dream. And, shackled as we were by the finitude of our expected fortune, we could not help but brood, neither able to forget that the other had gravely vowed to undertake his project. With equal ire, we felt each other in default; we had both put second a deed we had sworn to make our prime concern.

Ever more smoothly and skilfully did we set our larvae draining: fifteen on our second day, eighteen on our third. At that day's end we took some wine and hardtack and had a strolling meal, supping and wandering the chamber at large; it was a practice which, for one, helped divert us from our provisions' vile taste, and, two, which constantly added to our knowledge of our hosts.

We were agreeing, with some complacency, that we really had the hang of this work now, and could call ourselves pretty tolerable tappers, on the whole, when Barnar interrupted himself to cry, "Look there!"

A flux of larval feeding was just then tapering off—an after-ripple, no doubt, of a wave of Foragers returning to the Nest with their plunder. Everywhere the larvae's jaws worked furiously with a wet noise of mastication. This meaty murmur was embellished by demon utterance, muttered or shrill, as tough subworld entities surrendered fragment by fragment to larval greed. What had caught Barnar's eye was a huge chunk of torso, a blackish meat marbled with veins of incandescent green, which still writhed in the jaws of the Nurse that staggered under its mass. The size of the creature it had been bitten from must have been immense.

"The Foragers are surely dire indeed," I murmured, "to have slain whatever that was part of." We had been told, of course, that members of the Forager caste were made on a scale that dwarfed all other workers.

"You there! Hu-u-umans! Help me!"

Barnar and I spun around. Another Nurse was just

then passing behind us, and for a dizzying instant it seemed that this giantess had hailed us with this reedy outcry. But after an instant's stupefaction, we saw that the voice proceeded from the wad of mangled demon-meat which she bore in her jaws.

From a hash of several demons chewed into one pulpy ball, there thrust out the head, shoulders, and one writhing limb of a still-living demon whose body had been mangled in with the others. It was this creature whose warbly voice accosted us. His head was encrusted with an opulent jewelry of eyes, whose glint pierced the fungal gloom as he was borne past us. "Stalwart tappers! L-u-uminous Heroes! Save me, and I will make you rich past the wildest dreams of avarice!"

Barnar and I exchanged a look. Did I appear as startled, as nakedly greedy, as he did? We both hastily assumed suitably grave and skeptical countenances. "What else would it say, after all?" I noted.

"Of course!"

"Still," I prevaricated, "As the old saw has it: 'Who knows the bournes of demon pelf?'"

"... 'Neither Man nor demon self.'" Barnar finished, nodding. So we trotted after the Nurse, reassuring each other we would merely indulge our curiosity by inquiring of the demon precisely what he was offering.

"We should keep firmly in mind," I urged, "that we already have a wildly lucrative enterprise in hand. We must not be seduced by desperate promises. Because almost surely, whatever this demon has to offer, the payment will lie in the subworld and will somehow involve our carrying him thither."

"Precisely," Barnar nodded. "On the other hand . . . what can be lost by interrogating this demon? His kind are studious of Behemoth lore. Demons know their conquerors in detail. We may learn a bit, if nothing else."

"Let's hurry, then," I said. "It looks like it'll have two grubs on it."

The Nurse had bestowed her burden between two larvae, which mouthed up to it on either side. The eye-jewelled demon writhed on the crest of this food-lump, his broken hindquarters inextricably anchored in the mass. His limb (a tentacle with a three-clawed tip) desperately signaled us. His mouth was a membranous vent in his throat, whence once more came his ululant voice. "Quick! Oh quickly, Exalted Ones! Wealth past telling I promise you! Oh, hurry! If they eat my head, I'll be blind!"

"That sounds highly probable," I told the demon. The Nurse had left—we had a clear field of action. "But I'm afraid we must require you to define precisely what you mean by 'wealth past telling.' And you'd best be quick about it, I think."

The demon gaped a moment. His eyes were a wild mix, each distinctly charactered, and a little multitude of individually evil minds looked out from these mixed eyes. His mouth-vent moaned, and then renewed his reedy plea:

"The Unguent of Flight! I can put in your possession the Unguent of Flight! If I prove to lie, feed me back to these brutes!"

Who would not have called us credulous, in acting as we then did? But what *is* great luck, if not highly unlikely? We advanced on the food-clump, sword and axe drawn. "Oh yes!" the demon cried. "Cut me free at the ribs! Oh, hurry!"

I reached the demon my left arm, which he powerfully gripped. The sucking larval jaws now scissored quite close to him from either side. I pulled him outward, and Barnar chopped through his chest's mangled axis with one shearing stroke of Old Biter.

We took our demonic fragment to a little recess in the chamber wall and laid him on the stone. The bleeding stump of his amputation scabbed over almost as we spoke, and in moments his stump was sheathed

in a tough, dry bark. Head and shoulders, one limb—
he lay there and glittered up at us his eyes of a hundred
different beings, a hundred alien hungers. His mouth-
vent, moist and urgent, pleaded, "Plant me! Just plant
me, anywhere in subworld soil. I'll root! The Unguent
of Flight, in return, is easy to be had, and not deep in
the subworld at all, by a safe path I know." Barnar and
I shared a knowing look here. The demon grew more
urgent. "Bear me for your guide, oh Radiant Ones, and
I will give you power to swim the air! I am your hum-
blest, most abject servant, your doting Ostrogall by
name!"

Well, sure enough, here was the proposition we'd
foreseen: a quick little journey down to the nest-mouth,
and out into the subworld. And for what prize now? The
Unguent of Flight, a priceless treasure in itself, and a
ready means to further wealth! The sheer, mad unlike-
liness of the prospect perversely made me feel it might
be genuine.

"We can promise no more than to think it over," I
answered our truncated interlocutor, this abbreviated
Ostrogall. "You will have to abide our leisure to consider
your proposition, and in the interim you must vow to
cause no mischief."

Ostrogall fervently agreed. He then set to slathering
us with effusive flattery, and though he was silent at our
command, his vigilant presence, riding in a loop of my
loosened weapons belt, still compromised our sense of
privacy. Thus, when we returned to our operations nook,
I popped Ostrogall (with his effusive assurances that he
would be "quite comfortable") into a stout leather supply
bag, and hung this from a peg on the wall.

IX

Through years and years a young lad flees
And whips his team that breasts the seas.

WE SAGGED into our hammocks, and into the silence
that had grown our habit at this hour. But tonight we
could almost hear each other's minds racing. "How
chances multiply, sometimes," I ventured, "and set us
branching off from our first intent!"

"Aye. Though surely we must stay on the branching
that leads to the Royal Brood Chamber, and the giants'
pap, for there our least doubtful fortune lies?"

"Of course! But in this pattern of constantly emergent
opportunity . . . I feel something here I scarcely dare
put into words, Barnar. I feel Our Time is coming!"

"By Crack, Key and Cauldron, Nifft, you speak my
very mind!" We both sat upright in our hammocks now.
Barnar's eyes revealed to mine a glint of cautious glee.
"We've both been feeling it, haven't we?" he went on.
"Here and now has come to us that truly golden moment
in our professional lives. When we came down through
that gangway—nay, when we first contracted to help my

feckless nephew, with that first inauspicious step—we passed through that Door that is only once opened to a craftsman in all his life. Luck herself invited us down here under the earth, and down here, Luck means to do us well beyond our power to imagine!"

"I have felt the same, old friend," I solemnly answered. "The very same."

One must not speak too much aloud of Luck, most especially when She hovers nearest, but when we'd lain back again, Barnar could not forbear giving his suppressed excitement some vent in speech. "Suppose we get even a little luckier than what we now contemplate? Say we made just one or two hundredweight more than six hundred? With eight hundredweight, we could forest the heights and the barrens as well as my clan's holdings, just as you said, Nifft. Then, if the Ham-Hadryan, and the Magnass-Dryan clans should, through some accord, unite their endeavors, our mills would reap such wealth from Shallows' shipyards, (See Shag Margold's Interjection) that your venture to the Tomb of Pelfer could be undertaken within a twelvemonth's time."

I was stung to find him still so placidly putting in second place the glorious exploit that I burned to undertake. "We would be prudent, I think," I sneered gently, "to bank nothing on the desperate promises of a demon. Lucky we may feel, but we might not prove so, stumping down to the subworld with that polyocular abomination tucked under one arm."

"I mean only," Barnar said patiently (but I could tell he was stung in turn), "that opportunities seem to be opening to us at every turn, and among them may well come something which makes us richer yet."

I was not of a mind to answer. After a moment, Barnar said, "Let me tell you a story, Nifft, about a man we both know—a man who is dear as a brother to my heart. This man is called Nifft the Karkmanhite, but though Karkmahn-Ra, Jewel of Pardash, herself the Queen of the Ephesion

Chain, is his chosen home, he was in fact born at the little harbor of Ladrona Bay on Samadrios, a lesser Ephesion and the southernmost isle of the Chain."

"Spare me," I complained, though I knew he must have his turn.

"Winds from the glacial maelstroms frost Samadrios' southern shores," Barnar resumed, "but little Ladrona with her cosy bay on the isle's northern coast had a brisk but temperate clime, and bustled with trade. Ladrona's dire fate in the end was conversely the making of Nifft. To know the man, you must know the boy who saw that city's death.

"His family ran a harborside hostel, and it was Nifft's fortune on the morning of his city's death to have driven his father's wagon up into the hills on the weekly trip to the brewery. The lad had taken on the casks of ale and small beer he had been sent for, and had just started along the ridge road back down to the harbor, when he felt the earth jolt under him. The whole island did several sharp dance steps on the ocean floor, and the wide sea around it convulsed like flesh that shudders.

"The lad stood amazed, fighting the reins of his rearing team. And then he saw the ocean rise into a single mountain of infinite width, and march toward his world.

"Now he lashed his team on again, plunging down harborwards, while his unbelieving mind still hung behind him, hawklike on the sky, beholding the sea's vast, glittery onslaught. In his blind haste it insanely seemed to him that if he just reached home before the wave smote it—if he could just burst into the hostel and cry, 'Father! Mother! The Ocean is coming!'—if he could just reach them with a warning, then the disaster would be halted.

"He was still high in the hills when the great maw of foam thunderously swallowed Ladrona Bay at a gulp. Still Nifft lashed his mad team downward, as if moved by the same unstoppable fury as moved the sea. As the road crossed a little upland valley, the leaping sea came avalanching up over the ridge and snatched him, wagon and all, up into a boiling cauldron of weedy brine.

"For long, unbelievable moments his team crested the boil and dragged his wagon through it, he wielding his whip like Benthodagon in his sea-chariot of Aristoz legend. It was the wave's highest reach; it receded, leaving in the valley a salt lake where, nostrils flaring, eyes glaring, the team at length drowned and dragged the wagon down, and Nifft, a lifetime older than he had been seconds earlier, swam dazedly to higher ground.

"Ladrona was scoured from the shore. Not even the foundations of his family's hostel remained. Not long after this, Nifft apprenticed himself to a travelling acrobatic troupe, and he has never once returned to the isle of his birth. But perhaps it is equally true to say that he has never left that foaming lake in the hills above drowned Ladrona—has never ceased lashing his team through the waves, to stay ahead of drowning.

"For when has Nifft ceased from wandering? When has he ceased to push restlessly from exploit to exploit? Whatever he has, he seeks always a further prize. And it is with just this in mind that his good friend, Barnar Ham-Hadryan, urges him: at some point even the greatest craftsmen must say of someplace: *Here I will abide—this place I will cherish as my own.* For what will Pelfer's Buskins and all the rest bring, but further wandering, further seeking? Whereas on Chilia, in my natal mountains, we have a paradise to resurrect, and then, inhabit!"

I had to endure in patience a ploy I'd used myself, but I was hard put to hold my tongue. When I answered, I struggled to hide my irritation. "Isn't it enough, Barnar, that we first vowed to seek Pelfer's Tomb, and that my vow of the Witches' Seed came second? Can we not lay this painful controversy to rest on this simple principle of priority?"

"Come to that, Nifft, why should not the more recent undertaking be the more binding?"

Discussion was useless. Silence fell again on us. Out in the nursery chamber echoed the whicker and whisper of huge chitinous legs most delicately a-dancing, and the sounds of grubs wetly mouthing, and of demons faintly crooning their annihilation. The murmur of the Nest's mighty life gradually, gently rubbed my thoughts away, and I sank into sleep.

But some time later, from the deeps of that sleep, a little noise tickled me awake. I lay for a moment listening to it. When I stealthily arose, I found that Ostrogall had got his whole limb thrust out of the mouth of his bag; his industrious little claws had almost untied the bag's binding.

I roused Barnar and we held judgement over the fractional demon. His gush of verbose apology was silenced by Barnar's gesturings with his axe.

"Already you have abused our trust," I told Ostrogall. "You now swear you will suffer any punishment to reinstate our tentative agreement. Very well. We must insist on precaution. You must be quit of that remaining limb of yours if we are to keep you here in our quarters. If this is unacceptable to you, we will be glad to return you to those grubs."

Ostrogall scarcely paused. "Agreed! Agreed, if it must be! I need only my neck, and just a bit of chest to be planted by, but that's quite enough, as long as you *will* plant me. I humbly accept the precaution. Just give me a fair hearing on the matter of the Unguent when you are so inclined. Question me, and I swear you will be persuaded. And once you are aloft—once, Oh Effulgent Ones, you have the Unguent, and are soaring at will high up among the winds, you will bless the day our paths crossed down here. You will see, my Benefactors!"

So he extended his limb, and Barnar lopped it off. We returned him to his bag, bound this double tight, hung it high, and went back to our hammocks, and our interrupted sleep.

X

Who goeth to the Mother's breast
Of greater Life to sup,
Oh, tread ye nimbly through the Nest!
Oh, firmly grip thy cup!

EARLY ON OUR FOURTH DAY in the chamber, I teetered atop a half-deflated grub, waiting to free the valve and ease the line back up to the ceiling. As the grub gently, steadily sank under me, I gazed over the larval shoals. Barnar, returning from signalling for suction on this our third larva of the day, came climbing up to keep me company.

"It's more than a momentary flux," I told him. "I'll swear it! The place is . . . seething! Look where one comes for the empty already." A Nurse, just a spearcast off, loomed down to devour the plundered bag of our second larva of the morning. The whole chamber bustled with activity; feeding was going on everywhere. Nurses and Lickers sped in every direction. We'd found things in this state on our awaking, and for hours now the spate had not slackened.

Barnar agreed. "It's all the pupae that impress me most. It has to mean a . . . population surge, does it not?"

We stood thoughtful as the grub deflated. What else could it mean? On our first days here we only occasionally saw the pupae carried out by Nurses. Pupae were constantly forming; matured, full-fed grubs grew quiet and developed a thick sheen of exudate which, in a day or so, hardened into the pupal husk. These pupae were carried off by Nurses to the eclosia (so we had been told), where the callows would hatch and be nursed up to adult size.

But now, any time and anywhere we looked, we saw more pupae being carried out. Correspondingly, new larvae were being incessantly brought in from the Incubaria. Barnar hesitated, before adding, "Our friend in the bag is most urgent for an audience with our effulgent selves. While I was signalling just now he was wheedling me through the leather, telling me there is a very 'significant stir' in the Nest."

This awareness in the demon-nub, bagged as he was, reminded us that demonkind possessed valuable insights into Behemoth's ways. "Well," I suggested, "let's go back and chat with him." We untethered the suck-line from the empty we stood on, and went back to the nook.

Hanging blind in his bag, still Ostorgall was aware of us, though we approached quietly to test him. "O Effulgent Ones! Dare I address you? Dare I share with you my humble concern for your safety?"

What could we lose by hearing his gambits? Unbagged and propped on a ledge, Ostrogall looked as healthy as ever. His recent amputation was smoothly and toughly scabbed over. An oily light of alien solicitude sparkled in his hundred eyes.

"Gentlemen, only my fears for your safety make me thus importunate, for is not your salvation also my own? As my liberation is your enrichment? I urge only this: if you mean at all to travel through the Nest, then undertake it boldly and at once, for past all doubt, I sense some great business is astir in this Nest. A yeasty ferment is at work, their numbers grow—I feel it! And at such times, sirs, the corridors thunder with traffic, and grow ever more perilous for travellers of our slight size!"

"You seem to imply," I answered, "that our carrying you down to the subworld is a settled thing, but I, for one, am far from decided. Tell me this, Ostrogall: Do the Younger Umbral's verses, describing the Flight of Forkbeard, accurately represent the Unguent as being obtained by squeezing certain tubers grubbed up from the garden of a giant swamp-waddle?"

"Forgive me," meekly fluted the demon-nub, "but I really cannot say."

"You really can't say?" Barnar raised his brows. "What of Cogiter's dactyls? Do these rightly report the Unguent as being the product of a hirsute, odoriferous fruit that grows on the walls of caverns in the floor of the primary subworld, as expressed in the couplet: 'Deep grottoes papilla-ed with bulbulous swellings—Fruits better for squeezing and draining than smelling'?"

"I must, with inexpressible regret," Ostrogall faintly piped, "profess myself powerless to respond to your query."

"Well, what *can* you tell us then?" I urged. I seized him up by the neck stump and we went out into the open chamber with him. "I so far find no reason not to tuck you back into the larval jaws from which we so imprudently plucked you! What think you, Barnar? Which one looks hungriest to you?"

"Gentle saviors! Sagacious paladins!" Ostrogall bleated. "I can do no other than cling to my sole poor means of purchasing your aid. Men of your bold make would dare the place without my guidance if you knew where and how to look."

"That grub over there," Barnar suggested, "looks extremely hungry. See how she works her jaws? We want the demon's end to be quick as possible of course—we're not cruel men. Let's pop him in there."

"If you are bent on doing so, Masters, I must suffer it," the demon cried. "The grub's loathsome gut will reduce me to a mash of quaternary spores, which will escape in its fecal matter. By little and little, some of these spores of mine will be tracked out in the tunnels, and thence to the subworld floor. It will take perhaps a century before I seed, and root, and bloom, and see again, but I will bear this long blindness if I must!"

In the end we rebagged him. Why not hang him up blind for a while, and see if his attitude evolved? Moreover, in the last analysis, we did not feel his desperate reticence was wholly out of character for one who had a true treasure to protect.

At the same time, Ostrogall had succeeded in persuading us, though not to the quest he craved. He had convinced us of the danger of this rising pulse in the Nest-life, this fermentation. If we were to explore at large, it must be done now before this tempo grew any quicker. Costard must rest content with the sap we'd sent him. We must be off on our own greater mission, for two jarsful of juice worth three hundredweight of gold.

Our equipage was soon assembled: our arms, oiled and sharpened, strapped to our backs; two bandoliers each, these hung with some provisions, but primarily laden with dozens of the little skin bladders of orange dye that all tappers carry on their belts for touch-ups of their invisibility. We brought a large surplus of these, for splashes of the dye on the walls of the Nest tunnels could also serve us as path markers. In addition we had two hundred ells of tough, limber climbing-line each, and, most to the point, two leathern amphorae, stoutly lidded, discreetly provided us by Bunt for filling with the giants' pap.

When all was ready, Barnar sent the "pause-for-rest" code on the signal cord. No simple acknowledgement came back, but rather an impatient clatter of inquiry. We disdained to answer, but we did grow mindful of the gold in our lockless provisions chests, should bumptious Costard be moved to come down if we were long on our errand. So we staggered a half mile or so along the chamber wall with our wealth, till we found a safe nook to bury it in.

And so we stepped for the first time out into a Nest tunnel. We stepped out cringing, recoiling in advance from monstrosities which . . . did not materialize. We stood in high-vaulted emptiness, scanning a cerulean gloom that yawned away in both directions.

"Well," said Barnar, "let's be off. What *is* the slope, would you say? It looks dead level here." We were concerned in our explorations always to move up-slope, following the principle that Behemoth's most protected chambers lie highest in the mountains. By this reasoning, the Royal Brood Chamber must lie at the Nest's apex, above even these lofty strata of the larval chambers.

"Doesn't this way seem just fractionally. . . ?"

"Yes, I suppose so. Let's cover ground while it's clear like this." We were off at a jog-trot, squirting arcs of dye every few rods against the gallery walls. The emptiness of the tunnel grew ominous, almost unbearable. Then . . . was that a tremoring underfoot? "Barnar, do you feel—"

"By Crack, Key and Cauldron!"

"Dive into this crevice!"

Thus began our introduction to the larger worker castes. That first one—for we came to recognize their features with some repetition—was a Digger, with huge, blunt, earth-breaking jaws. Its body had half again the bulk of a Nurse's. In moments, the unnatural void that had greeted our entry was obliterated by the thunder of repeated passings. Diggers, Sweepers, Carriers (whose immense crops made them provision-vessels to other castes), the colossal size of all these workers was only half their impact. Their speed was the other half—their speed and their reckless elan. Two workers running abreast might charge headlong at three others oppositely bound, and none would hesitate a jot. All of them would thunderously merge, and sunder, with not a bristle's width to spare, their glossy flanks whickering with glancing frictions, their giant, sharp-kneed legs pumping miraculously free of entanglement. Incessantly though these thunderous mergings occurred, they did not fail to awe us every time.

Equal to the awe of their onrush was the awe of their stopping. It seemed impossible such hugeness could come to such precise and absolute a halt as these giants could when confronted with a fellow worker's begging. We learned that an individual of any caste could detain any other by bowing, as it were, and, in a crouched posture, twiddle her antennae in a ritualized gesture of supplication. The accosted one then either shared with the beggar food she carried in her jaws, or regurgitated into the beggar's mouth the macerated nourishment she carried in her crop. By such exchange, of course, does a subworld harvest reach every hungry one of a Nest's million mouths.

These sudden pauses in the flux threatened our rhythm, and we learned not to slow down for anything—to run hard when we were in the clear, to read tremors through our footsoles, and to dive sharp or shin quick up a veining in the wall at the very first vibration of oncomers. We learned to guess the numbers and course of these oncomers, and move decisively before the danger was in view, for by then it might well be too late.

After what we judged a couple miles of this, we rested in a fissure, and took wine. "I'm damned . . ." Barnar said, breathing hard, "if I can tell for sure . . . but I think we're bearing . . . *down*slope."

" . . . this run-and-stop rhythm . . . I can't be sure either . . . but I agree."

We lay catching our breath a moment. Giants thundered

past. A few sour draughts of wine caught fire in our racing
blood. Courage blazed in us.

"Shall we retrace and try the other way then?"

"Why not? You know, Barnar, if this is the worst of
it, I think we can manage it."

"Aye to that and aye again! Look—here's a Licker."
She danced bobbingly towards us, mouthing the fungal
fur along our stretch of wall. We knew to sit still, our
crevice being sunk in a fungal bald patch. High as a
galleon's bowsprit, the Licker reared above us her spittly
kiss, the arched buttresses of her legs bracketing us in
that moment like some mighty temple's nave. Then she
danced on.

"Think, Nifft!" Barnar growled fervently. "With such
spawn as these, what must the Queen's dimensions be?"

We set to jogging back the way we'd come. "What if
she prove too big for mounting and milking?" I asked.
"What if we can't climb her? Is it not . . . serendipitous
how the Unguent, if it be real, would answer so perfectly
to this need? Surely we could turn the trick of getting
the pap if we were airborne."

"I tell you, I too feel the itch of that very thought,
Nifft! Ostrogall of course has every motive to lie uncon-
strainedly."

"Well . . . we must question him closer once we get
back."

Loping along pretty briskly now, we were feeling more
attuned to these tunnels with each stride. All at once we
sensed the tremor of a very big weight approaching, and
we looked sharp for shelter. A natural ridge of quartz
ribbed the tunnel wall just ahead of us.

"Let's shin up that!" I said. We swarmed our way up
it just in time to get above a fast-moving Sweeper who
veered under us. But even as we sighed relief, here,
oppositely bound, there surged titanically towards us a
Forager.

We were almost unhinged—it was the first we'd seen.

Still we kept our grips, and scrambled desperately higher, to get above her hugeness. Her jaws alone were half the size of a Nurse! Since the onrushing Sweeper never altered course, the Forager arched up accommodatingly on her legs, while the Sweeper crouched slightly and rushed right under her.

Unluckily, as the Forager lifted herself in this maneuver, she glanced against the tunnel wall just under us. The shock wave plucked us clean off the rock, and we plunged down toward the Forager's vast back, our hands and feet clawing thin air in a desperate, futile bid to be elsewhere, anywhere other than where we fell to.

Shag Margold's First Interjection

A LITTLE MORE than a decade before the time of this present narrative, Nifft and Barnar endured a subworld sojourn in the Demon Sea, to which Nifft alludes when they ride the bucket down the gangway. During that infernal submersion among demonry, the pair acquired the friendship-till-death of the shape-shifter Gildmirth of Sordon, whom they set at liberty from durance in that vile abyss.

Some five years after, and about as long before this present business, Nifft and Barnar had acquired—in the Great Shallows, at a gaming table in one of the raft-cities of the Hydrobani—a little flat-deck yawlp. With this and some rented harpoons, they went out next morning a-sculping. Towards mid-day, they harpooned (as they thought) a particularly large and fine-looking sculp. It was a solid hit, and took the barb deep, and they were already congratulating themselves on a very profitable venture. Then their sculp melted into the form of a giant marine reptile, who held their bloodless harpoon in one claw, and towed them for a long and merry ride through the Shallows, skimming at incredible speed above those

77

gorgeous reefs all aflame with life and color. The pair could neither quit nor cut the harpoon cable. They ceased to try when the reptile began to sing and warble melodiously in an unknown tongue as it towed them through their crazy course. Long before Gildmirth melted down to his true form, and climbed dripping aboard, they had guessed him for who he was.

From this merry, chance meeting of friends, weighty events developed which, while they may concern us elsewhere, cannot detain us here. But it was on this occasion that Nifft heard from Gildmirth a highly particular account of Pelfer the Peerless' tomb, and of the Buskins, Cowl and Gantlets buried there with that arch-thief. These Supreme Facilitators of Felonious Appropriation are of course a by-word through the world at large; even the uncouth upland brigands of the Ingens Cluster swear by the "boots, hood and gloves of the Pilferer."

But it was Nifft's and Barnar's rare luck to hear the full and detailed truth of the matter from Gildmirth of Sordon, and what they learned enflamed their imaginations. The Buskins are popularly credited with conferring everything from the power of flight to the power to run faster that the eye can follow; in fact, my friends learned, they confer the Blessing of Bounding Absquatulation, by which is understood the power to make one-league leaps. Escape, to the thief shod with Pelfer's Buskins, is never in doubt.

The Cowl is loosely deemed to confer invisibility. In fact, they learned, it confers on its wearer the Blessing of Circumambient Similitude, or an identity of aspect to the wearer's immediate surroundings, however complex. The Cowl's function is best illustrated in the tale told of Pelfer, when he had penetrated the Art Trove of UrrGurr the Grasping. That ghastly Elemental surprised Pelfer in the very midst of his Trove, but discerned him not, for the thief, beCowled, bore a simultaneous piecemeal resemblance to no less than three of that age's great masterworks in oils: Goob's *Battle of Trumpet Plains*, the *Smiling Mimostula* by Phasri Pedofilaster, and Quonsonby's epoch-making *Still Life with Rumkins and Prooms*. From this the finesse of the Cowl's power may be surmised.

As for Pelfer's Gantlets, they confer the Blessing of Loosened Locks upon the hands they ensheathe. With regard to these Gantlets, the popular conception does not so much err as fall short. Gloved with these, the thief's touch will cause any obstacle—lock, wall, weighty door, or mass of earth—to fall asunder, so be this obstacle interposed as a barrier between the thief and the prize she craves.

From this, the fervor of Nifft's mercenary motive will be readily understood. A thief accoutered as great Pelfer was, would soon abound in wealth.

But Barnar, on his side, cherishes no merely sentimental enterprise. His family feeling, and his romantic interest in a certain beauty of the Magnass-Dryan clan, are foremost in his motives, of course. They cause in him an intransigence to match the force of Nifft's greed for Pelfer's Facilitators. But dense-wooded Chilia lies of course in the Great Shallows, just off the mainland of the Kolodrian Continent. And, like that forested Kolodrian coast, Chilia serves the timber needs of the Great Shallows—a vast broth of cultures and of thriving trade, populous with vessels of all makes. Shallows' boatyards are a bottomless maw for lumber. When the saw-mills of Barnar's clan howl at full capacity, they turn a golden harvest, and Chilite tree-jacks with lush mountain holdings, though their palms be hard with doing their own axework, grow seriously rich.

—Shag Margold

XI

Now saddle my mount, I am riding to plunder
The Ur-hoard encoffered in caskets infernal!
Swift my mount bears me, her footfall as
thunder,
Where hell sweats its lucre in fever eternal!

THE HORROR of being on the Forager's back made us stagger and stumble at first, now to port, now to starboard, where her legs pumped in their high-kneed ranks. But we found that our footing was not really difficult, no harder than finding your sea-legs on a big vessel that is riding a steady swell. I mean a big vessel indeed, though, for the biggest galleon we ever shipped on was less than half her size. Her abdomen bulged sternward and we could not see its tip; the immense bowsprit of her jaws loomed half eclipsed beyond her head's great spheroid. The blue-litten walls tore past us, blurred to the look of sea-foam with the speed of her passage.

"Dye!" Barnar shouted—and the sense of it brought my wits back to me. We rushed as near as we dared to her pumping legs, I to port and Barnar to starboard, and

from our bottles of dye jetted out arcs of pigment against
the streaming tunnel walls. These little banners of liquid
we ejected grew tattered as they fell, torn by our velocity.
Just so would our bodies be if we leapt or fell while
moving at this rate; we would at the very least break our
legs.

"If she's begged for food and she stops," I shouted
back over my shoulder, "jump on the instant!"

"Do you think her crop is full?" Barnar shouted back
after a heartbeat's pause. Amid the confusion of the
rushing walls and the flaring cyanic fungi like sea-foam
cut by a swift keel, the question hung full of significance
in the air between us. If her crop was full of demon
harvest, our Forager would be returning from forage, and
could well be bound to our very own destination: the
Royal Brood Chamber. If, on the other hand, her crop
were empty, she might equally well be bound to the
subworld, to re-fill it.

For a dreamlike, indefinite time, we sped along poised
on this uncertainty: If another worker begged food of
us, and our Forager's crop proved full, then *should* we
jump down? Might she not go on up with her offering
to the Queen?

But all too soon, our descent grew unmistakable.
"Downslope she goes!" Barnar cried needlessly, as
suddenly the pitch grew steeper. No other Behemoth
detained us, nor would, we saw. Her nestmates would
sense our mount's emptiness.

We dared not let the horror of where we were going
slacken our sinews. Complex branchings of the tunnels
flowed unpredictably past us, and at such intersections
we must spray a frenzied profusion of dye, not to miss
our turning when—luck grant it!—we might come
trudging back. Dispensing dye like dervishes, we fren-
ziedly blazed our path, as our Forager, unaccosted by
any oncomer, thundered on down to the mountainroot.

Our descent was long enough to astonish us with the

Nest's immense extent, yet so inexorably were we carried
whither every fiber of our souls recoiled from being, that
it seemed no time at all before I was crying out, "Can
we doubt any longer? Do you see ahead there? A red-
dening of the light?"

"Yes!" Barnar's voice seemed to mourn, and I know
he, with me, experienced an irrepressible qualm of pure
loathing, a slither of revulsion climbing up and down the
spine.

"I suppose," I called, wanly attempting optimism, "we
could scarcely go down there any better guarded than
we are."

"No doubt," Barnar boomed glumly.

"Ah, look there now friend! We're close! Hammer in
some pitons—let's string some rope to hold by!"

Convergent tunnels had broadened to a mighty gallery
which was flooded with an ever redder light. Now another
Forager ran to port of us, two more to starboard . . . and
now we ran amidst a thundering flux of Foragers, an
outsurging armada of rampant titans. Kneeling, we hammered into the ragged, tough chitin of our Forager's
dorsum several of the spikes we used to dog down spike
valves. I paid line off my coil, and strung it between these
spikes for hand- and foot-holds.

"There!" I shrieked. "There's the foul hellgate itself!"

The Nest-mouth framed a ragged oval of ruby light.
It was a hole in the hell-sky. To exit it seemed a plunge
into thin air. A rushing moment later, and the yawning
portal framed a vista: far below spread the subworld
plain, threaded with red rivers, and looking strangely
empty and quiescent, compared to other parts of it we'd
seen.

We flung ourselves down and gripped our ropes.
"Hold on!"

"I am!"

The Forager erupted from the Nest-mouth, and dove
down the vertiginous subworld wall. We clung to our

ropes, jouncing and jolting against the rough carapace.
All the plain and all its stony sky, revealed to us in crazy,
shaken glimpses, dispread around us its vile grandeur.
Both hellfloor and hellvault shocked us out of our
expectations. The rolling plain was all but denuded.
"Behemoth's scoured it clean as bone!" cried Barnar—
but we cried out indeed when we looked above us.

"By the Crack and by all that crawls from it!" I yelped.
"Look there! What Thing looks down on us?"

For this part of the subworld's stony sky was gigantically inhabited by a monstrous crimson Eye, socketed
in the earth-bone and staring immensely down. Its pupil
was a ragged fissure of utter blackness faintly measled
with stars, while within the scarlet hemisphere of its half-
translucent ball, pearly shapes of cloudy tissue writhed,
or languidly convulsed. But most hair-raisingly, the orb
attended, turned torpidly to focus here or there. It was
framed in a gasketing of ophidian scales that merged with
the stone. And unceasingly it bled tears that ran in
branching, impossible rivers across the hell-ceiling, and
down the hell-walls near and distant, to weave in red
rivers through the plains' rolling denudation.

Indeed, the only things abounding on those plains
were Foragers. Their multitudes tiny with distance,
everywhere they rushed in broad fronts or phalanxes. As
we surged down onto the plain ourselves, and the
mountainroot we'd emerged from fell away behind us,
we saw how poxed it was with Nest-mouths like our own,
and how these bled a ceaseless stream of demonkind's
nemesis.

We ran in a wide invading wave of Foragers—sparse,
perhaps, here and there, but stretching from horizon to
horizon. Finding our legs again, we scanned awhile in
awe the waste we crossed. "It's a desert!" I breathed.

"Like a spider-hole swept by a giant broom."

"Do we not owe them"—I indicated our mount, and
her congeners sweeping across the plains—"our gratitude?

Even our love? Look at what they have wrought in this unclean dominion! Look at the purging they have worked!"

Not that demon vitality was utterly absent. The hellfloor was a crazy-quilt of living tissues, hides, mantlings and tegmenta: wet, barnacly stretches yielded to tough knolls and swales of plated scale that reeked like a bull Titanoplod in rut, these in turn yielding to meadows of black thorns as thick as fur. But all these anatomical terrains sprawled alike deserted. Nonetheless here and there we saw other Foragers stop, and set their jaws against this ground. We failed to draw warning from this behaviour, and thus were we knocked nine-pin-down in our doltish unreadiness when our own mount stopped dead, and drove her jaws' spiked tips against the ground she trod——a terrain of black, glassy slag. She pried up a great, groaning section of the stubborn stone, and we danced lively for footing in the heave of her labors.

The flap of stone she lifted proved flexible. It was a huge *lip* in fact, for fang-rimmed jaws appeared beneath. But the jaws were slack. From the black gap between them a stench of putrefaction rose like a geyser's effusion. Our Forager began, in a probing, testing way, to pull this laired being apart a bit, ripping up fang-crowned chunks of jawbone, and plucking out a huge, tri-forked tongue. But apparently her appetite recoiled. She dropped the tongue to lie reeking like a long-beached whale, and reared up and rushed on.

"Live demons will be swarming somewhere," gloomed Barnar, "if she scorns to take carrion in her crop."

I was squinting at the horizon when Barnar almost stopped my heart by booming, "Look out for your foot, Nifft! Jump back!"

I stumbled in my alarm and was too late, for a cold, slimy pressure slid across my buskin top and my bare calf above it. A dun-colored hemispheroid, of the approximate size and form of a Jarkkelad battle-casque, then slid hastily away across the carapace, whose mottled hue it almost precisely matched.

And in moments, our instructed eyes discovered that the Forager's rugose and fissured thorax swarmed with these creatures; they were especially thick around the oily junctures of the Behemoth's huge legs with her armored flanks. Our brief inspection proved them harmless detritivores, grazing on the giant's dermal oils and scaly debris.

A scarlet river streamed ahead, a wide, sinewy torrent, exhaling a nimbus of lavender mist where it tore itself against its living banks. Our Forager surged solid-footed through the flux, and when we crested the farther bank, we saw our goal: a distant acropolis, swarmingly besieged.

The landscape surged upward toward that embattled height, the ridged terrain converging toward it like corded sinews. We followed a crestline, and had broad vantage of the far-flung multitude of Foragers running confluently with us. They spread to sight's farthest reach beneath the bleeding, grieving gaze of our cyclopean sun.

The fortress's form and circumstance grew steadily clearer. Her tiered walls towered half a mile high, and three leagues or more in breadth. The ramparts, rising in recessed plateaus, seethed with furious war. We could just make out the roiling mantle of Behemoths that those bulwarks wore, and the splash of fire and hail of missiles hurled down by the demon defenders.

"Duck!" howled Barnar. I fell on my face, astonished— we were nowhere in range of the fray. But here indeed attackers came swooping down upon us, battering the air with sinewy wings.

But by the time our wits were regathered, our blades drawn, and ourselves afoot again, the harmless truth of the matter was plain. For these winged shapes, a croaking, stenchful flock of them, were wholly unmindful of ourselves. They were demon parasites feeding greedily upon the lice we had lately discovered infesting our great mount's leg-joints.

Big, leathery wings these new parasites had, and scrawny bodies of just under human size. Their heads were monocular, with tripart branchlike mouthparts adept at seizing the lice, as were their nether pairs of scrawny, spindle-clawed legs; with these appendages they deftly plucked up their prey, winging acrobatically amidst the hugely pumping thighs of the Forager. When any of these Harpies had a brace or three of lice in its jaws or claws, it winged up into the clear and, hovering, broke open the lice like glossy melons and greedily sucked out the pallid, oleaginous meat. Just between their haunches, where a human would be sexed, these harpies bore little, thin-lipped secondary mouths that did not feed, but spoke in shrieks and gull-like shrills to one another.

"They're pretty alert-looking vermin, wouldn't you say?" Barnar growled in my ear. I nodded. The single, pentagonal eye that crowned their skullish little heads looked quick and sharp. Concerning ourselves, they seemed both aware of us, and incurious about us. We studied them, however, with growing interest. I began toying with one end of my rope, just as Barnar murmured again in my ear. "Just suppose," he said, "that we might do a little . . . fishing with one of them?" I thrilled at the genius of the notion, for it was my own as well: I had just finished making a noose in the end of my line, and we leaned close together to hide it.

The ramparts loomed nearer now. The stench of scorched tissue and blood reached us, and the din of deathcries. We could see that a writhing, tentacular forest of demon limbs sprouted from the stone of the ramparts, and seized on the legs of the assaulting Foragers.

In moments we would be in the thick of the fray, our footing uncertain. . . . Suddenly, one of the harpies swooped carelessly close to us, rising with a just-snatched louse in its claws. With an unpremeditated snap of the wrist, I put the noose up neatly in the harpy's path. The batwinged parasitivore thrust its head home, and we yanked it down and piled onto it.

Grotesque strength lived in this loathsome pterod's scrawny form, but because we pinned its wings as it half-folded them in shock, we were able to bind those powerful pinions tightly shut, while my hand smothered the mouth between its haunches. As we bound our captive, its fellows, seeing our predation, recoiled slightly, creating a zone of safety between themselves and us. But having done thus much, all of them studiously returned to feeding on the lice.

I unmuffled our captive's nether mouth and knelt to speak to it, while Barnar stood with his axe poised to clip the demon's mouthparts from its head.

"We don't know how long we'll be stuck on the back of this beast," I told the Harpy. "Meanwhile, we've grown hungry, I'm afraid, and unless you can suggest an alternative course of action, we're going to have to eat you."

"No! No! Don't!" hissed the mouth between the Harpy's leathery haunches. It appeared that this demon could use human speech only in a ragged whisper. "I can bring you better eating, heavenly eating! I could bring you gold!"

"Excellent!" Barnar replied. "As it happens, we consider several hundredweight of gold, or a like value in gems (which are lighter and perhaps preferable) to be a completely satisfactory alternative to eating you."

In truth we would have died rather than eat one bite of that scabrous hyperparasite, but its fervor in accepting the exchange suggested that the creature did not know this.

The ramparts loomed just ahead—we could see the barbed and suckered demon tentacles get death-grips on assaulting Foragers, and break their backs. And we could see these fallen Foragers, though detained in death, still lend their backs as footing to their following sisters. Chaos would swallow us in moments. . . .

And yet at that imperiled moment, as I gazed upon that Harpy trembling in its bonds, I experienced what I can only call a kind of transformation of the spirit. Here lay this Harpy, a winged and willing agent of our enrichment, and here about us spread the subworld. The subworld, much as it breathes of horror and harm, breathes equally of wealth. The dizzying muchness of gold and gem, of sheer, raw lucre pooled and coffered there, puts intoxication in the air. Demonkind sweats gold— gold is demonkind's shite and vomitus, and lies heaped everywhere. So now a lustful hope of wealth blazed most hotly in me.

But at the same time it was more than avarice I burned with; it was a sense of miracle as well. We began to climb those ramparts atop our stupendous living vehicle, with that Harpy lying bound and compliant between us, and I *believed* that we even now rode on the crest of the greatest wave of fortune our lives would ever know. I felt then a kind of ecstasy of cosmic attunement. This was our Moment, our hour to be loved and doted on by the universe! We were now, at last, fated to have enrichment thrust on us at every turning.

"Look even there!" hissed our desperate captive. "Where we ascend the ramparts here—I know this sector! I'll find you things of value!"

We rode in giddying surges upwards across the backs of luckless Foragers gripped in the forest of demon-limbs. The Behemoths' legs smoked and crumbled wherever they were firmly in the grip of those prodigious paws and tentacles, and our own mount's legs, though they tore free of capture at every other step, were ridged with fuming welts from the contact.

"Duck!" Barnar bellowed. From the battlements, rags of green fire came flapping down around our huddled shoulders, and boulders hurtled through the rubescent gloom. Weaponry too rained on us—darts, arrows, javelins whirtled and snickered down, while everywhere the million-voiced banshee of War raved and wailed and roared, a conflagration of noise that consumed our thoughts.

But did I, in this boil of risk, this great melee of swooping doom and arrowing death, falter one instant from my ecstasy? I did not! I knew my time. Now was Fortune mine, not harm. Now were power, and sweet ambition's pinnacles, and my wild will soaring at full wingspread—now were these all mine! I could not die!

Our Forager attained the crest of the battlements, where giant batrachian demons, welded at the waist to the stone, seized the jaws or legs of the invaders in wrestler's grips. Here and there, seized three on one, Foragers' limbs buckled—they faltered and were broken, limb and skull. Elsewhere the warty titans were scissored to a spew of green tissue by juggernaut jaws. A tentacle seized our mount's foremost portside leg. She heaved and struggled, and we were shaken as by earthquake. Acid smoke hissed round the tentacle's grip. The leg was sundered, and fell away, and we surged across the crest of the ramparts.

We were through. We were over. Smoothly we plunged down toward the broad, wall-girt plains all aswarm with demonkind, and the rhythm of our mount's onrush seemed unaltered by the lost leg. "This is our time!" I bellowed to Barnar. "Our greatest hour commences with this exploit!"

XII

Harken me Harpy, and answer me clear:
What might you find to fish out for us here?

OUR FORAGER sped through phalanxes of demon
defenders, and torn demonmeat sprayed like wake, the
flying fragments trailing entrails like comet-tails. The
terrain dispread before us might be called city here
and there, where domes and ragged steeples seethed
with tiny-distant shapes in turmoil. Jungle it was elsewhere, where towering tracts of foliage thrashed and
tremored with veiled struggles. There were walled
gardens where grew rows on rows of things in glittery,
bright-hued soil, things with eyes and voices, and neck-
cords straining with their desperate utterance. On flag-
stoned highways caravans fled amid armed escorts,
their multibrachiate mounts all saddlebagged with
bundles that twitched and bulged. Red rivers snaked
through it all, plunging here and there into caverns,
and all these foaming red rapids were thronged with
demonkind, whether in vessels or their own aquatic
nakedness, all woven in the subworld's red-clawed

trafficking. And all was grievingly, weepingly beheld by the great alien Eye in the hellroof.

Foragers cruised everywhere, smiting down domes and towers, scissoring down tall-crested jungle skylines, bursting through the great plantations' walls, devouring caravans and guards and packbeasts alike, churning into the wild red rivers and rising with broken galleons dripping in their jaws. . . .

"Harken, Harpy," I cried to our captive. "What might you fish up for us here? We favor high value and relatively light weight. Gemstones come to mind."

To hear its hissed answer we had to lean low to our Harpy's hindquarters, and smell the creature's personal scent, which was not unlike a putrefying lizard's. "Use reason, sires! Can I *pilot* this monster? Gemstones and their like are easily had, they're common mulch in gardens—if this Behemoth but carry us there."

We sprawled a-tumbling, barely keeping a grip on the pinioned Harpy, which might else have gone rolling off our mount. The Forager had stopped short, and violently assaulted the earth with her jaws.

This was a stretch of rolling, rocky ground all studded with stone and steel trapdoors, burrow-mouths hugely hinged and barred, squat-built turrets, and bunkers of massy iron. Our mount began to rip out the lintel and frame of a trapdoor.

There were other Foragers assailing the many-portaled ground, and we saw one of them in particular—a silhouette at some distance—rear up to encounter an attacker. Shaken as we were by our mount's convulsive tearings at the stone, this remote encounter gripped our attention, for now we could make out the silhouette of that other Forager's attacker; it was fully as large as the Behemoth, and resembled an immense 'lurk, or running-spider.

But now beneath us gaped a corridor, deeply branching and sulfurously lit and thronged by multibrachiate creatures fleeing ever deeper. Into this, our mount plunged.

Down green-litten echo-y hallways we chased hordes of scaly, hooved brutes which, as they fled, deafened us with the trumpetings of their brazen, funiculate mouths. We swerved through a turning, and thrust into a high-vaulted chamber, richly carpeted, with facing rows of splendid doors and grand statuary. Amazingly, our mount attacked the carpet, seizing up huge flaps of it. The carpet bled copious purple gore where it was torn. She pulled mightily, and the heavy, hemorrhaging fabric slithered twitching through her jaws and into her crop. And as the carpet tore, a wave of mutation rippled down the magnificent corridor walls; doors and statues and ceiling vaults all shuddered and melted from their form, revealed in their upheaval as one continuous anatomy. Statues became probing papillae, doors the wet membraneous valves of mouths, floor and wall and ceiling all one unified, sinuous, cloacal tube of carnivorous tissue. Ridges of annular muscle swept peristaltically through the glassy demonmeat, whose labyrinthine veins surged inky-black in its death-throes.

If the weight of our Forager's huge meal had slowed her, we failed to note it, and were knocked sprawling once again by the suddenness of her wheeling round and surging surfacewards.

"List! Oh, list!" the Harpy malodorously hissed, and we crouched hearkening. "Her crop's half full now. She'll feed more, but will be soon enough returning. If you mean to use me, let us stand ready!"

We tethered the demon by the neck, and bound its legs, which, though skinny, had strength and flexibility to uncollar it once on the wing. Our mount was speeding now towards a walled orchard. "Do your gathering with your jaws," Barnar told the Harpy. "A false move and we'll break your neck. Bring us up wealth enough, and we will set you free."

Barnar and I traded a covert look here, for we had both, in the same instant, seen a further way the Harpy might be useful to us.

"Agreed!" the Harpy gasped. "Look how she makes for that plantation—your wish for jewels may well bear fruit, oh Honest Masters! I hope I may without offense, and fervently, ask you for solemn assurance of your intent to reward my earnest endeavors with the restoration of my freedom."

"We would not dream of denying you such assurance," I told the demon distractedly. Our course towards the orchard was bringing us nearer the silhouetted combat we had glimpsed just before plunging underground. But it was combat no longer. The Forager crouched paralyzed. The spider straddled it, the tip of its abdomen waggling as it bound its prey in shadowy shrouds of webbing. We shuddered at the sight, but were soon enough distracted, as the orchard wall towered swiftly near. "Down!" I bellowed. "Hold fast!"

We dropped, and gripped our harness. The wall exploded; its huge ashlars tumbled across our dreadnaught's dorsum like giant dice. We were through the wall, and speeding across a soil of purest gemstones that crunched like gravel underfoot.

True demon jewels, their colors blazed completely unaltered by the vinous hue of the subworld's light—colors for which no earthly names exist, colors like lascivious caresses, prurient osculations of the optic orbs.

From this dazzling soil of gems grew rows of taut-muscled saplings, each one rooted at the groin in the brilliant substrate. These trees were multiply headed, though every head mouthless; their branching necks strained to give utterance to a voiceless woe; their polyglot limbs futilely grappled the air.

Our Forager was not bent upon this crop itself, but toward a cluster of huge shapes in the middle distance. Finding her steady in her course, we unbound the

Harpy's wings. "We can work off her shoulder at the gap in her legs!" Barnar cried. Though her seared-off leg-stump rowed powerfully in rhythm with the other limbs, its truncation gave us a gap to play our line through. The Harpy took to the air, and we paid out some two hundred strides of line, about as much as we could easily manage the drag of.

"Don't let the line foul in its legs," I shouted to the Harpy, "or you'll be pulled in and trampled." Disdaining to reply, the demon executed an out-arcing, in-sweeping dive. It seized up jewels in the ample grip of its jaws, and we hauled in slack as it swooped up and back.

Again and again our Harpy angler dove, and with each return it streaked low in front of us and spat down a hefty spill of gemstones. While Barnar managed the Harpy's tether, I began to collect the gems in the leathern, lidded amphorae we had brought for the giants' pap.

Our mount neared her quarry; the demon agriculturalists, or at least harvesters, of this infernal orchard. They were giant slugs, moving in slow formation, inching down parallel lines of the struggling trees. Their slick, mottled hide was just such flesh as we had seen being fed to the grubs in our larval chamber. Each slug glided down one line of plantings, feeding. It slid sudsing along on a tongue of slime, engulfing its slow, savoring way down its row, leaving behind black stumps where movement and struggle had been, and every so often, emitting from its anal pore a flatulent spew of fresh, bright gems.

"We're closing," rasped the Harpy, hovering near us. We allowed it to alight, till the first shock of impact was past. The foremost slug, its stalked eyes thrusting belatedly toward our Forager, was jolting ponderously to a halt, trying to reverse direction amid a great froth of agitated mucus, but our mount was upon it, shearing off half the huge molluscoid's back in one bite, exposing the wet work of its globular heart, toiling nakedly in its broken cavern of innards. The Harpy, looking behind us, was flapping furiously, and hissing.

A huge spider approached us, abdomen bobbing amid the graceful arches of its dancing legs. Above the twiddling, shaggy-sleeved horror of its fangs, its eyeknobs were mounted like a wall of merciless black gems, the biggest topmost.

"Batten down!" Barnar and I shouted at each other. We lay flat and hugged our jewels. The Harpy spread a wing to help contain the heap that was as yet unbagged. Our Forager, though a leg light on her port side, nonetheless wheeled majestically to do battle.

Looking up some thirty degrees of inclination along our mount's lifted head, we saw the rearing spider loom above us, saw it strike.

And as it struck, the Forager's great fighting jaws scissored. They seized the fangs crosswise and sheared them off. The fang-stumps bled venom which smoked ruinously down on the Forager's jaws, melting great wounds in those huge, spiked mandibles.

Our Forager, unfazed, ducked and thrust more deeply under our attacker. The spider, seized at the waist where flat thorax joined bulging abdomen, was lifted off half its legs; the foremost quartet of them trod the air, all tractionless.

But hoisted thus, the spider could reach down along the Forager's ridgeline, and strike her carapace with its sheared-off, unequal fangs. Had these been undamaged, they might have punched through even our mount's adamantine exoskeleton. Even as it was, when the wounded fangs struck, the splash of poison fanned hissing and smoking across her back, and some of her armor cracked deeply with a stress-groan like a ship's hull half stove in by a rock.

We scuttled frantically back to the Forager's waist, dragging as best we could our spill of jewels. Our little world heaved as the Forager flexed her abdomen for leverage and counter-thrust. In her jaws' slow, grinding pressure, the spider's mid-joint crumpled. Still the monster's fang-strokes fell, their strength and venom dwindling, though the relentless murder never faded from the eight black ice-moons of its eyes.

Then the arachnid broke; its legs crumpled into a crookedly twitching bouquet. It was flung down. The hairy bag of its abdomen, undefended, our Behemoth ripped wide open with her poison-scarred jaws. Thrusting her head into the bristly bag, the Forager guzzled long glutinous coils of pallid stuff which appeared to be connected to the twitching monster's spinnerettes. Apparently, our Forager feasted on that which would have mummied her, had she fallen prey.

At length, she turned from this feeding back to the sundered slug, and fed on this molluscoid until her crop could hold no more. We made a few more passes with the Harpy, but once the Forager set out on her return, her sole aim was to bear her precious booty of nourishment back to the Nest, and such was the undeviating energy of her onrush, that Barnar re-bound the Harpy, and set to helping me cut lengths of line, and weave them into a sturdy net to hold our swag, which now formed an effulgent pile of heart-stopping bigness.

"It's as if . . ." he marvelled at our dazzling hoard while we worked, " . . . as if we've snatched a piece of the sun!"

XIII

Behold them kiss their mother's side,
A-suckling of her pap.
They wash against her like a tide
That at its shore doth lap.

THE RAMPART was crossed, and fell away behind us, almost unregarded, so raptly we gazed on our lucent loot. Our mount surged over the plains unopposed, like the embodiment of our henceforth triumphant fate. Three hundredweight of demon gems! I felt immortal. Wherever my desire turned its eye, obstacles toppled, while stern Impossibilities bowed obsequiously, and withdrew. We could now afford a fleet of ships, and five hundred picked mercenaries. More! A flock of Gaunts could now be hired from the Astrygals—even Stregan or Hagian gaunts could be hired, damn the cost! And with these obedient horrors on the wing for us, Pelfer's tomb could be sacked in a single day's siege. I might stand actually *shod* in the Buskins of Bounding Absquatulation before two months were out!

And then, with Pelfer's triad of Facilitators, how swiftly

could we plant our names, Barnar's and mine, among the very greatest in the Annals of Thievery! So bright could we shine that, when we were long gone to dust, our names would be sung in admiring melodies, by tongues whose languages are yet unborn.

I lifted my jubilant eyes to that looming, lunar Eye that wept its red rivers through every corner of this piece of hell. An indecipherable passion blazed from that eye, and bathed all below as in a warm mist of blood. How could I hope to read the emotion in that awesome orb? The black gulf of its pupil was a World-leak, a hole in the shell of the Cosmos of Man, where the winds off the stars breathed through.

Yet at that moment, I did feel I could read it. I thought I saw in that Eye a glee like my own. I thought I saw glee, along with that fierce absolute hunger of a hawk's eye that is reading a far field for food: the gaze of a power both random and absolute. I saw in that Eye in the hellroof the gaze of Luck herself telling me: "Yes."

I stole looks at Barnar, afraid to confront the different dreams I knew were enkindled in him. And he seemed on his part unwilling to encounter my gaze.

The Harpy, its legs still bound and its neck short-tethered to a piton, began in its ragged whisper to entreat us for its freedom. Barnar answered it kindly.

"Regrettably, oh Demon, we find that we require your help in one small further matter. You have but to render us this bit of additional aid, and you may expect your freedom with perfect confidence, and every—"

The Harpy interrupted with a heated burst of obscenity. It hissed some personal remarks so grotesquely disparaging to Barnar and myself, that I drew Ready Jack and clipped off a punitive inch from one of the creature's elaborate mouthparts. The Harpy's pentagonal pupil contracted in pain. "You have my silence!" it humbly hissed. "I wait to do your bidding, for I must."

Barnar and I traded one quick look, and spoke no more.

Why compound the mad extravagance of what we hoped for, by speaking it aloud? Yet no hope seemed utterly mad for men who had just been carried through the subworld on a Behemoth's back, and laden with jewels, and brought back out again. Already the hell-wall loomed nearer, the mountain-roots darkly mouthed with Behemoth Nests.

"In this abyss we find our apogee of Luck." I whispered this to myself, like a prayer. We gripped our harness and our bale of gems. Our Forager surged up the mountain-wall.

"The instant she branches off our blazes," was all Barnar said, and "Yes," was my only answer. The mountain-wall snatched us steeply upwards. We hung gripping the harness and our gems, our sinews cracking. In the Nest, the instant our mount left our marked path we must grip the Harpy's tether and jump, and let the sturdy demon slow our fall as best it could with its wings.

On the other hand, our Forager's course might lie straight back up to the apex of the Nest, perhaps even by the path it had brought us down. . . .

Here was our Nest-mouth, vomiting and swallowing giants, looming larger, larger, yawning to ingest us. . . . We were in, and cruising through the multitudes in its entryway. We jumped to our feet and dragged our gems and the Harpy over to the gap where the Forager's foremost portside leg had been. I wrenched the Harpy's neck to have its whole attention.

"If we jump, demon, wing it hard for the tunnel wall. If you let us break our legs, we'll see that you're crushed to death with us on the tunnel floor."

"Is that our blaze?" Barnar cried.

"Yes, by Key and Cauldron! And she turns!"

Silently we watched the miracle unfold. The Forager hugged our dye-blazed path at every turn. Up and up she sped, never diverging, till at length we ceased to fear she would. This Nest, this vault of Power—our Forager was its key, a key delivered into our hands.

And at length, when we did branch from our marked trail, we'd followed it so high we knew the point of our divergence must be very near our larval chamber. Why dismount now, when the Forager's goal was so sure to be our own? With jets of dye, we blazed this newest path.

The tunnel climbed more steeply, and began to yawn bigger and bigger, as gallery after gallery merged with ours from every side. The multitude of workers was even greater here than down at the Nest's entry hall, but this throng was more various in make and size, for workers of every caste were here, converging—we could not doubt it now, surely?—upon their millenial Mother.

Still we worked gently up-slope, the thousands thronging around us in rivers of opposing flow, till there ahead of us we saw the yawning portal of a chamber which dwarfed even this great concourse of confluent tunnels. And within that colossal cavern yonder, nested in its cyanic gloom, there lay a pallid, breathing hugeness that was Awe itself.

A central current in that titan throng caught us, and snatched us through the portal. And thus were we swept into the purview of the Nest Mother's glittery eyeglobes, and into the reach of her Royal jaws.

The Queen! Living immensity, more than planetary! Her abdomen's ribbed ellipsoid, all marbled white-and-black, bulged away in the blue shadow. It was a great island at whose shores whole seas of her progeny lapped. Her Royal head, black as a lacquered battle-casque, at first appeared a stranded thing, resembling, in its relative smallness, a different being that had been half swallowed by that abdomen's egg-laying mountain. We approached the Presence on the river of other Courtiers and Supplicants.

We learned the true hugeness of the Royal head as she received her daughters' kisses. Forager after Forager, lifting her offering, was utterly dwarfed by the Queen's receiving jaws. For an interval of awe and rapture, time vanished in our stupefaction as we drew nearer. And then our own mount lifted her filial gift up to the Royal visage. The daughter's regurgitation shook us like a silken earthquake; she cast her demon-spoil into the sky-clasping arc of the Royal mouthparts.

The Nest Mother's nearness breathed a gust of eternity on us. These jaws were the Appetite of the Nest itself, a great furnace door through which armies of demonkind marched, that Behemoth might breed and brood and build, and scour still cleaner the upper floor of hell.

Then the Royal head reared—dismissing us, summoning the next. Our mount slid aside, and cruised in a current of her sisters that coasted down along the Royal flank. We sailed past hundreds of supplicant workers, all lifting their hungry jaws to the Mother's bulging side.

And it was their jaws that helped us see something that was hard to discern at first in the densely marbled whorls of white and black that blazoned the abdominal integument. But all at once, cued by the nursing brutes, we saw them everywhere: arrays of pores across the Royal flank, pores round as a potter's jar-mouths, each delicately lipped where the chitin came up in a slight circumferential ridge.

These pores, as I say, in their harlequin mottling, played seek-me-out with our eyes, but in a short time we began to find pattern: pores of a given size lay in roughly horizontal clusters; smaller pores lay low on the abdomen, while the strata highest on the flank comprised the orifices of greatest diameter.

"See them, Barnar?" I trembled. "Each caste has its level. Is Bunt's gamble won, then?"

"See their delicacy," breathed my friend, and I shared his wonder. To drink, the Behemoths closed their mandibles, and lay the tips of them to the pores; the closed jaws, like quills' nibs touched to ink, pulled down the fluid in their cloven points.

"What tenderness," I shuddered in my turn. The nursing giants reared up, forelegs gently resting on the Royal flank, and delicately, delicately drank, as still as statues.

"Ah, look now, Nifft. Look, old friend. Foragers every one, is it not so?"

He referred to the cluster of pores that our mount now approached. Only Foragers nursed at them, drinking perhaps an ichor exclusive to themselves; drinking giants' pap, perhaps.

We'd already lashed our netted gems to the pitons. Our mount reared high, her dorsum a steep, glossy hill now. With some scrambling, we found our footing, as she softly sank the point of her closed mandibles into a slow, stickly exudation, like white honey, that we could now see oozing from the pore.

"Now, Demon, attend!" Barnar barked—and he faltered a moment, both of us startled by the strangeness of a human shout in this measureless chthonic broodhole of the Mountain Queen. Before Barnar's exclamation, it had not seemed to be a silence that surrounded us; the march of tarsal claws on stone, the susurrus of whickering legs, the wet whisper of feedings, the slow thrum of the Queen's majestic heart—all this had not seemed to be silence until his human voice rang so sharp and alien in this speechless smithy of giants. We harkened to his echo which still hung in that vastness—distinct, eery, melancholy. It was the echo of a phantom's voice. We were phantoms, a race undreamed of by the titans; thirsty ghosts that haunted them.

"Quick then," I muttered to the Harpy. We had already emptied the gems from our amphorae into the net. We now had these leathern jars dangling from ropes, whose ends I put in the Harpy's elaborate mouthparts. "Your legs must stay bound," I told our captive. "But with your jaws you can easily manage these ropes. Drag the jars into the outflux of the ichor; if you once sink their rims in the pap, you can scrape the jars full of the stuff. You should contrive to fill them with a couple of passes. Remember how close your freedom is! Only do this well, and liberty is yours. Up now, and away."

The Harpy cringed obediently, not yet taking wing. The creature tremored with what was perhaps outrage. "Pitiless masters," it gasped, "I obey! I obey! But oh this is cruel! Do you not see the dangers—"

"Harpy," I answered, courteously gripping the imp by the throat, "had we wings of our own, we would brave these dangers ourselves. As it is, do now, or die at once."

The Harpy took wing, its malodorous pinions seizing the air like big, sinewed hands. Up it climbed, the amphorae dangling from its jaws. When it gained some two rods' altitude, we held its tether short. It tugged and gestured beggingly for more line, but we were loathe to give it more than we could firmly manage, lest the demon contrive to snag it, and work itself free.

It hovered, studying the pore where our mount still nursed.

"Oh no!" gasped Barnar. "We didn't dye it!"

It hit us like a blow. There hung the Harpy, wings toiling, high, wide and hideous, directly above our nursing Forager's glittery blue eyeglobes. In our shock we stood doltish, staring, like casual spectators.

And nothing happened. Still the Forager funneled down pap, unperturbed.

The Harpy winged cautiously lower, and eased the leathern jars down on the pore. Then it winged lower still, to tilt the jars' brims down into the pap; in a moment, it had sunk the brims into the cloudy lactescence.

Now came some delicate wingwork, as the Harpy tugged the lips of the jars deeper into the exudate. To manage the oblique angle needful for this work, the demon hovered even lower, hanging not quite two fathoms above the Royal abdomen, and tugging, coaxing the jarmouths into the pap.

Something moved, something huge and sudden and night-black surged up from the abdomen. A ragged piece of blackness hugged bristly limbs around the Harpy, and snatched it from the air.

Even as it dined loudly on our hapless subworld servitor, the monster—doubtless some Royal ectoparasite—remained more than half hidden in the pattern of the Royal hide. We made out barbed fur, like a Sucking Star's, and tree-thick palps or tentacles. The Harpy lifted once more that eerie, gull-like voice it had used with its own kind before we captured it; in this melancholy demon-song, it briefly declaimed the agonies of its demise.

We slashed the lead and flung it free. Our mount, as if dismissed by our failure, instantly ceased to imbibe the pap, and backed down from the Royal flank. She wheeled, and slid out into a current of sated workers that were out-bound from the Chamber. Throughout our long withdrawal from the Queen's immensity, we scanned the terrain of Her abdomen, and though detail faded in the murk our alerted eyes discovered—now here, now there, much that lived, and moved, upon the Queen.

Somber and silent, we crouched by the gap in our mount's legs, ready to jump, feeling broody, and rebuked by Luck, whom we had thought so wholly ours. The three hundredweight that we had just failed to earn from Bunt by obtaining the pap was more than made up by the value of the jewels we had captured, but this did not comfort me. Failure had flawed our fortune's smooth ascent. I felt betrayed. I blush now at this petulance, but so it was.

We had gone not a quarter mile out of the atrium of the Royal Chamber, when an oncoming Licker bowed low in our path, and with stroking antennae, begged our mount for food. Her crop was not empty, it seemed. She stopped, and leaned down to comply. Barnar and I tossed down our bale of gems, and jumped after it.

XIV

See how faithless Fortune bleeds!
Our lustrous Future fast recedes . . .
See how Fortune's healed again!
Our purses wax! Our dolors wane!

HOW EASILY had our Forager borne this bale of gems! How cruelly this same bale taxed our little bodies— for we had shrunk, as it seemed to us, as small as tiny, toilsome beetles, inching down these vast corridors we'd so lately bestridden like giants. Grunting and sweating, staggering and stumbling, and cursing continually, we carried our weighty fortune. Thanks to our blazes, our route was never in doubt; our death by a misstep due to exhaustion, however, seemed highly likely.

The toil was least when we shared the load between our shoulders; we could hustle it along for good stretches this way. But this mode made us dangerously awkward at ducking, and dodging, and diving for cover. We were soon covered with bruises and lacerations, and had several near collisions with oncoming Behemoths. Each time we took cover, we lay long minutes gasping, powerless to move till our hearts slowed down.

Grimly, we lurched on. And, amazingly, towards the end, our sheer determination seemed to prevail, and we found ourselves wielding our burden with new strength and stamina. Jaws clenched in a fury of resolution, we actually jogged the last mile to our larval chamber without a single pause for rest. Jubilant, we staggered through the portal, and sprawled against the wall, gasping and exulting.

"What stamina . . . for two old dogs . . . eh?" Barnar beamed.

"By Key and Cauldron!" I wheezed boastfully, " . . . as if the bag . . . grew lighter as we went!"

We paused. An icy finger touched my nape. We seized the bundle.

It *had* gotten lighter—by fully a third of its weight! One corner had been slightly ruptured, probably upon dismounting. We scrambled back out into the tunnel. A gemstone sparkled from the tunnel floor. When I recovered it, I saw others winking beyond. Barnar groaned, "They'll be strung out all the way back!"

Was our Luck wound on a spool, to be spun out, and then reeled back in again? The remnant gems, which we soon cached with our gold, were of course worth a fortune, but the bitterness of our setback consumed us.

We sought out our hammocks, but lay sleeplessly brooding. "We'll have every stone of it back," I growled, "first thing on rising. . . . Do you know, Barnar, that Harpy was a luckless brute, but what power there is in a pair of wings, eh?"

Barnar nodded thoughtfully. "I believe I take your meaning." Lowering his voice, he added, "You know, Nifft, I find myself inclined to venture for the alleged Unguent. At least this part of the subworld does not seem overpopulous with demonkind."

"Just so. My very thought. Let's have our friend out of his bag, then."

So we unbagged Ostrogall and propped him on a rock. Though we brusquely silenced his obsequious effusions, the loathsome jewelry of his eyes still wooed us with a hundred oily glints of adoration.

"We wish to explore a bit further your proposition regarding the so-called Unguent of Flight," I told him. "I will begin by observing, I hope without painful bluntness, that only a fraction of you remains. How can you then yearn so vehemently to survive?"

"But I do so yearn, Masters, most strenuously! Only plant me neck-deep in my native subworld floor. In days I can release ocular spores, breeze-borne on gossamer, that will slip through the orifices of my countrymen. Soon I'll be peeping from eye-pustules on a thousand demons I've infected, and shall see many wonders as my vigilance steals outward through the subworld."

"Enough!" said Barnar. "Lead us not too vividly to know what saving you accomplishes. Nifft and I have been debating a point that wants some clarification. Vitrol the Gelded, in his *Fabulary*, reports of the Unguent of Flight that it is: ' . . . demon slime and demon sweat/which man by demon hand-clasp gets,/and otherwise has ne'er got yet.' We wish you to comment on the veracity of this passage."

There was a silence, in which a myriad of apologetic glances overswept Ostrogall's eyes. The silence was broken when the signal cord set up a vigorous clacking— something it had been doing, with scant respite, since our return. We ignored it. "Oh beneficent saviours," the demonstump wheedlingly began, "it torments me that I must, perforce, deny—"

"Silence!" I told him. "We do but test you. We are disposed, soon, to essay the venture you propose to us. In what manner must we prepare ourselves?"

"Oh bounteous, blessed, beautiful benefactors! Your doughty weapons, and the peerless courage that courses through your veins, are all the preparation such men as yourselves—"

"Enough! You are advised of our intent. Be sure that any treachery attempted, when once we have set out together, will be decisively repaid. Since it appears that even in fragmented state you are capable of regeneration, we propose, in the event of your malfeasance, to smear you with pitch and burn you to a crisp. Silence! We seek no further discourse at present."

"I only beg that you set me on some secure ledge, unenveloped, that I may see a bit while I await your pleasure."

There seemed no harm in this. We set him where he had a bit of a view out into the chamber, for which he effusively thanked us. It crossed my mind that his craving for vision must be great indeed, to be so glad of a view which, to him and his kind, must surely be like a vista of ultimate Nightmare.

Barnar sent a terse message on the signal cord, using the signal indicating that the tappers were shutting down for sleep. This must vex Costard, having had no work or word of us for longer than we could estimate. Bunt might at least surmise that we had been about his mission; if so, he would calm the youth if he could. If he couldn't, let Costard seethe. We returned to our hammocks.

"Are we actually going to do it, old friend?" I asked drowsily. I knew we were, and the resolution, though fraught with uncertainty, somehow soothed the anguish of imagining our spilt jewels lying strewn along miles of tunnel floor.

"It would be craven, for one setback, to cease pushing our luck. This is our time, Nifft. We're meant to win. . . ."

We both drifted toward sleep. The knowledge that divergent ambitions must still divide us, once we had all our plunder back up in the world again, was something we were tired enough, and rapt enough in imminent exploits, to put aside in our hearts for the moment. Out in the chamber the whickery whisper of Behemoth legs, the soft, wet sound of a thousand feedings, the faint gibbering of dying demons . . . already, these sounds seemed soothing music to us, home sounds. Great Behemoth, nursing Her own, cradled us like her own children in the bounty of her strength. I slept, a bright orange flea snug in the lair of the tolerant colossus who both fed and protected it.

Ostrogall's voice woke us up. His tone was urgent, wheedling, a low melody of hasty persuasion. When my fogged mind grasped that he was addressing someone else, it brought me bolt upright.

There, not five strides from our hammocks, three orange shapes crouched raptly around the voluble demon-fragment. The glittery pox of Ostrogall's eyes wetly solicited their credence, while his mouth-vent murmured busily.

We recognized two of his hearers: Costard and Bunt— both kilted and stained orange. Costard looked trim enough in the half-naked outfit of kilt, boots, and bandoliers. Ha'Awley Bunt was plump, and his ripply orange flab was not a little reminiscent of larval corpulence.

Our third visitor was a young woman with a handsome, strong-shouldered frame, big-breasted and robustly haunched. On her the short-kilt and buskins were a pleasing costume altogether, though there was nothing mincing in the way she bore her semi-nakedness. The back-sweep of her orange pompadour gave her strong-nosed face the crested look of some winged raptor, though there was an engaging candor in her eyes, which were quick to meet ours when she discovered us looking on.

"Good evening, gentlemen! Your deep sleep hints that

you've been hard at work—though not, we gather, at tapping sap." I knew the pleasant alto of her voice. This was Sha'Urley, Bunt's sister, who had briefly presented herself at our supper before we took ship from Dolmen Harbor.

"Uncle!" Costard piped, jumping up from where he crouched near Ostrogall. "Uncle, I've just learned! I mean, I've just learned what you're *doing*. How could you not *tell* me of giants' pap? How could you . . . *steal* from me?"

"You presumptuous young moron! How can I steal, you ask? I am a thief!" It was a measure of Barnar's fury and flusterment that he had no sharper answer than this, and I shared his rage. What an appalling intrusion, these three overwrought property-owners, fairly twitching with acquisitive impulses! Just now, as we gathered ourselves inwardly for a highly ticklish venture, here was this unruly, contentious little mob dropping down square in our laps.

"You simply refuse to grasp," Ha'Awley Bunt was reproving Costard, "that taking the pap *isn't* stealing." His weary contempt bespoke long battles between him and Costard since we'd come below. "A mine owner here owns his own apparatus, and owns the right to work his site. But no one *owns* a Nest, or anything in it! What's found here is the finder's, whoever he may be!"

"What might it be said that I own,"—Costard's voice was a croak of bitter sarcasm—"if I don't own whatever's in this Nest? I'd like you to suggest just what ownership might mean at *all*, if not—"

"I respectfully remind you," Sha'Urley Bunt told the young man, "that your acceptance of my investment, a substantial sum of gold specie now reposing in your vault above, grants us full partnership and right of entry here now. Let this fact suffice for the moment, honest Costard, and let us ask our tappers here," (she turned to Barnar and me) "about this new matter, this Unguent of Flight . . . ? Do you really contemplate entering the subworld to retrieve it?"

All three of them watched us. We, in turn, glared down at Ostrogall. "Effulgent Ones!" the fragment fluted, answering the menace in our eyes. "I had to speak, to account for myself, or they would have slain me. I had to explain my presence so near to your sleeping selves!"

I looked at our visitors. "If you will be so kind as to explain why you have come down here," I told them, "then perhaps we can proceed to a discussion of where we mean to go from here."

What we next learned was not had without trouble. In the verbal pouring forth that followed, Ha'Awley Bunt and Costard flared up at each other with a lively rancor. Luckily, Sha'Urley had the knack of silencing them both, and maintaining order amidst contention. Through her crisp narrative, with some vituperative amplifications from Bunt and Costard, we had the gist of what had transpired up in the mine compound these last few days.

Before Ha'Awley had even left Dolmen with us, Sha'Urley, ever alert to her brother's speculations (for she seemed to feel some affectionate contempt for his business acumen) had sensed that he had some costly venture afoot. She engaged two armed retainers, trusted swordswomen long in her service, and took ship for KairnGate Harbor the night after we did. She had arrived at the Superior Sap Mine bare hours after Barnar and I went rattling down the Gangway in the bucket.

Only her power to debunk Bunt's own false persona compelled him, at her warning glances, to a temporary connivance in her fiction. She presented herself to Costard as a businesswoman of Dry Hole who had heard of the Superior Sap Mine's fiscal straits, and had seen opportunity for investment in an industry she had long craved to assay.

Despite the eye-play and the awkwardness that must have passed between the brother and sister during this first encounter, and despite the improbability of a wandering investor seeking Costard out like this, that young man, implacably self-important, heard everything with judicious nods and complete belief. Sha'Urley, after all, shared her brother's polished manners and persuasive skill.

Thus we learned that the catastrophic handling, topside, of our first attempts at tapping, were caused in part by Costard's and Bunt's distraction with Sha'Urley's arrival.

Costard speedily accepted Sha'Urley's hefty pouch of specie, and tendered to her the freshly drawn up instrument of partnership in the Superior Sap Mine, which he had signed with a flourish.

Sha'Urley immediately expressed interest in a tour of the operations down in the larval chamber. Costard fatuously declined to subject one of the "fair sex" to those subterranean rigors. Sha'Urley, piqued, made Costard aware of fundamental realities—that she now had a legal propriety in the mine, and that she had as well, unlike Costard, two resolute young women, skilled at arms, in her employ.

The three retired that night on uneasy terms. Sha'Urley and her brother took a nocturnal ramble through the main building, and were shortly plunged into an argument that echoed in the empty structure. Bunt fumed that, for all his sister's doubt of his acumen, she herself had foolishly over-invested in the mine. Why secure a source of giants' pap before its worth was known? Sha'Urley, however, had ascertained the sum that her brother had withdrawn from the Hivery's assets to pay Barnar and me. She snapped that she had just secured partnership for a fraction of that sum, and that now, if the pap proved out, they stood ready to make a fortune at once—for if the pap worked, how could its effects long be hidden from competitors?

Meanwhile, she continued, if she and Ha'Awley now went down and harvested the pap themselves, before

Barnar and I went after it, they could save the huge second payment promised us.

The upshot was of course that Costard, overhearing, came discreetly out of his chambers, harkened, and learned all.

The three of them plunged into furious controversy, and arrived at stalemate, since Sha'Urley refused remittance of her investment, and had, with her armed retainers, the means to enforce her partnership. They quarreled for days. Our long cessation of tapping activity was what finally brought them to a concerted action. They imagined the pair of us down here, bottling the Royal pap; perhaps they began to picture us purloining it for ourselves by some contrivance. Costard, still denying them an iota of ownership of the pap, agreed to their all going down together, with the swordswomen posted above to protect the compound.

When we'd heard all this, Barnar and I excused ourselves, and retired a few paces to confer. "Here's a mess indeed, eh?" "Suddenly, everything we had in view looks ten times harder!" Barnar sighed.

"But perhaps not without added profit. Look at them. They came down all in a flutter and a clatter of contention. But see how they look uneasily about them? They're beginning to *feel* where they are. Suppose they saw the Queen for themselves? How much more do you think they'd be willing to pay us to get the pap for them, once they understood the task? Let's offer to guide them to the Brood chamber for a hundredweight of specie. We'll recollect our jewels on the way." This idea greatly cheered us; the prospect of easy profit warmed us like a sunbeam.

"What of the Unguent?" Barnar asked. "What if they want to come with us in pursuit of that?"

"Can you see them, any of them, actually walking into the subworld of their own free will? They are all administrators, adepts of accounts, of panelled chambers, and letters of draft."

The three of them had drawn together slightly as we watched them, unconsciously huddling up a bit as they felt the grandeur and danger of this place. Costard, moreover, was probably recalling the terror and indignity of that mishap which ended his very brief career as a tapper.

Barnar and I became the gracious hosts. We urged our vile wine and jerky on them, and anxiously saw to it that they were comfy on the bales and lockers we'd assembled to seat them. When they were settled, Barnar beamed. "Here is how Nifft and I have reasoned the matter out, my friends. The three hundredweight we have received of Bunt we consider fully earned by our entry of the Brood Chamber, followed by our attempt in good faith to execute your commission, at the near loss of both our lives. Naturally we are despondent at losing the second three hundredweight which was to have rewarded our success. Still, at present we cannot contemplate a second attempt on the pap. More obtainable goals claim our thoughts just now. Nevertheless we may yet have occasion to assist your own pursuit of the ichor. We will guide you to the Royal Brood Chamber for the sum of one hundredweight of prime specie, if you will all assent to leave at once, and to provide us with a fiftyweight of specie in advance . . . do I sense hesitation?"

"Honest thief," Sha'Urley answered, "my brother started by giving you impossibly large sums of money. Bunt Cellars is an old and prosperous House. We 'still our mead at no less than seven 'stilleries throughout the Angalheims. But to speak as casually as you do of hundredweights of specie is a wild exaggeration, both of our resources, and of this pap's real value. You must drastically scale down your expectations."

"But we won't, you see," I told her as amiably as I could. "We would as soon be on our own way, come to that, so I'm afraid our price is firm, and you must take or leave it. I hope you don't think me unpleasant. It just happens that my friend and I are in a very acquisitive frame of mind of late."

Some haggling followed, a twenty-fiveweight was offered as advance, more time was requested before departure, the price was vainly protested as inordinate, the doubtfulness of the pap's real value was urged, and the like. They already knew we would yield them nothing. At bottom, they dickered mainly for delay, as a way to ease into the fact of where they were about to go. When the talk wound down at last, the three of them seemed slightly dazed, trying to digest the fact that they had just agreed to pay a huge sum of money to be led on foot into the unimaginable dangers of the Royal Brood Chamber.

"Well, then," I said. "It's settled. Before we disperse, though, I feel I must say a few words about this alleged Unguent of Flight. We, who plucked this demon from a larva's jaws, regard him as strictly our own, along with any information of value he may possess about any Unguents real or putative."

"Luminous Ones!" fluted Ostrogall. "I affirm myself yours! It is only to your two revered selves I will divulge the Unguent's source!"

No doubt the demon was sincere in yielding himself to the most battle-ready of his potential escorts. On the other hand he had done his cause no harm by arousing the competing interest of our colleagues as a stimulus to commit us to his expedition. Costard piped, "Surely, Good-uncle Barnar, the demon had just been brought into my larval chamber by one of my Nurse Behemoths when you found him, and just as surely he is at least as much mine as he is yours! Moreover, this means in principle that, should he lead you to the Unguent, that Unguent too is at least as much mine as yours."

"One of *your* Nurse Behemoths," Barnar echoed him. "What? Will you call one of them to heel for you now? That one there, for instance. Is that Nurse *yours*? Make her do something, then! Bid her dance you a jump-up in obedience to your august ownership of her! What? You can't do this? Nephew, I will put the matter concisely. You will not be a part of our search for the Unguent. And, if we obtain it, we are keeping every jot for ourselves. Now, if you don't go up and get us our advance fairly soon, we will grow impatient, and go follow our own concerns."

So, back up the gangway bucket went Costard and Ha'Awley Bunt, to get our fiftyweight of specie and to alert Sha'Urley's two retainers to our setting forth from the larval chamber. Barnar sat down to oiling and sharpening his weapons. Mine I deemed still sharp enough from our preparations for our last setting-forth. And while I wished to be civil and hostly to Sha'Urley, I was anxious to have another look at my cache of gems and specie. So I airily excused myself, saying I was going for a ramble.

But a moment later as I strode along the chamber wall, here was Sha'Urley catching up to me. "Will you show me all this, honest Thief? Be sociable, good Karkmahnite. Negotiation's done for a while."

"Well, why not? Come, then, and let me guide you into the midst of our little sap-skins, and their wondrous Nurses."

So I showed Sha'Urley this and that. The chamber was still a-boil with the heightened activity that had moved us to our recent foray. New larvae were borne in, new pupae rushed out, and demon-meat distributed, in a turmoil that would have paralyzed Barnar and me had we confronted it on our first days down here.

I liked Sha'Urley for her unfeigned awe at the spectacle, when sharp dealing would demand that she should scant the challenges we faced down here. At the same time, I could not help but feel that her eyes, when they met mine, were playing a kind of smiling game with me. I wondered if she had noticed that, while we were all talking, I had forgetfully allowed my gaze to dwell upon the lovely abundance of her body. She gestured at the larvae, her eyes playing with mine again. "Are these sap-swollen creatures . . . hard to mount?"

"Some tremble when we set the Spike in them, but in the main they are at ease beneath us."

"Unlucky for them," she smiled. "Oh, what a piece of work they are, Nifft! We are blessed indeed to enjoy even the fraction of their bounty that we are able to extract."

"It's a miracle we can steal so much, yet never cause them harm. Indeed we cannot speak of ownership down here—only of lucky theft."

"Yes. And, since we are speaking plainly, Nifft, I see no reason not to tell you that I have always had a keen carnal appetite for men of your veiny, sinewy make." Now she was looking me straight in the eyes.

"Nor can I conceal," I croaked, "an equal craving for women of your opulent design."

"Indeed you cannot conceal it," she smiled more broadly, "short-kilted as you are. Are we safe here to indulge ourselves—here in this nook of soft earth perhaps?"

"Oh yes! Perfectly safe!" I answered her, for we had wound our way back out to the perimeter again, where a fissure in the wall offered its safety near at hand.

I think life's profoundest joys are just such simple pleasures, simply had, as Sha'Urley and I partook together while the Nurses wheeled and glided through the larval host, and those huge white loaves of living tissue baked and swelled in the great Nest's genial womb! We sang the paean of life together, none more surprised than I to be given this delight. We ended with some nuzzling and laughing together, and at length stood up with happy sighs, and regirt our loins. And I remember quite distinctly having at that moment a genuine glint of clairvoyance. For at that moment, the thought came to

me: *This is the most pleasant thing that is going to
happen to me for quite some time to come.*

Again we walked, and shared the marvels of the place.
Sha'Urley poked a friendly fist in my shortribs. "Let's not
be stiff and formal in our dealings now, Nifft. Let's talk
bluntly, as good friends should. Not to put too fine a point
on it, don't you feel you are charging us rather . . . stiffly,
for your guide services?"

"Sweet Sha'Urley! It's not that long a walk in miles,
but it is long indeed in perils. And when we show you
the Royal Chamber, you will understand the princely fee
we set."

XV

Behold thy babe, that doth beseech a crown,
And would go mantled in thy majesty.
Bestow on her an army of thy spawn,
Or else reweave her in thy tapestry.

WHEN THE SIX OF US finally set out (the fractional but loquacious Ostrogall, riding holstered on my hip and bagged for silence, being the sixth) the Bunts and Costard went in such awe of the tunnels, and of the titans that trafficked them, that they hung well back of our lead, and clung to the tunnel wall as they crept along. We also gave them the responsibility of blazing our course with additional dye marks, which task further deflected their attention. Thus for a while we recollected our dropped gems without being noticed by our newcomers.

But after they had experienced the first few surges of Behemoths, had weathered the terror of those encounters and caught on to the stop-and-start rhythmn of our travel, they began taking note of our gem-gleaning. Costard, spotting a gem we'd missed, leapt on it. Barnar roared, "Desist! Is it not plain? These gems, which you can see we have come equipped to regather, are *ours*, lost here by us scant hours ago!"

"Yours, Uncle!?" shrilled Costard. "Is every damned thing now *yours* down here in *my mine*?"

So we had to stop in a safe recess, and reveal to our visitors our recent foray through the subworld. "So you have seen it then," Sha'Urley mused. "The subworld. Is it, ah, lively?"

"We have seen it more than once," I answered stiffly. "In this sector, at least, wide tracts of it seem virtually deserted, save for the Foragers coming and going." I was uneasily aware that this determined young woman had far from abandoned her interest in a venture for the Unguent of Flight.

"Our main point, at least, is clear, is it not?" Barnar asked the three of them. "If you really wish to own demon jewels, as we own these, you must needs go down and get your own, as we did."

They respected our property after this, though they kept a tactless, sullen eye on us as we regathered it. I had for a moment the strangest feeling as they watched me; that, vigorously gathering my gems as I was, I cut a somehow grotesque figure—that there was something, well . . . piggish, even swinish about my thrifty diligence! The bizarre delusion quickly passed, however.

The traffic grew thicker, the galleries bigger, and the tremor of footfalls unceasing. Then, long before we thought we could be near that ultimate Chamber, the ground-vibrations grew sharper, and we breathed a gust of raw fecundity. The echo-y sound of a huge and thronging interior was audible not far ahead. We huddled for a penultimate conference, eye-to-eye in a narrow cranny.

"You are about to understand how much we have dared in bringing you here. You will behold, and cease to cavil at our fee," Barnar told them. "We will keep to the chamber wall, following it leftward from the entryway.

Wherever we are forced to cross open ground, you must keep moving. If you let the dread of where you are freeze your legs, you will surely be crushed."

And in the next moment, we were running all-out, caught in the contagion of furious momentum that surged around us. In heartbeats, the great antechamber of the Royal room engulfed us in a turmoil of legs that churned the gloom like the ranked oars of war galleys. High overhead, blue light corruscated across all those faceted Behemoth eyes, great ocular nets too coarse to catch the images of our little selves.

There was the Royal Brood Chamber. Within, the Queen's immensity lay upon the sea of her dwarfed, adoring spawn. We crossed the threshold, and plunged along the wall. Mad dodges, fierce, quick climbs above onrushers, footwork, footwork, footwork, and our hearts and lungs laboring, laboring—for a time these struggles engulfed us.

Then a ridged seam of harder stone jutted into our path. "Up this one!" I called, and up we clambered.

High above the Chamber floor, the rough stone gave us secure and even restful perches, whence we drank in the stupefaction of the Queen amidst her generations. For a timeless time, speech seemed impiety. I mutely pointed where the nuzzling workers nursed, in clusters of like caste. We gazed, and supped the vintage of pure Awe. Once Sha'Urley spoke, as she watched a stream of workers—issuing from the gloom that shrouded the Queen's caudal region—carrying the Royal eggs high in their jaws. These eggs streamed like pearls through the underwater light, rivering toward the Incubaria, whence the larvae would be borne to the Nurseries. Sha'Urley surprised me by reciting: "Great mother, deathless Demiurge,/Mankind's nurse and demon's scourge/Our hopes are hammered in thy forge!"

"By the Black Crack!" gasped Barnar. "What is that they are bringing Her?"

We looked where he pointed, and our jaws hung ajar. Something easily ten times the size of the largest Forager was being carried on the flood of workers. Lying on its back, like a rudderless vessel it moved veeringly towards the Royal Presence. It was surely a Behemoth but, apart from its great size, it was of a make we had not seen before. Its abdomen was tapered toward a caudal point; its folded legs were inordinately massive and long. It had as well, jutting from its thoracic segment, a pair of long, bladelike wings, and by these its bearers gripped it.

They staggered under their mighty burden. The throng melted from their path and closed behind them, seeming to urge them forward toward the Queen. The Queen, for her part, twitched her jaws and tilted her head as if inquiringly towards the approaching bearers and their offering.

I unbagged Ostrogall, and cut short his effusive thanks. "Tell us, Demon," I bade him, "if you know what approaches the Queen."

"By all the Powers," fluted the unctuous fragment. "This is the Presentation of the Scions! Do you not grasp what passes here? In the Mythos that surrounds our dire predators, this scene, most darkly figured, forms the central horror. And now I find it literally, fully true! O woe for my tormented homeland! Woe for all my murdered kindred! Woe and wail!"

"The Presentation of the Scions. . . ." muttered Costard. "You mean that's a, a *princess* there being carried to the Queen?"

"It is a Queen in bud," the demon answered. "Whether the Queen approves its investiture or not falls according to a law none understand. But somehow, in just such confrontations as we now behold, the Queen determines which of her Royal infants shall go forth with a conquering army to extend, by one more Nest, her species' empire in my helpless land! Now is the recent

stir in the Nest explained! The army of the New Queen
is a-forging!"

Now the Royal babe had arrived at the only point
in the Chamber where she might seem small; directly
under the Queen's jaws. Could there have been in actual
fact the ripple of tension that I sensed throughout the
host? Could the sea of giants, with their hundred
thousand individual aims and errands, have shuddered
as one—as it seemed to me they did—a restive rearing
of heads, a palpitant pause of pistoning legs, a stir like
the horripilation of a single flesh? We scarcely breathed,
our minds wholly given to this chthonian epiphany.

The Queen's globed head tilted left, then right, the
blue light flaring across the facets of Her eye-spheres.
Within those globes She seemed to view all Time, all
Space. Her mouthparts moved, tasting the air above Her
supine daughter, while that Royal Scion, with an infant's
unknowing urgency, wrestled in her bearers' grip. The
terrible beauty of her slender, bladelike wings cut my
heart—their veins pulsed with the insurgent sap of her
nascent power. Her great legs plucked gracefully at the
air. The Queen bowed Her head.

She bowed Her head, and declared Her Royal will
by plucking off Her daughter's head and devouring it with
a loud, wet crunching. She ate Her daughter's thorax in
three bites—ate it and its kicking legs, these uprooted
limbs jutting briefly from the Royal jaws and twitching
there before they were crunched into the multifoliate
maternal maw. . . .

"And so the young Queen is not to be," intoned
Ostrogall solemnly. So rapt was I in the spectacle I did not
even mind the demon's unsolicited declamation from the
podium of my hip. "The daughter is to re-sinew the Nest's
ever-multiplying body. She is to become jaw and leg-joint,
Forager and Nurse and gluttonous grub, her flesh re-fash-
ioned into theirs! The Queen disgorges them in their
thousands, and in their thousands She devours them."

Barnar, with an effort, broke our trance. "I suggest we bend our thoughts to the business at hand. We invite you to note a certain system in the pap pores' arrangement. By now you have surely perceived how different castes imbibe at different levels on the maternal flank?"

"It is most encouraging!" assented Ha'Awley Bunt. "Plainly, there is a pap specific to the Foragers' caste!"

"Whether that which they drink," I admonished them, "is as specific to their caste as the fonts they drink it from, is of course uncertain. And if the beverage be different, can we still be sure that bigness is a specific property that it imparts? Even to the Foragers, I mean— let alone to . . . other living things?"

I spoke with some sense of rectitude, for my profit, after all, did not lie in discouraging our companions' lust for the pap. In any case, their lust seemed unaffected by these reminders. "All these things," I continued, "about the pap are uncertain, while the dangers of obtaining it are past doubt. Firstly, how is the Queen to be climbed? And if she be climbed, how is the climber to survive? For I note that you three have been as slow to see your ultimate obstacle as Barnar and I were to see it. Study the Royal flanks more closely. Look for movement, especially in the black parts."

And just then, a brace of low-flying creatures made a fortuitous swoop above the Queen and, in the next instant, a ragged blackness surged up and dragged one squawking down. All now gazed with wakened eyes.

"By the Crack" gasped Sha'Urley after a moment. "She's crawling with . . . vermin! Look there! And there, in that tangle of marbling!"

The essence of the situation was soon clear to our companions: the Royal pap-pores might or might not be oases of liquid wealth, but they were most certainly environed by armies of monsters.

"Well, it seems our course is plain enough," Ha'Awley Bunt announced, his tone resolute, yet not without a quaver in it. "The Unguent of Flight would offer us the only feasible means of harvesting the pap."

"Why do you willfully misunderstand us?" Barnar barked. "You are not *invited* to join our pursuit of the alleged Unguent. This demon here is ours—he even affirms it himself!"

"What will you do, good Chilite?" Sha'Urley drily asked. "If we follow you, will you drive us back with your drawn blades? Will you kill us if we refuse to be repulsed from following you?"

What, in the end, could we do? "We have reached a juncture," I said at last, "where some sharp lines must be drawn. Of course we cannot prevent your following us on a subworld venture whose object we regard as highly dubious—be silent!" (This to Ostrogall's attempt at protestation) "—though naturally if you thrust your presence on us you cannot expect our protection on the journey, and must fend for yourselves in that regard. But you must understand that the Unguent of Flight is to be ours, mine and Barnar's, exclusively. If it is to be had in abundance, of course, then how could we object to your having some? But if the supply is limited, we most firmly declare it now in advance to be ours alone."

"Do you know, Nifft," Sha'Urley said, "leaving aside questions of claim and title, don't you feel it's a bit churlish, a bit knavish, a bit villainous of you not to grant me even a *little* of the Unguent, if only in affectionate acknowledgement of the intimacies we have shared?"

"Let the heavens witness that I cherish those joys as you do, my dear!" I protested. "But you are over-wrought. What assurance do we have of the Unguent's reality? And supposing it real, well, to speak plainly, there is a kind of fever that thieves are prone to—perhaps never experienced by persons of business like yourself—and this is the fever of concupiscence. Barnar and I, dear Sha'Urley, are in its throes. The augmentation of our personal gain is our obsession and all-mastering aim."

"Your charming frankness disarms me," she answered with a little bow and a cool smile. "I accept your terms because I must. As for lacking your protection, I can bear it. I do not wear this sword of mine for ornament alone. Brother? Partner Costard? Are we of one will in this?"

They were, though one wouldn't say they looked blithe about it. And what shame in this? Who lightly undertakes a journey into the subworld?

"Look there," piped Ostrogall, "where they bear another Scion to the Queen!"

Her clawed feet plucked the air, as her sister's had. Her wings twitched in the grip of her bearers—did she dream she was airborne? Leading her legions on their sweep of plunder to fuel the digging of a new Nest in the hell-wall? More awesome than this princess' size— and she might have plucked a town aloft and carried it away—was the limitless fecundity that could fashion such as she and, on a regal whim, swallow her up again. She drifted in her dreamy struggle till she lay beneath her mighty Mother's jaws.

The Queen's inspection, as before, was long protracted. With little movements of Her mouthparts, She seemed to feed upon Her offspring's aura. Then slowly, slowly, She brought down Her jaws and touched them to the infant's lesser mouth, sustaining for a trembling time a contact not unlike a kiss.

"She is chosen!" cried Ostrogall, his voice a croon of tender terror. "Chosen! She now imbibes the Mother's all-empowering regurgitation. She will be sequestered in a Royal chamber, and her growth to her full flying size will be swift. In not a score of days, flanked by royal consorts winged like herself, she and her army will stream from the Nest and scourge a path of conquest through my world, till they are fed to readiness, and she has mated. Then will they go to ground, and another Nest of Death be planted in my homeland. Oh my embattled nation! Woe to my fatherland, fair to behold!"

The coronation of her Mother's kiss complete, the Royal Princess—unstruggling now, as if sated or sleepy— was borne out. "Quick!" I cried, and Barnar in the same breath cried, "Let's see where they take her!" Thus did our ambitious thoughts leap perfectly together, for my friend and I had, in the same heartbeat, imagined the incalculable loot to be had by anyone who followed the wake of a conquering army of Behemoths through the subworld. What resistance could be left standing? What riches, unregarded by the giants, would not lie spilt from their shattered coffers, shining all unguarded?

"Peace!" intoned the knowing demonstump. "I understand your urgency to be on hand when she sallies forth upon her Nesting Flight. But be at ease, my benevolent masters! All royal Incubaria lie close at hand here to the Brood Chamber. She may easily be found again, and followed, when you come back . . . on the wing."

"Well then," I said. "It seems we are all bound to the same place now. Is there any reason we should not be on our way?"

XVI

Heliomphalodon Incarnadine
Did crave to clutch the splendor of the sun . . . .

NEAR THE NEST-MOUTH, we knew, the light of
the subworld discolored the light of the tunnels. This
was our greatest fear through that long downward
journey. Through the dodging, and dashing, and diving
for cover, it came back to us, and haunted our talk
when we rested. Would our orange hue, outside the
blue gloom of the Nest, remain invisible to Behemoth
eyes? Going out astride our Forager, Barnar and I had
invisibility by our position. Down on the tunnel floor,
where every Behemoth eye bent automatic scrutiny for
parasites, would our cloaks of dye still conceal us?
Before we must worry about finding cover in the
demonrealm, we must worry about managing to exit
the Nest at all.

We had a full "day" of trekking behind us, and a bone-
tired sleep in a cramped crevice, and almost another day
again of the quick-march (to judge by the weariness in
our muscles) when, as we crouched together for a rest,

Barnar said, "There's no doubt we're near. You can smell it, can't you?"

For the Nest-smell, though rank in places, was a vital fetor, an oven aroma of life a-rising; the poisoned carrion scent of the demon-realm came coldly twisting through this womb-smell like a venemous reptile.

So we trotted the last leg of our descent with a fated, falling feeling, that hollow-gutted sensation of knowing you're launched, a loosed arrow.

We passed a turning, and there was the atrium, thunderous with traffic, awash with purple light, and windowed at its far end by the Nest-mouth raggedly framing the blood-red void of the demon-realm beyond.

"Can you run all-out? A half mile and more?" I asked the Bunts and Costard. The three of them were in the condition to be expected: eyes glazed with weariness, blistered and breathing hard. They nodded gamely, even soft Ha'Awley, but still I silently cursed them. They must surely die on us! Because—Cauldron scald them!—Barnar and I were damned if we'd let them slow us up by even one stride! "Hold close to the wall then," I gritted, "have a scent flask in hand, and *run!*"

The downward pitch was helpful, and the terror like a wave that lifts you from behind. From the giants that rushed towering by us too there came a kind of impetus, as if the gust of their passage pulled us along. Even so we slogged through the wine-red air as if submerged, our limbs and lungs fighting the drag of a thickening dread. I couldn't believe we ran unseen, though the Behemoths rushed past unheeding, high knees pumping.

"Faster! Nearly there!" I looked back to bellow—and saw a Digger, overtaking us with her jaws full of tailings, suddenly drop her burden and tilt an alert eyeglobe at Bunt and Sha'Urley, who were bringing up our rear.

Horror thrilled me, stopped me, spun me round. The Bunts still owed us a fiftyweight of specie, and should we lose the pair of them, there was no hope of extracting the sum from feckless Costard. Doubling back, I bellowed "Faster! Faster!" and, meeting the Digger, I flung my flask of brood-scent. It burst between her eyes, as I doubled round yet again, and sprinted for my life after the others.

The Digger thundered after me, her jaws thrust almost to my back (I dared not turn, but felt the whelm of air their hugeness shoved before them) and then a mighty scuffling resounded behind me and I pelted on unseized.

Just short of the Nest-mouth's threshold, I dared to look back. Two Foragers had lifted the struggling Digger in their jaws. Almost comic was the labor that she gave them, herself not far inferior to a Forager in size. But the Foragers' strength prevailed as, staggeringly, they carried her up-tunnel, returning (as the scent persuaded them) a strayed babe to the safety of its nursery.

Out the Nest-mouth we leapt, and slid down the steep pitch of the hell-wall. For a short eternity the stone ate us alive. And then, as Ostrogall had promised, a fissure, transecting our descent, stopped our plunge.

It was just deep enough to hunker down in, and it deepened as we followed it downslope. At length we could crouch and catch our breath. The Foragers pouring out of the Nest overstrode us, their hard claws loud against the stone. I lifted Ostrogall from his holster on my hip, so that we might speak eye-to-eyes.

"Thus far, you prove a faithful guide, oh Fractional Demon. We urge you to remain so—else you suffer swift incineration."

"Ineffable benefactor! My adoration and my gratitude aside, you remain indispensable to my humble survival! I must be planted in some safe recess. Repose yourselves in my complete devotion. Press on, and trust those measures I've described."

There was nothing else to do, of course. The seam, as it descended to the plain, grew into an arroyo of moderate depth, which wound away as far as we could

see. While it sank us below the line of sight of errant
Foragers, this arroyo was no haven, for demon lair-
mouths, gates, hatches and doorways honeycombed its
walls. Yet Ostrogall had suggested a countermeasure, and
we implemented it at once.

Every tapper's equipage included jacks of brood-scent.
From one of his, Barnar wetted a clout-tipped knout he
had prepared for the purpose. Bearing this scented
cudgel aloft like a flameless torch, he walked in the lead
down the arroyo, while we followed, arms at the ready.

This scent-torch, while to an adult Behemoth it
signified specifically the presence of a misplaced egg or
larva, to be hastily returned to safety, signified to
demonkind nothing so specific. To demons it simply
declared the nearness of one of their devourers. And the
hellspawn's sensitivity to the scent proved quite extreme,
with the result that Barnar's flameless brand thrust, as
it were, a phantom Behemoth before us, an invisible
vanguard, as we advanced. Far ahead down the defile,
the invisible, olfactory Behemoth awoke panic in the
laired demons who might have hunted us. Far ahead we
saw vague, busy movement in the ruddy gloom. We heard
the boom of distant hatchways slammed shut and secured,
and as we advanced, long stretches of emptiness received
us, where we found every portal sealed up tight against
our coming.

Our ploy's danger was that the brood-scent summoned an occasional Forager from her quest for food.
But these randomly attracted few were always announced
by the noise and tremor of their tread. Barnar then only
had to fling the torch from the ravine. We would take
cover, the Forager would solicitously rush back Nestwards
with its minute wooden foundling, and we would anoint
another knout and resume the ploy.

Here and there were things that eyed us before nosing
us, especially airborne things. Harpies of a huger, more
wolfish make than our late assistant swooped shrieking

down on us. I swung Ready Jack in great, whistling circles, while Barnar's axe and Sha'Urley's surprisingly deft broadsword wrought equal havoc. That stalwart young woman, when it came to a stand-and-fight, made a very good account of herself. She swung powerful two-handed overhead eights, in the Jarkeladd nomads' style, and our attackers' lopped talons danced clattering down around her in showers of smoking blood; these stubborn claws still clutched at our feet when their shorn possessors had winged shrieking off.

Long and far we travelled this ravine. We slept, and woke, and travelled long and far again, till once more we most sorely craved our rest. Once more we found a recess in the ravine wall, and stretched out our leaden limbs.

Even the sour wine of the Supreme Sap Mine's rations glowed on our palates like the most exquisite vintage, such was our weary loathing of this place, and our craving for all things born beneath the sun. Barnar and I gave the others first sleep, and they dropped straight into it.

"The approach to the Unguent of Flight seems relatively easy," I said to Ostrogall. "Even, I mean, considering this admirable evasion of the brood-scent you have so cunningly suggested."

An evasive ripple moved through the jewelry of the demon's eyes. "The approach to Unguent," Ostrogall conceded, "does, as it happens, present few dangers from my kind—at least since the spread of Behemoth into this region. But the tunnels down to the Talons of 'Omphalodon—for I may tell you now that the Talons of Heliomphalodon Incarnadine are the source of the Unguent—the Talons of 'Omphalodon themselves are guarded by demons from the Second Subworld."

We bent our most menacing scowls on him at hearing this, and the demon hastily bleated, "Access to the Unguent is readily obtainable from the Secondaries, oh

Luminous Masters! They merely require a toll, you see, from suitors for that treasure. And while I confess I don't know precisely what this toll is, it is at least absolutely certain that one may pay this toll, and still live!"

Barnar nodded thoughtfully. "Yet this is far," he said, "from assuring us that this toll is slight enough to pay. Perhaps, good Ostrogall, you should now share with us all that you know regarding the Unguent of Flight."

"I assent wholeheartedly! The matter lies thus: Less than an eon past, Heliomphaladon Incarnadine, a demon of the Tertiary Subworld, was enkindled by myths and legends of the sun sufficiently to covet that world-bathing orb for his own. 'Omphalodon reasoned that the sun's radiance, once seized and brought below by a greatsouled act of daring, would melt away the binding spells and thaumaturgic toils that chained his giant nation within the planet's bowels. His folly was his faith that the sun, once had by daring raid, would enlighten and liberate his baneful, chthonian breed—would free them to do their awful will abroad upon the earth, and possess the planet entirely and forever.

"The demon knew, of course, the fate of his great compatriot Sazmazm (see Shag Margold's Second Interjection) and knew that his Tertiary dungeon was direful hard to rise from. Nonetheless, the lure of heroism, of one great shining deed that blazons forth one's being to the ages, still held 'Omphalodon's huge heart fast in thrall.

"All the Tertiary Ceiling's natural portals have been long eons sealed, but 'Omphalodon reasoned that a cunning egress might be found by a bold drive straight up through the lithic world-bone itself—by brute penetration of the superincumbent subworlds' floors and ceilings. He devised, with long and cunning brood-time, a balm which, once it bathed his limbs and his extremities, would imbue them with a melting energy, that he might swim through leagues of primal stone as liquid-easy as an eel through water.

"Wild was the will, ancient the art, and unbounded the bravery, of Heliomphalodon Incarnadine! When he broke sunwards in his daring surge, he veritably soared through solid stone, breaching the floor of the Secondary Subworld, and plunging upwards through its massy vault.

"But here alas, his furious energies bogged down, snared in the sinewy nets of Sorcery that Wizardkind have knit so deeply in your over-world's foundations. So utterly, however, did 'Omphalodon's will imbue his every part, that these sorcerous detentions sundered him, and fragments of him mounted higher than the rest, before they in their turn were snared by stasis. His sun-craving eye, lofted by most fierce desire, was embedded in yonder vault, and became itself a kind of sun to this region of our world. And one clutch of his Talons reached almost all the way up through our floor. This grim paw of his, now frozen in the stone just under us, is still besmeared, of course, with his levitative ointment, whose stone-spurning virtues lend, in upper air, the power to stride the sky. This, of course, is what the world has come to call the Unguent of Flight.

"My kind, you may be sure, were quick to dig down to it. Secondary demons, however, were nearly as quick to come up and usurp our diggings. And, while it may be contended that 'Omphalodon's Talons lie as much in our floor as they do in the lower world's ceiling, we have always found that when dispute occurs between us, our deeper cousins oftenest prevail."

We weighed Ostrogall's words through a long silence, in which we heard a distant, ragged noise of war, the ethereal chirring and shrilling of demon rage and death-cry. We became aware that, if we clambered to the top of our ravine, yet another embattled fortress would be visible far off.

"Your knowledge of this," Barnar said at length, "is so thorough, Ostrogall! Your vagueness as regards the nature of the toll stands in strange contrast with such detailed sapience."

"It also troubles me," I put in, "that you assured us that our journey to the Unguent would be relatively brief."

"Why, so it has been, Effulgent One!" fluted the Demonstump. "We are as good as arrived already. Let us climb above and I will show you!"

And so we climbed up to the rim of the ravine. From here we saw the source of the noise we'd heard—a far, embattled fortress, as we'd thought. But Ostrogall, with a tilting of his head, said, "Look that way, along the line our ravine runs. Do you see that high ground there?"

"Can you mean that low hill yonder?" I asked.

"Not hill, but bulge," the demon said, "born of the upthrust of the giant's Talons, which were stone-frozen just underneath it an eon ago."

Though it was surely wisdom to doubt our demon's every word, I will confess a thrill went through me, to think what might lie just beneath that hill, and what power we might be soon to borrow from it.

Barnar took watch to give me first sleep, but when I snapped awake (after who knows how long?) he lay snoring like the rest. Ostrogall—that spheroid of glittery eyes—had been our guard. Perhaps he had as much to fear from his countrymen as we had.

XVII

... Nor take no more than is alloted you,
Else huge Convulsions, and your deaths, ensue.

THERE WAS no need to mount even briefly to
the open plain. As we neared the low hill capping
'Omphalodon's stone-pent Talons, a shallow defile branched
off from our ravine. We followed this a quarter mile or
so, arrived at the flank of the hill, and thus quickly
confronted one of the portals to those talons.

More precisely, we confronted what *filled* the portal—
filled it utterly, and bulged forth from it.

This Tolltaker, or at least that portion of one here
presented to our view, was like nothing so much as a
giant bud, whose tight-clenched petals were of a viscid,
purplish meat that smelled like sun-cooked carrion. It
lay as still as carrion too, until Ostrogall, startling me,
gave utterance to a shrill ululation, apparently a greeting
in some demon-speech.

At this, the bud delicately shivered. One of its petals
stirred, and extruded from the rest like a great, reeking
tongue. Embedded within was a ratlike demon—more

like a captive than an anatomical feature, for it was netted to the tongue by purple veins that pierced and pinioned it. It opened a whiskered, edentulous maw and emitted an unearthly warble that answered Ostrogall's in pitch and cadence.

With an instant impulse of distrust, I slipped the carrying bag over Ostrogall's head, crying, "Silence, stump! We are the seekers here! Make known to *us*, oh Tolltaker, what we must do to partake of the Unguent of Flight." Assuming that this demon was tongued for human speech, as Ostrogall was, I was unprepared for the Secondary's readiness to meet all comers. The entire petal retracted, re-entombing the embedded demon, and another petal thrust forth.

Beside me, Sha'Urley gasped. Perhaps we all did. A beautiful young woman lay half sunk in this demon tongue, likewise netted in a piercing mesh of veins. The pallor of her face, her lovely breasts, had a womb-licked wetness, a natal sheen. I think the most piercing horror of this epiphany was her eyes, all dark and lustrous, knowing us, a living mind behind them, yet long centuries vacant of all hope. Her voice was an echo in an empty habitation:

"Each seeker's toll," she hollowly pronounced, "is one of his limbs. You are five, and might alternatively render one of your number entire, to pay for the other four." Now another of the Secondary's petals protruded—this one the lowest of the cluster. It split open, presenting us a steamy, fanged mouth that drizzled caustic drool. Evidently it was to this esurient orifice the owed limbs were to be tendered.

The proposition took us several stunned heartbeats to digest. I answered her. "You err, oh fair and luckless captive! We are six. And this demon here, though he lack a limb or two, is all entire of mind and wit. The life of him, the nasty devious will of him, the gist of him is quite intact. What if we render him? Surely he would pay for all of us? Or pay for my partner and me, at least?"

"His wholeness of mind is of slight import to my master," she intoned. "He is a head, no more. He would pay for one."

I had expected little more; meanwhile my offer outraged our companions, and woke a bag-muffled wail from Ostrogall. "Peace, all of you!" I cried. "One must test one's ground!"

Barnar leaned near me. What he murmured in my ear was purest inspiration. I beamed. I gripped his hand. Again I addressed our tragic interpreter, while Barnar whispered to our companions, taking something from each of them.

"Unhappy young woman!" I said. "I herewith make it known to your possessor that its hellish inflexibility awakes my wrath. I have determined to slay your master, and pay no toll at all!"

"My master hears you with indifference," she emptily reported.

"Well, we shall see," I huffed, unlimbering the quiver of throwing-steel I'd brought. This comprised four in-close javelins, heavy-butted for thrusting weight, and four spears, three-quarter hafted for carrying, with the plume-shaped head I like for penetration and the short bronze neck for resilience on impact that lets a rightly-thrown stick snake its way deeper into tough spots. I hoisted and hefted a javelin, making a great show of adjusting my throwing stance. Meanwhile Barnar and Ha'Awley incon-spicuously retired to where they could climb the defile's opposite walls and, unseen, re-approach the Tolltaker along higher ground. There they would deploy a weapon of their own.

"By all the powers, beautiful one!" It was Sha'Urley, just behind me—and by her tender tone I knew she did not speak merely to assist our distraction of the Tolltaker, but rather spoke outright from her heart. "Who are you? Ah my poor sister! How came you to this vile dur-ance?"

This in some measure seemed to stun the beauteous thrall of the puppeteering demon. Her startled eyes seemed to stare into wastes of time we could not know, as if, in melancholy horror, she only now remembered she had had a name, a native home, a soul . . . .

"I was Niasynth . . ." she said, wonderingly. "I was born in Saradown of world-wide fame for ships, and sailing folk. . . ."

"Alas, poor fair one," Sha'Urley breathed. Were those tears in her eyes? "It is a name unknown to me."

"I came to the infamous port of Bawd, renowned for decadence. . . . I lay with a handsome stranger, who drugged me and sold me to a demon-broker . . ."

"Fair sufferer!" I cried, "your liberation is at hand!" I knew as I spoke that I lied, unless her likely death were liberation. I pitched the javelin mightily. It slipped through the tiny aperture of the bud where the petal-points met, vanishing utterly, waking scarce a tremor from that mountainous demonmeat.

"My master bids me mock the paltriness of your power to do it harm," Niasynth emptily intoned.

"Indeed!" I raged, hefting now a spear. Now Barnar and Ha'Awley had crept into view above, and at opposite sides of, the defile. "Make known to that heap of reeking meat," I raged, "that I herewith repay its callous tyrannies!" I gave my spear-cast a goodly wind-up dance, to allow my friends to coincide their assault precisely with what slight distraction my weapon's impact might afford, lest the Tolltaker detect *their* weapon's approach.

I sank my shaft near all its length straight down the throat of the jaws the demon had thrust out to take our toll. The jaws engulfed the shaft without a tremor, but simultaneously my colleagues squeezed out the whole contents of four full flasks of brood-scent on the demon's dorsal surface.

I waited through several heartbeats, strung tight, expecting the demon's surge of panic at the whelm of

Behemoth-scent, and sudden withdrawal. Surely so
powerful a gust of spoor, coming from above and behind,
must throw the demon into an upheaval of escape. It
did not even stir. Though it were a secondary demon,
how could it be indifferent to Behemoth's scent?

Here came Bunt and Barnar tumbling pell-mell back
into the ravine. At a loss, I began deploying a third cast,
with further declamations of wrath and resolution. But
I had scarce cocked to throw when I sensed a fleet
approaching tremor in the ground. I flung my spear to
work what last diversion it could, and dove to hug the
ground. From overhead, huge jaws thrust down into the
defile, and seized the demon just where its blubberous
mass sprouted from the stone.

In the instant of seizure the Forager's aim had merely
been to lift and bear away what she had taken for a
misplaced infant. But the furious power of the demon's
reaction quickly galvanized her to an answering rage.
Undoubtedly some taste of demonmeat—for the Tolltaker
wounded itself with its struggles—counteracted the
delusion of the brood-scent. The hungry Forager pulled
mightily, her clawed feet shrieking on the stone. Three
rods of writhing demon was hauled twisting from its shaft.
Incredibly, such seemed its subworld strength, it balked
at further extraction, despite the Forager's mightiest
pullings.

And then a second Forager came pistoning up the
draw, and added its jaws to the demon's uprooting. More
heaving, bucking demon-thew came out.

A third Forager loomed above. We fled the ravine and
found more distant cover, while vast jaws tore, demon-
blood sprayed, and the vermiform Tolltaker writhed and
thrashed and hammered the stone with its ever-dimi-
nishing bulk. Did luck not love us? How we had blundered to success!

Soon, crops full, our huge assistants sped away.
Returning up the ravine, we found it sprayed with purple

gore and littered with torn flesh—and found the tunnel-
mouth open and unguarded.

"Look there!" Sha'Urley cried. "Niasynth lives!"

If live she did, it could not be for long. Poor demon-
thrall, poor human puppet! Though the slab of hellmeat
she was bound to had indeed fallen clear of the Foragers'
feast, it had bled out a purple pond already, and it
seemed that she, too, dwindled with the bleeding.
Sha'Urley, kneeling by her, began with her sword's edge
to shave the demon tissue from Niasynth, though still
that beauteous thrall bled her own blood from the stubs
of sundered demon veins that pierced her everywhere.
Her voice came dreamy with her waning strength:

"Thanks, dear sister, but I die apace. Hear me, earth-
fellows. Each of you may scrape off of 'Omphalodon's
uncovered flesh no more Unguent than will fill one of
the bowls you will find within the shaft. Should any one
take more, it will be known. The Secondaries' spells
enmesh the Talons. Huge convulsions, and your deaths,
will follow any act of greedy excess by any one of you.
One bowl each, no more. With all my heart I thank you
for this death's sweet . . . sweet . . . deliverance."

"We too rejoice for you. Away then!" I cried.

"First help me!" Sha'Urley urged. "I think she may
be saved!"

"Alas, fond hope!" I cried. Already my whole spirit
was below, in a rapture of near-achieved delight. The four
of us plunged into the shaft-mouth, while still Sha'Urley
knelt by bleeding Niasynth, plying her swordblade with
surgical tenderness.

An antechamber received us, where the light of
torches socketed in the wall mixed with dim, vinous light
leaking down from the subworld above. Here where his
eyes might help, and his treacheries could no longer
hinder, I unhooded Ostrogall. "Please, gentlemen!" he
cried, "Take her admonition firm to heart! For the least

excess in harvest of the Unguent will be known. And such
is the savage rigor of the Secondaries' spirit that they
have provided for these tunnels' ruin, sooner than bear
pilferage past what they prescribe!"

Half-hearkening, we scanned an inscription chiselled
in the wall, above a heap of carven stone bowls. These
lines of High Archaic were known to us. Their best-
known description is found in Finnik of Minuskulon's
Iambical Ditties:

> *Heliomphaladon Incarnadine*
> *Sunken in his Dark did long repine,*
> *And craved to clutch the splendor of the*
> *   sun*
> *Whose glow and grandeur, legended in*
> *   lore,*
> *The mighty demon ne'er laid eye upon,*
> *'Mured as he was in his Third Subworld*
> *   lair.*
>
> *Crouched where fang-tormented myriads*
> *   moan*
> *And Universe is but a rumored light,*
> *The demon gnawed Forever like a bone*
> *Whilst solar phantoms scorched his murky*
> *   sight,*
>
> *Till was more real this storied star to him*
> *Than were his world's inexorable walls.*
> *His molten hands did through the world-*
> *   bone swim. . . .*
> *Now behold where all disjoint he sprawls!*
> *On sunless hell his eye forever shines,*
> *Heliomphalodon Incarnadine.*

I hefted one of the bowls. It was capacious enough,
perhaps, if one but knew the concentration of the

Unguent's power. I could not repress the thought, however, that it would not hold half the capacity of one of the leathern jars that we had brought to bear our harvest away in. Perhaps Ostrogall sensed my disappointment, for he elaborated:

"The Secondaries, oh Luminous Masters, have involved the Talons in trigger spells. Take but an iota of excess and the Talons are fractionally released from the detaining sorcery ensnaring them. They surge upward. All this tunnelwork meets grinding annihilation in one clawtwitch. Believe me, none in all this time, not even the grimmest of my own compatriots, has ever dared to flout this iron limit. Should even one of us let greed over-rule him here, we all shall die together."

The four of us nodded solemnly at one another. "Well, then," Barnar said, scanning the several tunnels that branched from this chamber, "Nifft and I will take this way, you two that one, and the first to find our quarry can halloo the others."

As Costard's and Bunt's torches dwindled down the central shaft, we took the leftward one. We began going at a jog-trot, the pair of us moved by a wordless accord—Barnar, I am sure, mutely assessing distances and times, as I was.

Cut by demon art, the shaft walls had a melted smoothness, and were amply diametered to allow much larger beings than ourselves an easy passage. Our going down, though somewhat steep, was neither difficult, nor long.

The cavernous gallery we shortly came to was vaulted so high that our torchlight could not show us its upper reaches. And one entire wall of it was a glittery expanse of ophidian scales.

Barnar and I had once stood before the naked hugeness of everted Sazmazm. It may be that this stone-bound 'Omphalodon was a being less immense, but in the wholeness, the intact design of this grasping limb of his, there was an equal awe. Above, at the ragged limit of our torchlight, we discerned a seam in the scaly fabric, just such a fold as one's palm shows where it articulates. Fossiled in its sunward reach, this grasping extremity was the brute embodiment of the great demon's will; the very shape of his ambition loomed above us. Terror and exaltation filled us equally, as did simultaneous inspiration. "Let's try it out!" we cried, almost together.

"What must we do?" I asked Ostrogall.

"Besmear your hands and bootsoles. And please remember that this application must be deducted from your alloted bowl-ful."

Perhaps we feared the giant would feel, and move in answer to, our touch, for almost cringingly did we stroke our palms adown the waxy sheen that lacquered all its scales. But these scales were dense and hard as stone; ourselves it was who shuddered at the contact.

In our reaching downward to besmear our bootsoles, the Unguent's power was revealed to us, for the downthrust of our hands lifted us half a fathom off the ground.

"Without exertion of your conscious will to move earthward," Ostrogall told us, "your almost every movement spurns the ground beneath, and lifts you."

Our feet anointed, yelping and laughing with discovery like boys, arms and legs dogpaddling, we climbed into the torchlit gloom of the cavern. What fierce, rare joy it was! We quickly learned a swimming motion that drove us with increasing accuracy wherever we listed. "Let's try the tunnel, for speed," I cried. Were we preparing for what followed? I cannot think so—it did not seem so. We found we could swim up the tunnel we had come down much faster than either of us could run it.

Lust to possess this power in quantity soon turned our flight back down toward the cavern. The trick of swimming groundwards we brought off with some few bruises, discovering that we must will the specific rate of descent as well as the mere direction. Now, bowls ready, facing the scaly wall . . . we paused.

"You know, Barnar," I said, "what would be simpler for the Secondaries than to post a rumor of dire consequences? What could be easier than, by mere rumor, to minimize the taking of all seekers here, and thus prolong the cannibal profit of those same Secondaries' enterprise?"

"The very notion gnaws my thoughts as well!" my friend exclaimed.

Ostrogall's sharp bleat of protest was muffled when I sheathed him in his bag. "I'll be completely frank with you, Barnar," I went on. "I feel a powerful, unshakeable conviction that we are safe to fill our jars completely with this glorious ointment. How unlikely it is, after all, that the Secondaries would actually annihilate this huge source of profit, in punishment of pilferage!"

Barnar nodded vigorously, eyes shining. "You speak my very mind and heart, old friend! I will say more. I will tell you that in this inexplicable yet all-compelling conviction that I share with you, in this I recognize one of those moments of truth given to all men, one of those life-altering gambles that the soul must make to lift itself to greater destiny than was at first ordained it!"

Ostrogall grew shrill in his pouch, and I cried him, "Peace, thou hellish fragment! You have yourself allowed that none have dared to try this vaunted limit! It is a threat, no more, a bugbear whose sole potency lies in that none have ventured to assay it! Now be mute, or die herewith!"

Perhaps some half conscious vestige of caution led Barnar and me to trade a look, then swiftly act in tandem, abbreviating as fully as might be the act of harvesting the Unguent. With shaving sweeps of our swords' edges, we scraped off bladefuls of the waxen goo, and these in turn we scraped off into our jars. Twice, thrice . . . four sweeps, and we had filled and stoppered these containers, sheathed our blades, snatched up our torches, and swum into the air towards the tunnel we'd come down by.

This spontaneous haste of our departure proved fortunate. Almost at once, the vaulted stone entombing us groaned, and cracked, and hugely shuddered. A ripple of movement passed along the scaly wall of demonskin.

Madly we swam the air up-tunnel, bellowing, "Bunt! Costard! Make for the surface!" These shouts evinced more fellow-feeling than common sense, for the shriek of splintering stone, and the clamor of flying shards through which we flew, must render needless such verbal warnings.

Our tunnel collapsed behind us as we flew into the antechamber, and the gust of air it squeezed out after us set us tumbling, our torches blown out like candles. Here came Bunt and Costard sprawling out of their own tunnel, likewise collapsing behind them, as even now the antechamber shuddered and heaved and spilled out towering fragments from its riven walls in colossal slow collapse around us. We swooped towards the fallen pair. Their dropped bowls of Unguent skittered away across the convulsing floor as we seized them one-handed by their belts—I Costard, Barnar Bunt—and swam one-handed with them for the entryway.

Our flight proved only slightly hampered by the burden of our companions. We arrowed still quicker than a man might sprint on firm ground, which was far faster than any man might actually run across that heaving, buckling stone.

Yet the "O" of the entryway was still far, too far to reach. Then the gallery's roof and walls and floor heaved violently together like a clenching fist. Again a surge of squeezed-out air accelerated us—shot us wheeling out the collapsing entry, as a dart is powered from a blow-pipe's muzzle.

Ahead, across the dancing subworld floor, Sha'Urley

had got clear a hundred strides or so, though she labored with the slack and blood-bright shape of Niasynth across her shoulder.

"Get a grip on them as we swoop near!" I shouted at Bunt and Costard. With both their hands free, they got a firm though awkward hold on the struggling women, and we had all four of them aloft. We swam one-handed through the ruddy air, and dared to glance back. We saw the accursed hill of stone erupt, spraying wheeling boulders through the subworld sky.

Four black, titanic Talons sprouted from the subworld floor. Shedding stone, they thrust up, and up, and up—reached near a third the distance to the stony sky. There, though rooted at the wrist, they stirred and swayed, free, after an eon's burial, to move once more.

And it seemed the great star-pupiled eye, bloody sun to this fiendish domain, beheld with grieving joy this fragment of its former self, resurgent in its captive sight.

XVIII

Reach up thy claw!
To rise one world is given.
Live still in woe,
Still one stone sky from heaven.

"THUS," SHA'URLEY TOLD US. "Pluck them sharp like roots . . . see how her flesh heals whole and scarless where I've pulled them out?"

We had laid Niasynth in a recess of the ravine wall, having retreated some few miles from the Talons. These Talons of 'Omphalodon filled half our sky, sluggishly clawing the air, as if still disbelievingly testing their disinterment. The Unguent of Flight, for any others who might now come seeking it, must be a prize obtained more through a mountain climber's than a spelunker's skills.

The sundered network of demon veins that pierced Niasynth's body dribbled her own bright human blood until we plucked them out. We all worked intently at this, while Sha'Urley, with her poignard's edge, tenderly shaved off the last slabs of demonmeat from the young captive's limbs. As the Secondary's putrid substance fell away, Niasynth's skin, though still drawn and pale, resumed a youthful luster, a glow it must have worn long centuries gone when she was taken. Thus she resumed a beauty destined to be dust in ages past, but for the nefandous immortality that had engulfed it here, time out of mind. At length, her groanings done, her brow unknotted, clean and whole, she slept.

We moved away from her, as present business brought the five of us all eye to eye. Bunt had evidently prepared some grave remonstration, but Costard, forestalling him, bleated out, "Uncle Barnar, by the Crack, how *could* you?"—his very voice cracking on the question.

Barnar and I did trade—I do confess—one quick look that weighed denial. But we chose in the end a manly frankness. I showed Costard a condolent smile, and thwacked his shoulder. "We took a gamble, and lost."

"You took a gamble, and *we* lost our Unguent of Flight!" The petulant young dolt seemed really to be losing his voice, so badly was it breaking, his little ferret's eyes fairly popping under his low-slung brows. "*You two* came *flying* out! You can hardly keep on the ground right now!"

"It's hard getting the knack of willing oneself down, Nephew," Barnar explained to him. "With our extremities anointed, most casual movements act to thrust us aloft. We are just now learning to think ourselves steadily aground without being wholly occupied with the thinking."

"Let's just come to the point," urged Sha'Urley, managing a fairly friendly smile. "It's pretty plain you've come out packing a gluttonous excess of the Unguent—whence else the catastrophe? Whence *that*?"

She swept her hand towards the towering Talons. And just then, as we looked, three Foragers swarmed up one of 'Omphalodon's digits. We saw the flash of their comparatively tiny jaws, saw little bright rills of the

demon's blood—and then saw what we might have
expected, but were stunned to view: the Foragers swam,
legs flailing, into the air.

Airborne, a madness seized them—nothing in their
nature prepared them for this. Their legs pumped wildly
and they careened away into the ruby gloom, their frenzy
for the solid ground lofting them ever higher. Yet even
as we watched, a dozen more Foragers converged on the
Talons, drawn perhaps by the smell of 'Omphalodon's
blood. Of these, some two or three—treading where the
demon flesh was torn or washed with gore—maintained
their footing, and fed. Meanwhile, we saw in the wide-
spread flux of Behemoths—formerly converging toward
the distant fortress—a rippling directional change towards
a new cynosure: the Talons of 'Omphalodon.

Awesome though this spectacle was, narrow questions
of property very soon re-engrossed our companions. "The
only real question here, then," resumed Sha'Urley, "is will
you, or will you not, give the three of us some Unguent,
we whose shares of it your greed foreclosed?"

"Can we properly speak of 'shares,'" I asked, "of
something whose having lies wholly in the chance of the
taking? You, for instance, were detained not by us, but
by—most creditably, to be sure!—young Niasynth in her
extremity. Meanwhile, the esteemed Ha'Awley, and young
Costard here, were prevented of *their* so-called shares by
their failure to keep their footing, *and* their Unguent,
when the ground became unsteady. As you will readily
grant, we did everything we could to aid you during that
upheaval, but to put it bluntly, it is the first rule of
adventuring that each man must look to his own take."

Costard had more squawking to do, and the Bunts,
both of them, had further casuistries to propound. We
remained firm, though it grew increasingly difficult to
remain civil at the same time. Scanning about me for
some relief, I saw the Talons' lower portions now all
befurred with Foragers, while the upper joints were

beclouded with more Foragers in scrambling flight. The immense digits flexed furiously, and flexed again, and we could hear the faint splintery report of crushed Behemoths, whose minuscule debris fell from the workings of those giant joints. But still the flood of Foragers converged. I looked skywards.

Did 'Omphalodon's blood-weeping Eye up there, moon of this lower place—did his Eye move slightly? Scan more particularly this long-hid, new-born part of himself? And weep the more to see it freed but partly, still one sky lower than the sun-burnished heaven that was his ancient aim?

"Enough, Costard," Sha'Urley cried—for only he still harangued us now. "You deafen us all to no good! Is it not plain that our friends here would sooner leap naked into flames than surrender the least tittle of their takings?" She turned to me. "Do you know, Nifft, looking at you now, I almost have to smile, even to laugh. . . ." And indeed, first she smiled, and then she laughed—quite genuinely, it seemed. "You must forgive my saying it," she added when she could, "but I see you there, such an intense, crouched, piggish, greedy apparition at this moment, all tightened up right down to your bunghole at the bare notion of letting one tenth-pennyweight of your possession go!"

"I'm a little saddened," was my moderate response, "that you deem this crass turn of tongue to be warranted with me. I can only declare the simple truth, that Barnar and I have acted at every step with the best intentions toward yourselves. And we stand ready even now—that is, if we fail not of your standards of transportation—to carry you all back to the Nest's comparative safety. There awaits, after all, that first endeavor we stand contracted for, and from which, I believe, you projected the only profit that *we* engaged to bring you? For now, indeed, we plainly have power to earn that further payment you stand sworn to, Ha'Awley? Eh? While we stand dithering, the milking of the Royal Mother remains to do."

This moved them, though it did not silence Costard, who cavilled as we tied our climbing line into harnesses. "It's just so un*think*ably un*fair*, Uncles! You steal a piece of demon from *my* nursery, you use *my property* to locate and obtain this marvellous Unguent, and then (ignoring for the moment how you greedily *ruined* everybody else's takings) then you *refuse*—"

Here Barnar gently clamped the young man's mouth and the back of his head between two huge, scarred hands. "Hear me now, Costard," he said with an almost tender urgency. "You do not own the Nest. Once and for all, you own only the shafts and hoses and pumps wherewith you *rob* the Nest. And had you been presented with this piece of demon, you would not have thought to make any use of it whatever. And had you learned from it of the Unguent, you would never have survived the going after. And had you survived the going after, would you have paid an arm or a leg to the Tolltaker?

"So hear me now. If you speak a single word more— a single word!—I will set you afoot and let you walk back by yourself as best you can." Experimentally, he took his hand off Costard's mouth. At last, nothing came out.

We tied loops of line that the Bunts and Costard could sit in. For Niasynth we tied a more complex harness that she might lie in. Her eyes came open as we laid her in it.

She took Sha'Urley's tenderly proferred sips of wine. At the feel of terrestrial vintage in her throat, Niasynth's face convulsed as with a painful sweetness. At the taste of the wine, her wondering gaze seemed to remember earthly soil, and sky, and sun. Tears swelled and spilled from her eyes. "Oh sweet powers, what have I become in this Eternity? Have I not grown most loathsome to look on?"

Sha'Urley leaned near her smiling. In truth, that comely Dolmenite had a warm-hearted streak in her, whatever cross-grained tempers she might show.

"No, sweet Niasynth, you are lovely still. A lean and

vulpine beauty's yours, as though you'd not passed thirty summers' age. Drink more. Thus. Now rest. You are with friends. You will go up and live under the sun once more. . . ."

I tied the men's two lines to the front of my belt, as Barnar did those of the women to his. I stood aside a moment to unbag Ostrogall, and though ill use and outrage flashed from his hundred dissimilar eyes, his speech was flutes and hautboys once again. "Ineffable ones! We now may equally rejoice, may we not? You to have the marvel I promised you, and I am to be re-planted in my natal soil—in some suitable little streambed not far from here, perhaps?"

"We do rejoice, estimable demonstump!" I answered. "And we regard you with the fondest gratitude. Up and away then, Barnar?"

"Up and away with a will," Barnar cried. We had begun learning how to stay aground by maintaining a half-conscious thought of doing so, a kind of mental anchor in the earth that yet let us turn our thoughts elsewhere. Now, with one swimming motion and a will to soar, we smoothly climbed up through the wine-red gloom. We flew along the ravine, at perhaps a half a furlong's altitude above it.

"Please note, my Masters," Ostrogall quaveringly ventured, "how I've served you. I've brought you here safe and enriched you, O my luminous benefactors! Surely you would not dream of denying me the simple, easy re-plantation I—"

"Peace, Oh Fractional One!" I answered. "The fact is, Ostrogall, now that it comes to the point of honoring our contract, we find an insuperable revulsion arising in our hearts at the bare notion of doing *anything* to prolong your execrable demon life for even one instant, now that we securely possess the Unguent we craved, and can find our own unaided way back to the Nest."

"It is a deep instinctual loathing," Barnar elaborated,

"of human for demonkind. We find that we cannot, even with the best will in the world, withstand its atavistic ferocity."

"On the other hand," I added, "it seems unfair to inflict on you anything other than your true fate, the one we saved you from. Therefore, in a gesture of decency, and respectful acknowledgment of your honesty with us, we will bear the labor of carrying you back to the Nursery, and the jaws of your destined grub."

I will confess that Barnar and I were not entirely without a certain policy in saying what we did. The eye-studded demon seemed extremely upset. His vocal oboe had a cracked reed. "I must say, oh most effulgent Karkmahnite, most august Chilite—I must say, and of course I apologize most abjectly for doing so, I must say that you—and I say it in all cringing humility—that you take a really vile, verminous, villanous, odious, shameful and despicable advantage of my relative powerlessness in your hands. I say this with the profoundest and most reverent respect for yourselves, of course."

"Of course." I nodded as I swam, as though we were speaking face to face. I was growing quite used to conversations with this monstrous eye-crusted head that rode on my hip. "Nonetheless, I don't think I would be judged *over*-villainous by anyone who studiously reflects on this question: What could I rightfully be said to *owe* to the headpiece of a polyocular balloon of demonslime like yourself, whose pestilent life I plucked from death's jaws in the first place?"

A Forager hurtled above us, mad legs milling the air. Far ahead of us, two others plunged, describing long, flat parabolae toward the plain. Their smattering of the Unguent, acquired by climbing up 'Omphalodon's palm, dwindled in power, it seemed, with use. And indeed we ourselves could feel a diminution of the lift engendered by each stroke of our hands and feet. Though we carried a pair of adults apiece, and some fiftyweight of gems each, the work of flight had been at first easier than swimming. Already we felt that we breasted a more laborious medium, and were stroking harder for the same buoyancy.

"It would seem," Barnar offered, "that the Unguent is consumed proportionably to the weight it bears." And with this discovery, it panged me to the heart to think that we must surely dip into our precious store of the marvellous ointment to finish our present journey. But I can report with some well merited pride that I resisted the very powerful urge to set our companions afoot and thereby conserve our treasure. We toiled on—and more and more toilsome it grew—and at length we did indeed dip into our treasured hoards, and re-anoint our hands and feet

Meanwhile Ostrogall had not fallen mute. "Only consider, venerated ones!" he urged, "how I have produced for you that which I promised! Have I not undeniably benefitted you? See how you fly! Consider what other treasures you now have power to take unscathed! How, therefore, can you not feel some shred of . . . let's not call it *honor*, let's call it simple *equity?* Eh?"

"We grant we are not unmindful of this perspective on the matter," Barnar answered him. "But Nifft and I, you see, are simply overborn by a native loathing for yourself— your very race of being! For instance, by way of illustration, I would venture to hazard that the cycle of your life thus far has been one unbroken sequence of the most appalling parasitisms and loathsome plunderings of other beings. Please correct me if I err in this."

"Well," said the demon impatiently, "how *else* would I have reached adulthood? The larval forms which bore my spores across the desert, these tunnel to the fore-brains of their hosts, and their little eyes feast as directly upon their hosts' nightmares as do their little jaws upon their hosts' cerebral tissues. Then too, my cercarial shapes for aqueous transmission strip the host's spinal cord as they ascend it. The predators that devour the emptied husks of these hosts engulf as well my nymphal instars, and these eat those second hosts as well quite hollow, before we fly out like thistledown across the wind and light upon our rooting places.

"But what of this, gentlemen? Surely all things that live and breathe are entirely fed, shod, garbed and girded with the bodies of their many victims? What being lives, down here or in the over-world, whose blood is not the stolen sap of other lives?"

"I grant," I said, "you say no more than truth. But, you see, you offer mere reason to confute in us what is not reasoned, but is a brute, unarguable revulsion. And yet, do you know . . . ? It now occurs to me that this sullen and retrograde emotion of ours, though it can't be argued with, might be appeased, might be *bought off* so to speak, if you could think of some further service you could do that would increase our profit from our sojourn here below."

This produced, at last, a silence in my subworld side-piece. And indeed it scarcely needed further talk to assure us Ostrogall's guidance would be ours on our return to the Royal Chamber's awesome precincts.

Now the terrain rose towards the mountain roots. We turned to take our last look at 'Omphalodon's Talons. Even thus distant from them now we could see they swarmed, wholly furred with Foragers. The great claws struggled with awesome and undiminished vigor— clenching again and again, crushing hundreds with each grip then flailing side to side, smiting the plain with distant thunder. But though whole armies of Behemoths died at each stroke, their convergent tides neither slackened nor diminished.

"Have the Foragers ever before brought Tertiary meat back to the Nests?" Ha'Awley Bunt mused below us, with a note of something like fear. No one had an answer.

We turned a parting look to 'Omphalodon's Eye. Its ragged black pupillary hole seemed contracted in agony, while its glossy orb bled even more copious crimson rivulets across the seamed ceiling vault, and down to the stream-netted plains.

Then we turned our flight up to the mountain wall, and began to swim through the air with a will, gathering speed for the perils of re-entry.

XIX

What say we sally forth once more,
A-scouring the subworld floor?
What say we cast our nets again,
And bring more shining riches in?

OUR LARVAL CHAMBER—how homelike it seemed to us now, after the greater terrors we had tasted! Barnar saw to our companions' entertainment in the operations nook while I discreetly added our re-collected gems to our cache. We then wasted no time in coming to business.

"Here's how we reckon relative values," Barnar told them cheerily. "For two amphorae of giants' pap, we will require no more than the stipulated three hundredweight of gold specie, in consideration of your misfortunes with the Unguent. In addition, however, it seems only fair to require an annual tithe, in perpetuity, of all your earnings from the pap's use."

I think they literally gasped in unison, so equal were they in the little arts of haggling. We did not budge of course, and of course, ultimately, they had to agree.

Nonetheless, they really made quite a convincing display of outrage and vexation, and, for all that we knew it was mere art, we could not help but find these remonstrations a bit offensive.

Their reckonings among themselves were fierce. We courteously abstained from eavesdropping, but it was clear from his half-muffled bleatings that the cashless Costard was inexorably squeezed down to yielding outright what we knew to be his only asset, the mine itself, in consideration of the Bunts' providing his share of the specie, which we, of course, required in advance.

It happened that the Bunts' Hivery had many casks of mead warehoused in Dry Hole, and these could be liquidated within a day or so. The requisite sum might reach our hands in a little more than three days, " . . . if we ride without sleeping," Sha'Urley concluded, rather stiffly.

"That is highly convenient," I told her warmly. "We don't mind waiting a bit for you to muster the gold, but we don't want to cool our heels down here any longer than necessary." In fact we had a further, far more lucrative enterprise in mind, and this was the real reason for our impatience.

As Costard and Ha'Awley Bunt trudged toward the gangway bucket, I gave Sha'Urley a tender little signal to draw her a bit aside. Her face inscrutable, she came a few paces away with me. "Oh beauteous Dolmenite," I smiled to her, "is it overbold of me to remember the joys we took together here, not so long ago?"

She gave me an indefinable look of shock, and stared a moment, emotion struggling in her face. Then she laughed—a little stridently, I thought.

"Dear Miser," she grinned at me. "Can you actually suggest lovemaking? Let me try somehow to express to you how little I am inclined to make love to you. Let me describe what I would *rather* do to you! Not beat your head repeatedly with a knout or cudgel, no—not actually crack your skull, I suppose. But let's say, tie you on your knees, and then take a good two-handed grip on the tail of a large, dead fish—a fish some two or three days dead—and then spend a leisurely half hour or so smacking your long, broken-nosed, greedy *face* with it."

"Forgive me. I've chosen an unpropitious moment."

"Come, please, and help me get Niasynth into the bucket with us. We'll be back with your gold as fast as we can."

Niasynth, the pallid sojourner-below, sat upright now, and her eyes saw us more steadily, less often lost in inner vistas of nightmare. Looking in Barnar's eyes, and mine, she said, her voice shaking slightly, "I am going to see the sunlight again." She gave us her hands. Cold and infinitely frail they seemed, those sun-starved hands of hers!

When they were gone, I wished I had gone with them. How I craved the sunlight, longed for the wide cerulean sky and its sweet, cool breath against my face, for the night's jewelled black, sailed by a slim-hulled moon. . . . But Barnar and I were agreed that our attunement to these subterranean realms was a precious asset, and that it would be folly to interrupt our acclimation here with a heady but disorienting sojourn in the upper world.

"Now for a good long sleep," Barnar enthused, readying his hammock.

"Yes, " I said, "I suppose I should feed the rest of this demon back to the grub I took it from."

Ostrogall, in what for him amounted to a transport of rage, had been absolutely silent since our return to the Nest. We had placed his stump in his usual nook where he could look about him, and he had sat there dead mute from that moment.

"You might as well," Barnar boredly assented. "Mind your hands putting him in—you might get them bitten off."

"Well bethought. I know! If I skewer him on a spearpoint, I can poke him in from a safe distance."

"Excellent idea."

I made a business of choosing my longest spear. Then
I tucked Ostrogall in his holster on my hip, took up the
spear, and strolled off down the nearest lane-way amid
the larval shoals. At last Ostrogall broke the silence.

"In mere point of information, I must remind you that
if you . . . consummate that larval meal you interrupted,
then I will emerge in the form of minute eye-spores
mingled with the grub's feces. I can then exist as an
exiguous brood infection till some adult, or series of
them, tracks me out again to the subworld's floor. In no
more than a century I will be growing on the plain once
more, greeting the Eye of 'Omphalodon with my gladsome gazes!"

"I rejoice for you!" I answered. "In your present
extremity, what comfort you must draw from this reflec-
tion!"

A pause. "I will not conceal," Ostrogall sighed, "that
I'd prefer a quicker restoration of my interrupted life,
and one that did not involve the workings of those
loathsome larval jaws upon what remains of my person."

"Do you know, Ostrogall, your saying this is most
opportune! Barnar and I were only lately musing how
your expertise in matters Behemothine might be of use
to us in our upcoming venture. And we even agreed we
could offer you your restoration to your native soil as
recompense for this service. What stymied us was our
fear that you would now mistrust our offer, and refuse
it!"

"Mistrust?" fluted Ostrogall, his voice quavering as he
strove for a honied tone. "Mistrust your irreproachable
selves? I won't deny I *hesitate*. I won't deny your . . .
recent decisions give me *pause*. But how could I mistrust
such paragons of rectitude, such patterns, such epitomes
as your peerless selves? Still, may I humbly hope that
you really *will* re-plant me, if I aid you in the, ah, milking
of the Royal Mother?"

"Ostrogall, if you aid our enrichment in this next foray,

there is nothing on earth or under it so firm as our
intention of re-planting you!"

Barnar and I slept—how can we say how long, beyond
that it was long enough to purge the poisons of fatigue
from our muscles and minds? When we woke, and
ravenously breakfasted, we found our thoughts not so
much engaged by the milking of the Queen, as by that
even more lucrative project we contemplated—dared to
contemplate!—after the milking was accomplished. To
follow the Young Queen, and her conquering army, across
the hell-floor. The question that consumed us was, in
essence: how much wealth could we fly with? At the
outset, we burned with a delirium of possibility, for we
had seen the Unguent put Foragers aloft.

So we looped some line around the tapered ends of
a grub, and strove to fly with it. We could not budge
it from the ground. At this juncture Ostrogall warbled
from his perch, "It is said that the Unguent allows the
flier to carry ten times his own weight into the air, and
that, be he light or heavy, this is the limit of what he
may bring aloft with him. I forebore to speak before
you'd tried it for yourselves, feeling sure you'd insist on
a personal test."

It galled us to find our hunger for gain thus tram-
melled, but we made our peace with it at length,
reflecting that with selectivity, more than a ton apiece
of subworld plunder could amount to a wealth vast by
any standards, especially when added to what we had
already won.

But any thought of what this wealth might purchase
led us straight to that gulf that yawned between us. Some
airborne exploration of the Nest seemed preferable to
reopening this controversy.

Hovering ghosts, we haunted our way through another
nursery, then through several Incubaria, where lay pearly
troves of eggs, which Nurses incessantly turned, and

groomed of parasites. The hatchlings from these eggs, smaller versions of the grubs we knew, were fed up to size with lumps of a pale food of cheesy softness. We tracked a Nurse to the source of this substance—chambers full of a fungus unlike the growth which gave the Nest its light. This stenchful mold sprouted obese fruiting bodies like giant, hairy strawberries, which, macerated in the Nurses' jaws, became the hatchlings' nutriment. This fungus crop grew from a substrate of demon mulch, a coarse mash of chopped bodies, of bone and limb, talon, wing, fin, skull and thorny muzzle (some of it still a-twitch and astir with stubborn vitality) which melted slowly, consumed in the slow fire of the fungal growth. Here and there melting mouths still muttered, and fragmented visages alertly flashed at us their shards of eyes. . . .

"This fungus perhaps provides a kind of predigested demon pabulum," Barnar hazarded.

"Can we wonder," I answered, "that a diet of demon meat must be eased up to?"

We were chary of our Unguent, or we might have pushed exploration further. We found besides that, once returned to our operations nook, we were more than ready for more sleep, such had been our recent exertions. And when we awoke for the second time, it was to the voices of our returning partners.

XX

Airily wander the Royal terrain
Where profit and pasture so vastly abound.
But warily plunder when findest thy Gain,
For the taking may break thee, and drag thee
a-down!

THE QUEEN'S abdominal surface was oceanic;
between the broad, glossy undulations of her major ribs,
were endless local texturings of the mottled hide, lesser
vales and knolls, troughs and tumuli. We flew, and viewed
the wonder of Her planetary scope.

The abdomen's harlequin puzzle of black and white
was—as we had been prepared to find it—alive with
parasites and hyperparasites. "There now!" warned Barnar.
Side-stroking through the air, we veered leftward above
a little valley-bottom whence, with a glittery ripple of their
jointed backs, a host of hound-sized crustaceiods arose on
glassy wings. These airborne lice moved in a low, mazy
cloud to a neighboring swale, where we knew they would
resettle, for they grazed on the sebaceous oils the Queen's
back sweated out, and these lay thickest on low ground.

Their flight had the slow-rolling movement you see in flocks of starlls when they're gleaning the winter fields, blowing like gusted leaves from plot to plot.

The spectacle did not lack a certain ghastly charm. Indeed, it was not these creatures themselves we avoided, but rather their larger, grimmer predators, a triad of which now surged up in pursuit of the flock. Of reptilian make, with jaws extravagantly fanged, these hunters dined on the wing, and when they struck their flustered quarry, fragments of the sundered lice—body plates and bleeding legs—drizzled down.

We were learning as we went. Not many moments before, flying incautiously close to a flock of these lice, we'd been attacked by one of these same predators. I lopped off half the brute's jaw for him with Ready Jack, and Barnar clove his pate with Biter, but we were both set spinning and whirling by the violence of our own battle-blows. We tumbled so helplessly at first it seemed our weapons must fly from our hands, and Ostrogall wailed with terror from his precarious holster on my hip.

So we paused aloft to practice executing sword and axe strokes. We learned that any blow required a simultaneous countering, cancelling blow from an opposite limb, otherwise we were left spinning, or see-sawing madly, like skiffs in jumpy water. Shortly, we caught the trick of standing on the air, and pulling up with our legs as we down-swept with our weapons; this gestural symmetry let us chop hard, yet be left standing steady enough on the air.

We cruised, wary, taking a look about the Queenly terrain and consciously putting off—perhaps even pointedly putting off—our task at hand.

In some measure we were still peeved (if the whole truth be told) at the Bunts' poor performance of their bond. For they'd come back down with only two and a half hundredweight of gold, alleging that they'd found mead prices depressed in Dry Hole by a momentary glut of the beverage from other Angalheim hiveries, and in consequence they had liquidated their warehoused stock at a loss.

"Surely this won't be a sticking point, gentlemen?" Bunt blandly urged. "The lacking sum, which you may confidently expect within a week, is but a scant sixth of what is owed—a paltry fraction."

"This proportional way of viewing the deficit," I replied, "gravely misses the point." I was finding it hard to keep a civil tone. "A fiftyweight of gold is first to be considered in its absolute value, in concrete terms. With a fiftyweight, for instance, a man might hire a quartet of Stregan gaunts for siegework on the Cidril steppes."

There was a pause. Bunt seemed to find the example baffling.

"Or the same fiftyweight might," Barnar put in with equal heat, and an oblique glance at me, "buy the service of a brace of bog giants for a four-month, to manage the shackles of a gryph-gryph, and see the monster has water to sustain its micturations."

This left them all staring. Sha'Urley, recovering first, reasoned, "Surely the lacking sum is as secure in our temporary keeping, as it would be if added to your cache here with what must be another half a ton of gems and specie—safely buried no doubt, but nevertheless reposing in a place where restless giants continually dig the earth. Meanwhile, we may be infallibly trusted for payment. I have rightly called your demands exorbitant. I have never said Bunt Hivery cannot meet them, and handily. We are even extending your nephew a twentyweight or so to finance the venture he envisions with his giants' pap."

"And what might that venture be, Nephew?" Barnar asked.

"Alas," snapped tight-lipped Costard, "the harshly mercenary mood you've shown me warns me to guard my secret."

I had a qualm, just then, thinking that if giants' pap proved potent in upper-world applications, then selling Costard some of it was reckless folly. It was at the very least a serious disservice to the young man's immediate neighbors. I then dismissed the notion. Thus lightly, sometimes, does prescience touch our thoughts with her wing-tips.

But it wasn't just the fiftyweight that peeved me as we cruised above the Queen's abdomen, far inland from her busy flanks where the pap pores were. "It galls me! I cannot shake it!" I burst out at Barnar. "Look how we fly. See what effortless access we now have to these wonders, and to wealth that outgoes computation! And in the midst of it, in the very blaze of all this fortune, all this glory, I cannot rejoice! I am tormented by bitterness, when my heart might otherwise be lifted on the wings of joy! And why? Because your damned, ox-necked *stubbornness*, Barnar! You won't even grant two months—three at the very most; three paltry months! Your sullen, bovine, belligerent balkiness will not grant even so tiny a delay of your seed-whacking, tree-tilling obsession! How can you be so selfish!? Only think what your madness defers! Pelfer's Buskins! His Cowl!"

Barnar snorted, sounding, I felt, exactly like an ox. "Oh, in truth you are a nervy weasel to upbraid me with my honor's core, my love of kith and clan and hearthland! I'm truly sorry to find you can be such an odious reptile, Nifft, with all your selfish, supple twistings to wriggle loose of your bonded word! To slither out of the obligations of your own sworn oath!"

"Barnar, I was half drunk! How many sentimental, half-drunk quests have you sworn to? You *hold* me to this one! And in truth, I do acknowledge the vow, I will perform it! But why does it have to come first?"

Below us, in the pale parts of the Queen's hide, a subtle blue network of veins, sunk in Her oily translucence, grew visible. For some moments now a running pack of brutes, back-legged like grasshoppers, their jaws bouquets of thorny tentacles, had run beneath our line of flight, studying us with glinting, metallic eye-bumps. We dropped down across a rib crest in the dorsal topography just as these creatures, cresting it, sprang up at us.

Their legs had hellish thrust; we must needs wheel back hard as a brace of them surged up ravening at our legs. With my feet thrusting for counter-purchase on the air, I two-armed Ready Jack wide left, wide right. Tentacles and twitching leg-stumps rained back down on the marbled valley, where, with a liquid slide, a half-transparent amoebal mass engulfed and dissolved them.

"How," I asked Barnar, "can you have missed seeing what the possession of Pelfer's Facilitators could bring to us!? With the Buskins, Cowl and Gantlets, we could break into Mhurdaal's Manse. We could steal . . . *his library.*"

I know I shuddered at my own words; I had scarce, ere this, allowed myself to look in the face of my own greatest ambition—an ambition steadily a-kindling in me (I now realized) since our capture of the Unguent of Flight had shown me the scope of wealth that we might aspire to. Nor could Barnar hear so fine and wild and moon-drunk a scheme as stealing the Library of Mhurdaal spoken without visible emotion. But in his selfish impatience he shrugged it off, striking the noble thought aside. "You are addicted to chasing legends, Nifft! It is a madness that can yield no final fruit!"

"Gentlemen! Luminous Benefactors!" the demon-head oboed from my hip. "With your forbearance, I beg you to be wiser! All this fury for futurities? Gentlemen, look where you are! Even to me, for whom this is the very hearth of Hell—here, where the armies spawn who sack my kindred's habitation, and 'spoil us of our lives—even to me this is a mighty hall of wonder, and my every eye most avidly imbibes the Muchness and the Suchness of it all! Let me urge you to be where you are, in the moment, and partake of its magnificence."

"You urge a truth there, I suppose," I had to concede. Down in the terrain's crevasses, around licks and ponds of Royal sebum, flocks of winged things jostled amicably enough with multibrachiate competitors, like plains life at the waterholes in the Lulumean savannahs. Big, black shapes crouched half-distinguishable in the blacknesses, with an occasional twitch of importunate hunger. Where the Royal dorsum was white, the buried veins were visible, and down there in the cloudy luminosity of the Queen's deep meat, huge forked arteries convulsed with the slow, implacable authority of Earthquake as somewhere, far deeper, Her colossal heart propounded her relentless vitality.

"How do you, then, Ostrogall," I musingly asked him, "believe that Behemoth came to be?"

"My race, sire, generally feel Mankind could not have fashioned any weapon of such power as She. And therefore we also believe, that as Behemoth is Earthborn, so it must inevitably come to pass that in Her time, She shall be half-conquered, half-possessed by demonkind, as Earth herself has been."

"It makes me love you less to think on this possibility, oh fragmentary demon," Barnar said, "though of course we thank you for your candor."

"But gentlemen," our cephalic cicerone melodiously remonstrated, "we are Life, and live its laws! Why, look here! Is this not living proof leaping thus directly to our gaze? These nastra-haagen, do you not see them? They are demonkind! Living on the very flank of our nation's destroyer!"

He referred to a greenish patch like a thick scab of lichen all forested over with stalks that ended in starburst clusters of sticky red droplets. These honeydew clusters thrust and darted, snatching winged lice smartly from the air with their instant adhesion, and then bending to feed ragged mouths gaping open in the lichen-scab. As we drew more directly overhead we saw some of these adhesive droplets contained inhuman eyes, and only the look of these eyes was needed to prove them demonkind. Ostrogall uttered a crickety, chitinous yodel, and down in the demonpatch ragged lichen-mouths opened, and warbled answers.

As we hovered to allow this colloquy, two large shapes rushed over the next abdominal rib-crest. They were a pair of miniature Behemoths, roughly like the Digger caste in jaw and build but not a tenth the size, though still a match for the biggest parasites. In an instant they had set upon Ostrogall's interlocutors, ripping up great shaggy mats of lichen, crunching the adhesive honeydew stalks like sweet confections. The ragged mouths made a shriller music. A third of the patch was devoured at once, and two more of these little abdominal-patrol Behemoths rushed hither over the rib-line.

I could not help exulting a little. "So! See how rich in strategies and powers abound is your mighty Nemesis! See how Behemoth outgoes your deepest inroads, how she finds you and feeds on you after all!"

Still, I didn't at all like seeing demons flourishing on the Queen's very back—it gave me that sick-kneed, rotten-flooring feeling one gets from brooding too much over demon invasiveness, demon infiltration.

How long can one wrestle such imponderables? "Come on," said Barnar. "Let's go a-milking."

The milking of the giants' pap went swimmingly, until we committed a stupidity that I writhe and blush to report.

We hung above the Queen's flank, looking down on the lapping tides of her spawn. We identified a stratum of Forager pores, both by location and by the succession of Foragers that drank there. Selecting a pore which a sated Forager had just withdrawn from, we came circling carefully down to some five or six fathoms above the abundantly lactescent orifice.

Carefully, we dangled our slender, lidded jars of reinforced leather (dyed orange of course, as were the lines we lowered them by). I dipped mine first into the slow flux of viscosity. I lowered the jar's lip into it, and pulled straight upward. The jar grew heavier, and easier to dip, with each pull. In four passes, my jar was full.

Barnar moved into position and began following suit. Then another Forager reared up to the pore, and began drinking, just below where Barnar was dipping.

Barnar still had just enough room to work, and he did so with wonderful coolness; but in his instinct to work away from the Forager's huge eyes, Barnar began to drop back a bit over the abdominal wall, and pull at his jar more obliquely to fill it. He was working too low, just as our Harpy had done, and I was not alert enough to grasp this right away. Almost at once, one of the same species of spiny horror that had devoured our Harpy, vaulted high in an explosive bid to seize Barnar's legs. Ostrogall's shriek of warning gave Barnar an instant's lead, and he swam powerfully ceilingwards.

But he was just a blink too late, for, with the slender, utmost tip of one of its arms, the parasite threw one wrap around Barnar's left ankle.

I flew to his back, seized his collar, and added my power of ascent to his, and very slowly, with terrible effort, we lifted the stubbornly gripping parasite upward, outward from the Queen's flank. Barnar wore stout buskins, but the pain of the monster's grip was unbearably urgent for him.

"No use! Drop down and cut it through," he grunted.

The instant I let go to fly lower, Barnar began inexorably to sink with the parasite's huge weight. I dropped down to hang near the gripping tentacle, and I swung a one-handed stroke against the tentacle with Ready Jack. I maintained my balance, but could not deliver the power

I would have managed braced on firm ground. Jack bit only two fingers' depth. The dangling monster writhed, Barnar groaned, and toilsomely swam, and inexorably sank yet more.

The jaws of the nursing Behemoth were scarcely two fathoms below us, and we were sinking dead upon them.

I swung another stroke—a deeper bite but still the tentacle would not sunder. Then the Forager sprang up under us.

The parasite of course was not invisible to her—it danced before her eyes and now the great black sabers of her jaws closed slicing through the air. I somersaulted backward, and Barnar rocketed ceilingward, suddenly gripped only by a lightweight fragment of one tentacle. So hard had he been pulling to ascend, that he almost brained himself against the Chamber ceiling before he managed to stop his climb. I chopped the tentacle's writhing remnant free and it plummeted into the Forager's jaws after the rest of the parasite. The Forager consumed the morsel, and returned to her nursing, and Barnar dangled his jar down again, and this time drew it full, and sealed and secured it.

"Oh radiant Benefactors," Ostrogall chirruped, "may I now make bold to beg that you will take me straight from here to the Nest-mouth, and out to my re-planting? I know the straightest way from here, and then you would have done with that little matter, and thenceforth be unencumbered with my humble self."

"You know," mused Barnar, "on this foray, you gave us a bit of moral advice, some theorizing, and a warning that was not untimely. But we made our own way, mostly. You did not even translate for us your squawkings with that mold patch of your kinfolk back there."

"A thousand apologies! They said that takings were rich on the Queen, that there was nothing here to threaten them, and that their kin were colonizing the Royal Dorsum everywhere. I gathered from their dying exclamations that the little breed of Behemoth that devoured them was not previously known to them. It seems as you said, Effulgent One, that the Queen truly abounds in strategies, and swiftly molds her progeny to the great Nest's needs. But most revered gentlemen, I remind you that I shouted you first warning of the thorny star, and I earnestly beseech you not to deny me the replantation which my sharing of your dangers here has earned."

We made him, for a while, no answer, rapt as we were in our slow flight out of the Chamber, taking our last leave of this hall of titans. We began to negotiate the tunnels, feeling quite practiced now, deft as fish dodging through rapids. Ostrogall had grown tremulously quiet. "We just don't feel that you really, substantially *added* to our profit," I told him gently.

"Gentlemen," said the demonstump after a silence, in a tone of ineffable melancholy, "permit me to anticipate you. May I presume to . . . hasten ahead in this conversation, as it were? For somehow I feel there is a question you wish to come to. May we entertain this question at once, without a preliminary visit to the jaws of some loathsome grub?"

In part, I was almost moved to smile at this, and in equal part the demon's cynical certainty irked me. "I'm afraid," I began, "I find your tone a bit—"

"Please, Oh Effulgent Saviour! Only hear if I do not touch your very thought!"

"Speak on, then."

"The two of you rightly imagine great wealth to be had in the subworld by such airborne privateers as you now are. And you have also, I venture to guess, rightly seen that you will shortly have a unique opportunity for such a plundering tour of my world. For soon a New Queen will go forth on a Nesting Flight, with her own terrible army of Foragers and other castes thundering in the van.

"Their pillage and rapine will leave a raw and bleeding swathe, fertile like a furrow cut in rich soil. Naked wealth will sprawl from broken walls and toppled vaults and hoards exhumed, and all this wealth's defenders will be gone, consumed as in a ravening holocaust. It is an opportunity beyond the wildest dreams of any thief, if you will pardon the expression.

"The question, then, that I have mentioned, is: might not my company on this plundering tour, and my expertise in demonry, greatly speed your self-enrichment on this foray? My answer, revered Masters, is Yes! And might I not agree to *do* this, you further ask? And again, I answer Yes! I will do this, if only you will at last and in earnest swear to plant me in my native home again! May, oh *may* I beg you to promise this *sincerely* at the last?"

Nettled by something unflattering in the way the demon framed these propositions, we were very slow to answer, though we knew at once, of course, that we would strike the bargain.

When the Bunts and Costard had brought down our payment, Sha'Urley had brought Niasynth with her, for aboveground the sunlight had exhausted her, carefully though they shaded her, and she craved this brief respite underground. We found her at the ancient-young woman's side in the operations nook when we returned with our Royal plunder. Bunt and Costard snored in our hammocks, worn by days of hard driving and hasty dealing. We paid our respects to Niasynth, who lay propped at a resting but wakeful angle in a bed Sha'Urley had improvised for her. I felt a kind of kinship with this pale, resurrected woman, lying just-delivered from the gulf we were bound to. We both knew what Time was in the worlds below.

"I rejoice, sister," I told her low, meaning it, "that we have worked your liberation."

"You have worked mine as well, I think," Sha'Urley smiled. "Will you believe that I am suddenly weaned of this strange ambition of my brother's? For one lump consideration, I have relinquished to him all further revenues from our familial holdings. So let's say good-bye, Nifft, as friends only, with no business in it."

And indeed we embraced most sweetly, though I confess that her defection cost me a qualm. Was Bunt bound for mishap, and his sister sensing it? Should I not, after all, get the remaining fiftyweight in hand before yielding the pap?

We helped her get Niasynth into the bucket with her; she supported that frail escapee in her arms, for Niasynth seemed barely strong enough to stand unaided. "I know it is hard at first to bear," I told that antique nymph, "but is it not glorious to feel the sun again?"

She took my hand between her own and kissed it. So cool her hands and lips! So smooth! "It is a joy so severe," she said, "it fills me with terror that I cannot hold such life, that it will tear my heart!"

Before Sha'Urley bade us close the hatchway on them, she nodded toward the snoring Bunt and Costard. "They are close as death about their projects for the pap. My brother's is perhaps not hard to guess, though henceforth I'll know as little as I can of it. Costard, in making much of his own secrecy, has let slip enough to indicate that he is interested in the 'cattle-raising business' as he puts it. I would not wither enterprise in bud by speaking words of ill omen. I'll just say I'm glad we have other fish to fry, Niasynth and I."

When we had pulled the lever that sent down the counterweights, and the bucket had climbed rattling away, we stood gazing on the sleeping Bunt and Costard. Slick and shiny in their dye, they seemed to sweat through fevered dreams. I felt the strangest little touch of fear to wake them, to put them in possession of our jars of Nest-Magic.

✧   ✧   ✧

And when we had wakened them, still we temporized. We nagged them about the fiftyweight still owing; we reiterated our right to a tithe of their future revenues; we stressed that we wanted caretakers topside to assure we could make our eventual exit without trouble.

"We've hired two men from a neighboring mine," Bunt soothed. "Hatchways and pulleys and lines and such will be ship-shape. They know of your eventual emergence—we've told them you'll be bringing up larval scrapings, for sale to the perfumeries of the Great Shallows. Come now—may we hold what we've so dearly purchased?"

"Yes Uncle!" Costard chimed. "Come now—fair's fair!"

There was nothing else to do. I felt the jar's heft—I saw a stickiness about its lip that breathed out a breath of the Brood Chamber's awe to my nostrils. Sheer, delirious sorcery! It felt like doom, it felt like danger, to surrender it to these men—to Bunt with his urbane smile of thanks, ambition burning deep within his thoughtful eyes, to Costard with his bright vindictive gaze, his smile of youthful triumph. . . .

"No fakery here," Bunt beamed at us, too elated for complete tact. "I *feel* it past doubt, the Mother's power humming in this ichor! You are remarkable men, my friends—the things you have accomplished!"

"Our greatest deeds, we hope," I bowed, "are still to come."

"So, indeed, are ours!" Bunt answered, bowing in his turn.

XXI

The Chosen One's wings cleave the air like
*   bright swords*
That scythe down a harvest of doomed demon
*   lords.*
The Chosen One's jaws carve her empire-to-be.
Her glittering eyes possess all that they see!

IN THE LAST few hours before setting forth on her
Nesting Flight, the Young Queen was courted by her
suitors. These males had a madcap air. They weren't a
fourth her size; they were blacker, glossier-bodied, and
more tapered and slender than she. Their wings (which
would lift them, or one of them, to the raptures of actual
mating during the Nesting Flight) were like the blades
of slim poniards, and their bodily movements were
darting and veering and hectic to a degree conspicuously
surpassing all the handmaids seething round the young
Monarch, though the suitors in their turn dwarfed these
worker castes.

On the whole the young Princes put one in mind of
court-gallants at a Jarkeladd wedding feast, with their

caps raffishly aslant, the bright, chased hilts of their shortswords conspicuously agleam on their hips, their eyes bright with wine and readiness for a wrestle, a sprightly jump-up, or some other such jovial exploit.

The Young Queen, by contrast, seemed to sit in state. She all but filled her half of the titanic chamber alloted her pre-nuptial growing time. And grown she had, till her passage through the tunnels looked in doubt. But the Princes were not shy of her. Incessantly they courted her; each in turn proferred a gallant obeisance, and shared with her a quick, lascivious antennal touching, then darted down along her body, touching her further, tasting her, it seemed, with little lovers' nibbles at her legs, her thorax, her elegantly slender abdomen. They were powerless, it seemed, to get enough of her divine effluvium.

It was a relatively subtle thing which first signalled the imminence of the Nesting Flight. The Young Queen's wings began to vibrate. The amplitude of their oscillation was minute, but immensely powerful. A faint hum sounded through the chamber.

The seethe amid her servitors quickened. So did the circulation of her Suitors.

The rate of her wings' tremoring increased. They gave off a silver-blue sheen, flashing ever so slightly in the cyanic glow. Still more her Suitors quickened, and her retainers—among these, Diggers, who surged into the tunnel and began to attack its walls with shovelling strokes of their huge jaws.

The note of the Young Queen's wings rose higher, like a plucked lute-string now, a thrilling, silvery tone, while the wings themselves were ablaze with reflected light. The Suitors now began to rush among the mob of retainers, herding them, hastening them, it seemed, toward the tunnel. And there the mass of workers now surged, an auger with a thousand jaws. Filling their crops with earth, they chewed away the tunnel walls with incredible speed, leaving a grander corridor in their wake.

The Young Queen stirred. Her immobile legs arched, and lifted her. She stood a moment, a marvel of nature and yet so burnished, so sculpted, that she seemed also like some great and ingenious engine of war. Then she ran in the wake of her army.

She plunged into a half-darkness, for her servitors devoured half the fungal light source as they carved a larger way for their mistress. The boiling vanguard of workers and Princes gnawed away at the rim of light far ahead, and the Young Queen was a running shadow eerily sketched here and there in the following dark: a flashing thigh-joint, the glinting hull of her tapered thorax, the cerulean corruscation of one eyeglobe.

Until the tunnels in their descending confluence grew grander. Then under the high, blue vaults, the Young Queen ran with her army coalescing around her. Shoulder to shoulder, dense like some glittery fluid, the army of workers poured flanking her, trailing her, running ahead to the limit of vision. She ran high-prowed, towering amid them, her silver wings shimmering, two mighty swords about to be wielded. Diggers and Foragers were prominent in the legions most closely surrounding her. In the vanguard where the Princes ran, the army was a perfect mix of castes, all moving locked in their single furious rhythm of onslaught.

Here came the onrushing Nest-mouth, a crimson window on a rolling plain. The army poured out of it unhesitant, a mad cascade. The Princes plunged out onto the air, which their wakening wings, militant sabres, assaulted.

The Young Queen swept toward the portal. 'Omphalodon's Eye appeared in the distant vault. It had turned, by an unmistakable fraction, and its alien immensity—undeniably, inscrutably—noted the Young Monarch mounting on the subworld air, her imperial wings coming alive with the hum of a million bowstrings.

And out we flew after her, Barnar and I, though we swooped down the face of the hell-wall, hanging close above the army itself. Out in the gulf beyond us the Young Queen, in what seemed a dance of pure exuberance, swept through great arcs and counter-arcs, flew arabesques across the demon sky. The Suitors, nimble black acrobats, streaked near her and away, near and away, like boys vying for notice, seeming to woo her with a kind of comic verve. Their gamesome hectoring inspired the Young Queen to even dizzier sweeps. The Royal rout of courtship rolled out across the plain, as the army poured glittering below, a pursuing river.

This was how to harrow hell—we had the trick of it at last! We each had coils of line, and stoutly tied swagnets, and we had all our limbs free for flying because of the stout leathern harnesses round our middles, to hang our bags from and our other gear. This included a quiver of light harpoons and fishing tridents, furnished from Dry Hole by Sha'Urley's swordswomen, a small service deducted from the fiftyweight still owed us by the Bunts. Thus geared, we had sought out the Nuptial Chamber, and lingered there through seven sleeps before this hour had arrived. We took our ease, and stored up rest, trusting Ostrogall's vigilance to wake us at need.

Now the army rivered below us out onto the plain. High behind us it still poured from the Nest-mouth. Two miles of Behemoths branching across the subworld floor. "You behold the most dreaded catastrophe that can befall my race," wailed Ostrogall from his holster on my hip. "Look! Look to the Talons of 'Omphalodon!"

Though far down along the horizon, the Talons towered plainly visible, the more so in that they were all white bone now—that is, wherever they could be glimpsed through the enveloping boil of Behemoths. The colossal skeleton still clenched and thrashed, and now around its wrist the Behemoths' heaped dead rose in a small mountain of crushed debris. Slight slaughter! Behemoth's fecundity, as we now understood, was inexhaustible, and, although the Tertiary demon's claws displayed a powerful vitality that seemed undiminished by their decortication, we could see where the swarm was beginning to gnaw chunks from the very bones themselves.

"Every Nest in a hundred leagues of here's drawing meat from it," Barnar said. "That Tertiary flesh will have been coming to our own Nest these five or six days past."

"I think we can trust Behemoth's stomach to conquer whatever her jaws have conquered," I answered.

Yet who could know? I believe we both rued an accident of which, though wholly innocent, we were the unwitting causes, and which had brought such perilous sustenance to the jaws of the Behemoths we had grown to hold in awe, and almost to revere.

"Oh luminous masters," cried Ostrogall, "how can you think demonkind profits from this meal? Behold 'Omphalodon's Eye—do you see triumph there?" The great Eye's bloody leakage was profuse—indeed, everywhere on the plains, the rubescent streams and rivers seemed to be in spate, and thickly foaming within their channels. It was only later that this facile riposte of Ostrogall's began to echo unpleasantly in my thoughts. What, after all, were it best for him that we should think, if not that Behemoth had demonkind in full retreat, and that there was no ultimate harm in letting a certain particular demon be re-planted and continue his existence?

At that moment, though, prodigious 'Omphalodon's grieving gaze calmed our fears, buoyed our hearts, even as his Unguent buoyed our bodies. We'd stolen this bliss of flight from the Tertiary's very hide—what else could live down here that we need dread?

The forces thundering below us mantled the open plain like a shuddery, glossy garment. The army's first plunder was a league-long caravan of giant wains. The cargo of each wain was a single huge cottony sphere, each one perhaps twice the size of an Angalheim mead hall.

This caravan's course had been head-on to ours. It had wheeled about at the army's first appearance, but so sudden was the legions' onset that only now was the last of the great line of vehicles sluggishly wheeling round, its scaly drovers lashing their huge batrachian teams to a retreat.

"These A'Rak eggsacs are purchased from the Secondary Subworld, for the defense of fortresses," Ostrogall told us.

"Purchased with what commodity?" I asked.

"I, ah, frankly do not know."

"Purchased with human captives then, I'd guess," said Barnar.

"Candidly I tell you, I do not know, effulgent ones!"

But already the vanguard of Behemoths broke like a wave on the wains; the great cottony spheroids spilled out and were overswarmed. A thousand jaws sliced the slack bags to ribbons—and a spill of infant spiders, each no bigger than a war chariot-and-pair, leaked wiggling and twiddling out. "They grow to hunt my countrymen and Behemoth indiscriminately," enlarged Ostrogall, "but we tolerate them because, one time in four, they can bring a Forager down."

What a feast ensued upon the hatchlings! The Behemoths seemed to find their prey a choice confection—each spiderling just three bites large—and they gorged with every evidence of gusto.

Above, the Queen and her eager consorts were unconcerned, showing appetite for love alone; gigantically they cavorted in the subworld sky, the Suitors still swooping close to their belusted, then away, while the young Nest Mother in her mad majesty impassioned them with ever more dizzying aerobatics. We watched enthralled the plenipotency of our great guides and allies. Above us great Heliomphalodon wept. All demonkind, it seemed to us in that moment, lay belly up, surrendered for the taking.

Shag Margold's Second Interjection

SAZMAZM, A GREAT DEMON WARRIOR of the Tertiary Subworld, was betrayed by the wizard Wanet-Ka, whom he engaged to convey him up to the Prime Subworld, past the immemorial locks and guards that constrain his titanic ilk to their benthonic bastions. Once elevated to that lesser hell, Sazmazm purposed to win easy empire, thence afterwards to scourge the surface world. How the wizard tricked the demon is related in *The Fishing of the Demon Sea*.

Sazmazm's lust to rise from his domain was, like 'Omphalodon's, a lust for light. And monstrous though these Tertiaries were, who can fail to find a grandeur in their doomed upward striving? Some authorities aver that these ambitions were in any case suicidal; that sunlight would be instant death to these deepest-born of demonkind. We have not as yet—Thanks be!—had occasion to test this proposition.

Arguably, Nifft's fever to enter the Manse of Mhurdaal is a species of just this sort of light-lust. Mhurdaal, in the austerest, ice-blasted heights of the Kolodrian Ghaanack range, Earth's awful pinnacle, built his Manse

near the end of the Amber Millenium. This awesome
citadel he conceived expressly to house his precious
Library.

The rare and ancient tomes which this legendary
bibliotrove of Mhurdaal's comprises are only half its
fabled wonder. It holds as well no less than a hundred
of the Peripatextual Parchments, also called the Nomad
Books and the Vella Viatica. These folios of immortal
vellum, blank of any permanent imprintation, are haunted
by the ghosts of great works lost in lost millenia. Between
these Parchments' undying bindings those epochal,
obliterated books find intermittent housing, and take the
form of print again. More, the reader, on beholding, is
instantaneously endowed with perfect comprehension of
whatever vanished tongue the migrant tome is writ in.
Thus what is said of Mhordaal's Library may be credited,
that it is our world's deepest labyrinth of lore, a maze
of windows looking out upon a wider cosmos, whence
the raptured reader may gaze out across the rooftops of
a thousand histories.

Nevertheless Nifft's ardor for the Library does not
seem entirely bent upon scholarly illumination. Indeed,
I must blush for the predominantly commercial ambitions
which those catacombs of sapience seem to awaken in
my friend.

But he is, after all, a thief, and one in the throes of
a transport of avarice.

—Shag Margold

XXII

Darkness fell about my feet,
A mantle I had shed.
My face the gladsome breeze did greet—
I'd lost hope of a joy so sweet
Among the worse-than-dead.

I CANNOT describe us as footsore, when at last we swam the air wearily Nest-wards again from that foray, from that ransacking of whole demon nations, from that long, delirious fugue of discovery and plunder, the like of which I know life will never again afford me.

Since our setting-forth in the Young Queen's train, nigh on two months had passed, as we later learned to reckon the time. All we knew at that juncture was that the interval we had endured below was a series of little eternities, each one nested in the next like those cunning boxes crafted in the Minuskulons.

No, footsore we were not. But sore in every other fibre of ourselves we surely were. For we flew laden to the very limit of the Unguent's power to lift us. From our middles hung our hempen nets bulging with ten times our weight in demon-loot. We looked like the loaded booms of cargo cranes, dangling our pendant bales of infernal swag.

Flying this heavy was a labor every bit as hard as swimming, and swimming, I might add, in cold water that saps your heat, for both our physical strength and the lifting power of the Unguent were burned off us at a fierce rate. Our only way of resting was a liberal reanointment with the Unguent. When we re-smeared our hands and feet, we could, for a while, tread air with little labor, and regain our breath.

But the drag of our weight wore down the Unguent merely in keeping us aloft, whether we trod air, or swam full-out. Rests were relatively brief, then, and toil was the rule, for we were loathe to use up Unguent unless we were near the limit of our strength. League after league we grunted through the ruby gloom, pulling with our solid sinews at the melting substance of the air, the two of us like a pair of laborious apes clambering along miles of invisible vines.

This was most unlike what one thinks of as "flying." How clearly, at moments, did I recall that stab of delirious jubilation in the heart when we first climbed the air beside the wall of 'Omphalodon's buried palm. This long labor was nothing like that joy.

Now we again had, not too distantly in view, the wall of the Broken Axle Mountain-roots; indeed, we even now began to discern in that far wall the particular purplish smudge of darkness that might be the mouth of our own Nest.

Such was our anger with one another, however, Barnar's and mine, that I might almost say we were indifferent to this vision of our journey's accomplishment. I scarcely saw the actual mountain wall because my erstwhile friend's brute, immovable will was like a wall before my eyes. I'd been hammering at it for weeks now.

"Of the Corcyrene Codex, I will cease to speak," I told

him. "Let us forget the fact that, among those who know, there is absolute consensus that in the Corcyrene Codex the Star-Ladder is to be found. But let the Star-Ladder pass, I say! We have no interest in walking the Galactic Path, nor in going to the Mill of Time, the white-hot engine where Eternity's ground out, and a skilled thief can scoop up years of new life with his hands. . . .

"But let that pass, I say—it is perhaps too slight a thing to be prized. Let us rather consider a different volume that is, like the Codex, also to be found 'in Mhurdaal's Library. Let us confine our computations to one sole volume—the Handbook of Hapidamnos. Inscribed therein by Dastardosthenes is the command spell of the Auric Plague.

"Just weigh this with me a moment Barnar, please! Picture it with me. An entire town—a city stricken with the Auric Pest. This plague strikes all, in hours! Not a man or woman standing, all lying helpless in fever, all of them, sweating gold! Little nuggets bead out from their pores! They lie sodden for days, shedding a bright golden gravel till their bed-slats groan with its weight! Now picture ourselves, with some choice companions, going round, filling pokes and bags and bales with purest gold, tidying the citizens' beds and collecting the municipal effluvium of wealth. It's incalculable, the yield of this plague! And all the stricken fold heal, they stand up fine and healthy—though gaunt and hungry to be sure—after three days' time. What a beneficent form of pillage, and how stupendously lucrative!

"Barnar, with all respect, I merely urge you to weigh more carefully the kind of wealth you so peremptorily dismiss! The Auric Plague is costly to deploy, I grant this candidly. It must be windborn, and so we must engage a witch to capture an elemental in the Harakan Hills of Hagia. But once deployed—"

"Have done, Nifft! Will you not desist? How your voice has come to grate on my nerves! Spare me these

mad fugues of ambition. To squeeze gold from others
is the thief's vocation and essential art. The difference
between us, it seems, is that I am a Thief-for-a-time, a
Thief-while-I-must-be kind of thief, while you are a thief
down to the least lizardly bone of you!"

We swam—with already toilsome strokes—across a
wetland of red pools fringed by polypous stalks and
plumes and tentacles which were freckled with eyes and
writhing ceaselessly. Airborne shapes—a polyglot rabble
of pterid demons—haunted the wetland, swooping down
at the crimson pools, spearing up swallows from the wine-
red lagoons. Jawed things leapt out of the pools and
dragged down careless drinkers. We swam a bit higher
in the air to get above the buffeting of the the thirsty
prey's wings and the din of their cries.

"With a little help from you," Barnar resumed, his eyes
not meeting mine, his tone resolute and tired of the
whole debate, "I can summon the means, and deploy the
seed, to make all northern Chilia, every foot of her most
barren heights included, into an unbroken garden of
majestic timber. This is a different art from the Thief's,
Nifft, and in choosing this art, the art of cultivation, I
have done with, put away and depart from, the Guild
of Thieves. And in so doing, I dower the world around
me. The city-conjuring, ship-launching treasure of Timber
is bestowed by me—not stolen—bestowed on the whole
Great Shallows. The largesse of lumber, from a Chilia
re-garbed in her mantle of green. This feat, you see, this
grand reforestation, would be a getting and a giving.
Meanwhile look at your obsessions! I can't help it Nifft—
I must really think less of you! Look at these deliria of
insatiable greed that possess you, even to the point of
reneging on a personal vow!"

My temper snapped with his. "You bull-necked—"

"Gentlemen! I beg you! Mercy!" So shrill was Ostrogall
we startled, at first thinking him injured somehow. "My
awe is yours," he resumed, "my reverence, my utter fealty!

Yet please tolerate my humble, most apologetic suggestion—Though I am utterly dazzled by your virtues and excellences in all else!—my suggestion that you lose the profit of your recent travels when you are so absorbed in a debate about the future! Your nets bulge with your loot, of course, but what of all the sights and sounds, the spectacles you have beheld? Distracted as you are, will you even remember these wonders? You have seen so much of my world—far more than I had seen, even through my most far-flung eye-spores. By the Crack, what things we have *seen*, eh Gentlemen? I never guessed the multiplicity of my nation! May I be frank, revered benefactors? You even lose the, well, glee of having these riches, by being so embroiled in recrimination."

The dreariness of this world was all I could see of it now—I saw no wonders. We overflew a new terrain, a great prairie of huge tubeworms, their ciliated mouths making incessant, lascivious osculations. A winged parasite of our Harpy's make—though a bigger, more carniverous breed—infested these tubeworms, hanging above them like carrion flies, diving to get past the worms' darting, seeking mouths. When they got down among the lower stalks, they battened on the tubeworms' undefended root muscles and sucked their blood. Perhaps every second or third Harpy was caught and devoured by the worms as it plunged. A sufficiency survived: everywhere, studding the worms' root muscles like warts, shone the pallid egg-clusters which the Harpies laid.

"What I mean, Effulgent Ones," Ostrogall ventured, sounding both encouraged and worried by our silence, "is that you haven't even, well, *gloated* over this wealth. You haven't laughed and exulted and run your hands over it, you've neither cavorted nor capered nor crowed. You are fabulously rich, but—I grovel in apology!—you don't seem to know it! Surely you are glad of these incredible riches, gentlemen? And surely you feel now that I have truly benefitted you, enriched you beyond the shadow of a doubt? By any sane reckoning of your present abundance, and my unstinting assistance?"

Seeing his drift, I found myself to be instantly and peevishly disposed against it.

"Oh inexpressible ones," diapasoned Ostrogall, "oh my Rescuers, wise and just and mighty, oh dare I, in my utter humility, frame the word?—*friends!*"

"Forgive me," I snapped, "but you may not frame the word. You are a demon, part of the Quintessential Excremescence from the Cosmic Bowel. I think you presume most offensively upon the bond of obligation placed on you by our saving of your odious life!"

"Oh please, Effulgent Ones, I utterly retract the term, how could I have *presumed*, madness took me!—but *please* Effulgent ones, do not now again show a relenting of your good resolve to honor our bargain! Think not of returning me to those remorseless larval jaws. Please bethink yourselves how at every turn I have guided and enriched you!"

And indeed he had. But perversely, at that moment, our wealth seemed as much a burden as a boon—a dangerous, arduous cargo we must shepherd over many miles, through many nights in the open, with leisure and peace of mind a thing of the past, till we could make our little mountains of loot secure. And to add to the onus of it all, we must be very careful—more than careful, as a matter of fact—in using the Unguent of Flight once we had brought our treasure to the upper world. For if thieves saw us in mid-air, they would not rest until they had our courses marked—marked and, likely enough, followed to whatever destination Barnar and I might have in mind. It was one more burdensome accountability.

We paused above the tubeworm prairie; we trod the air and unlimbered our jars of Unguent. We had to reach deep to dip with careful, sparing fingertips, and freshly anoint our palms and our bootsoles. It was clear our jars would be half emptied by the time we reached the

surface world. Chance thus cunningly cozened us of the
extra flight we had filched, for our remainder looked to
equal the two bowlfuls formally allotted us by the secondary keepers of the Talons.

"You are right, demon," I answered at last, "in noting
that I am not ecstatic. And frankly, I feel no grateful
warmth toward you, though your advice on some occa-
sions has been arguably fruitful, I suppose. . . ."

"Oh please don't waver from your good resolve,
gentlemen! We are so near my natural home. Those
plains not one mile hence beyond these leechfields, just
rightwards there a bit from your course. But set me
there, I beg, and I'll take instant root! We'll be quits!
I'll bless your holy names eternally, my radiant saviours!"

And indeed the plains he indicated were not far off
from the field of tubeworms we still overflew. "Your
language is really quite shamelessly fulsome," I reproved
him, though I won't deny I felt the demon had a way
with words. Sensing a pause in our resistance, Ostrogall
gushed, his voice all flutes and oboes, "Oh do not
extinguish me, I beg. Gentlemen! Is not my Being like
a fine-wrought bowl of crystal that brims with the cosmos
around me? Do I not hold life's brief drink of wonders—
hold it in my senses like a chalice, as do you? What boots
inquisition into our individual deeds? We share Life's
brief excursion from the vasty dark. We soar a short
trajectory through wheeling infinities of form, and then
plunge gone again!"

Well, I will confess, he moved us. In a word, we felt
for the demon. Is it not amazing, what mere prolonged
association can inure us to? But in that moment Ostrogall
struck a true chord; life, after all, is a short flight, a few
centuries long at the utmost. Barnar and I traded a look,
and found, with surprise, that we were agreed to relent.

"Very well, then," Barnar said. "Give him here, Nifft.
I'll veer over and back—no need that we both waste
Unguent."

"Right," I said. "Here he is."

"Oh you paragons of human beauty!" the demon-stump ululated. "Oh you Archetypes, angelically strong and wise—*Aieeeee!*"

Our weariness, coupled perhaps with a failure to adjust to the new lift of our freshened Unguent, caused me to falter, and fumble the transfer of Ostrogall's head; I released it before Barnar had quite securely gripped it. It plunged.

The demon squawled with rage as he plummeted down through the harpy-swarms thick as flies: "Rot and roast you, human scum!" he shrilled. "Better the grub had me! Now I'll wait three hundred years for my spores to—" Here a tubeworm flickered up, and swallowed him.

We flew on, a little bemused. "There is something poignant, isn't there, about his mishap?" I asked Barnar. "How he loved seeing things! Such a devoted witnesser. Now he'll be blind three times longer than if the grub had eaten him."

"The irony is poignant, as you say."

We swam along in a silence somehow loud with the unspoken bitterness between us. The demon's absence seemed to throw our tacit controversy into stark relief. A last recrimination burst out of me: "I would never have believed it possible that Barnar Hammer-Hand might tell me he was not a thief, or that, hearing him say it, I might fail to swear he lied. But now when you tell me you are not a thief, I am shamefully compelled to nod assent, and say, 'In truth, no thief is he!'"

Barnar answered nothing. Far to our left, like a winter-slain tree, the stark, branching bones of 'Omphalodon's Talons, gnawed down to stumps now, still valiantly battled the living mantle of Foragers feeding on them. I looked up briefly at 'Omphalodon's Eye. We had flown close to that Eye not long past, and glimpsed things in its gulf that I disliked to remember. Now in that bloody orb I thought I saw a glint of the demon's grief for a part of himself too briefly resurrected; he seemed to pity that ruined limb which once had burned to seize the sun.

After a time, I said, "It won't be long now," meaning the black constellation of Nest-mouths we swam toward. There was deadly-hard work ahead of us, getting our plunder back up through the Nest.

It was a nightmare of toil. High in the vaulting of the Nest's great entry chamber, we webbed one of our bales in a crevice with pitons and line. We flew up-Nest one-handed, a shared grip on the second bale between us. Shifting and veering our burden's bulk clear of sudden traffic was killing labor. Our dye blazes were half worn off the tunnel walls, eroded to nothing in places. We blundered and groped, sweat-blind, through miles of tunnel.

We reached our larval chamber, and stowed our plunder. Then we flew back down, and did it all again.

When it was done at last, we fell into our hammocks. We could go up the gangway right now if we chose, breathe the wind and see the sun again. . . . We didn't move. We were stupendously rich men, and above us lay a world of thieves. We would sleep first, and come out careful. In truth, we felt like troglodytes still, twisted and stunted to this underworld, the sun and sky alien things we knew only from tales. Through another long dark we slept safe in the earth, lullabyed by Behemoth's unsleeping maternal bustle.

XXIII

Adhesions of the hell just left,
A feeling that the will is cleft
A taste for darkness in the soul
While hideous images unscroll
Before my staring Inner Eye.
Am I still I? Did I not . . . die?

ALL WAS PREPARED. I was armed. Our fortune was assembled in the nook, and Barnar standing by it, where I would send down to him packing materials, and whence he would send up our bundled wealth when I had transport secured above.

He watched me standing before the gangway hatch, watched me still hesitating to step into the bucket. I think he understood. I gestured at our netted gems, glinting bitterly like captured beasts' eyes, their other-worldly lusters biting through Behemoth's cyanic hue, and at our bales of infernal artifacts, bulging and jutting against their shroudings like the little bundled corpses of alien monsters. "I half feel it's real only down here in the dark," I told Barnar. "I half believe that when

194

we raise it up there, it will vanish, evaporate into the sky."

"Be comforted, Nifft. I've seen demon gems traded in sunlight, right enough. In the Shallows' bazaars I've seen one of them buy a whole ship, with its cargo and crew!" Barnar smiled as he said this, knowing it was something deeper that was giving me pause. Knowing that what panged me now was a fear that I myself—transformed by too long and lustful a sojourn below—might evaporate into the sky, no longer a proper citizen of the sunlight.

I had—we both had—faced such a return a decade past. But that reascension from the Demon Sea was an escape from constant battle for our lives. We had hewed and hacked and dodged our way through the subworld, and the desperate toil of it purged us of that realm's infections.

Now we were coming from a long, delirious bacchanal of plunder. From the great red furrow of ruin ploughed by a conquering army, we had gleaned obscene riches, hanging for the most part free and clear of the unspeakabilities we viewed. Here, at little personal risk, we plucked hell's fruit and savored it. In consequence, our hearts and souls were deeper-dyed with the demons' lurid gloom; half my will still swam in that dark like a hungry eel, nosing for infernal wealth.

"Well," I said, heaving a sigh, "I'll send down a warning, if the sunlight starts melting me." I stepped into the bucket, and Barnar winked at me, and slid the hatch closed. Down came the counterweight.

The clank and rattle of the climbing bucket put me in mind of a windlass weighing a heavy anchor. I fancied I was some stubborn, millenial root that could only with great mechanical force be pulled free of the earth.

And my will *clung* to the earth, to the dark. The smell of stone was like a home-scent to me; my heart rebelled at leaving it. I prayed it would be night above; that the stars, like distant demon eyes, might greet me with their gentler scrutiny—anything but the great fiery eye of the sun!

The sun! When I did step out into it at last, flinging back the hatchway with a desperate abandon, like one who steps off some high brink, my sick hesitations were in an instant burnt and purged away. For one heartbeat, light was pain—and then it was pure joy, was itself my heart.

I had emerged into early morning, and this first sunlight that I saw came in golden spears, piercing the rafters of the main building's vast roof.

I stepped out onto the rampway; the smell of open air overwhelmed me. A breeze, scented faintly with sun-warmed stone and skorse trees, moved through the building. Then tears of happiness sprang to my eyes. Tears of relief. I ran down the ramp, ran a beeline to the gaping bay doors nearest me, ran out and stood under the open sky again.

I climbed a half mile up the mountain side, and stood gazing for a long time at the sweep of the mountain ridges, their canyons and crevices brimming with velvety purple shadows, and their high ground all burnished with the young sun's slanting gold. Above them all the big blue bell of the sky rang its soundless peal, its reverberant azure note of boundlessness.

For a while I was wrenched out of time by the raw beauty of it all; I utterly forgot where I had just come from, and where I meant to go next. I wholly forgot that I possessed wealth to awe kings. I was filled with a floating freedom, newborn into a new world.

Faint music reached me, and I collected myself. It was a frail thread of melody, a jump-up falteringly rendered on a pennywhistle. I went back down to the compound.

Out below the balcony of Costard's office, where Anhyldia had planted a little greensward, two men at arms lounged, one man's cape spread between them with loaves and cheese on it. Two hefty fellows they were, taking their ease, their pikes and bucklers laid by. They were men of only middling talent in the trade of arms, perhaps, since they appeared wholly oblivious to my approach. Still, we could use them on the road. They would have orders to stand to their posts, but then, I reflected, these men had been hired by miserly Costard. I smiled, and eased open one of the smaller pouches of my money-belt.

"Greetings, stout fellows!" I heartily cried. They jumped; the musician nearly swallowed his pennywhistle. "The ineffable Costard," I told them with a courtly salute, "sends me to you with the first installment of your augmented salary, and with your new instructions."

They stared at me, a bright-orange savage in a brutish nomad's kilts and bandoliers, and armed to a perhaps disturbing degree. I had Ready Jack's pommel at my left shoulder and Old Biter's haft at my right, four javelin butts sprouting from the quiver aslant on the small of my back. I had besides, on my belt, a poignard, a knout-and-knuckles for close work, and a sling and a poke of lead shot. Their eyes moved toward their weapons, and abandoned the thought. They looked relieved when I placed hefty stacks of lictors in their hands. "Costard sends you with our new instructions," one of them echoed, nodding hesitantly. I could see him almost ask me if Costard was down in the mine I had obviously just stepped out of. But he felt of the weight of the gold, and nodded more decisively.

This was Klaskat, the calmer of the pair. Both he and Klopp were tonsured in the severely barbered style of the young stockyard bloods down in Dry Hole, their hair sparingly confined to the crown of the head, like a treed, short-furred cat. Klaskat allowed that Master Costard had mentioned a couple of associates still down in the mine. "But he didn't mention, or rather I'm not sure he mentioned, ah, new orders. . . ."

"Banish your doubts. This additional stipend—Oh you're quite welcome!—is to remunerate you for the travel involved. We'll be taking a wagon of heavy freight down to KairnGate Harbor. You'll be riding escort—and it's wonderful weather for journeying, don't you think? So fresh! So bright!"

"The, ah, day is fine indeed. And what shall we call you, sir?"

"Nifft, call me Nifft. And you'll call my associate Barnar, for that is his name. Our first task is to send him down some baling canvas and cinching straps. He'll be sending us back up the bundles we'll be carrying. These contain a waxy exudate we have scraped off of larval hides. Exotic pomatums and perfumes are manufactured of the stuff." They nodded knowingly at this. I resumed, "I will tell you frankly our load is worth almost a hundredweight of gold—You see how I trust you?—and this is why we want a couple of stout men-at-arms with us."

"Well, Honor Nifft, Klopp and I have been twice or thrice around the corral," Klaskat modestly smiled, by which he meant, in Dry Hole's cattle-town parlance, that they'd had some taste of doughty deeds and peril.

"I knew it when I first clapped eyes on you," I said.

XIV

Gravely is old Dry Hole smitten:
Toppled, trampled, and beshitten.

KLASKAT AND KLOPP had many Dry Hole kin and acquaintance working for neighboring sap mines—whence, indeed, Costard had hired them. They went over to the Lucky Gasket Mine across the ridge and leased a dray team and some mounts; with their cattletown savvy they brought over nine skinnies, six for yoking to one of the Superior's freight wagons, three for mounts. These light-built plods are quick afoot, but big in the shoulders for heavy pulling.

Barnar and I knew the joys of a bath in fresh mountain water, and the intoxication of the sky and sun, which draped our bodies like royal garments whose splendor we could not get used to. Even after we'd set to loading the wagon with the bales Barnar had bucketed up from the mine, we could not stop interrupting ourselves to stop and gaze about us, wave our arms and exclaim at the glory of the morning. Klaskat and Klopp gave us an odd look or two, but proved both discreet and industrious. Though

Barnar and I did all the loading, the massy bales of precious artefacts, wrought metals, gemstones, coin and bullion, were noisy in the handling; they knocked and rattled and chinked as we hefted them in place and tied them down. They sounded most unlike bales of larval skinwax. Klaskat and Klopp politely disattended, but acted a bit more impressed with their work thereafter.

By late afternoon we got rolling, Barnar at the reins, I riding point, Klasket and Klopp flanking behind. My fortune, my stupendous, fever-inducing wealth, now had wheels under it. Any child who could manage a team could possess it all in one opportune moment. Now I knew in full what it was to fear thieves. I felt more danger on this sunny, empty mountain highway than I had in any corner of the world of demons.

We'd hired two mediocre men-at-arms to help us guard a fortune that might buy an island chain: villages, fortresses, trading fleets and all; a fortune that—if not halved—could accomplish the wildest reachings of my imagination. The mediocrity of these hirelings of ours meant there was less to fear from them should they prove treacherous, of course, but it also meant less to hope for from their prowess if we should be attacked.

Ah to take wing with it all—what safety we'd felt in the air! But we grudged using any more of the precious Unguent for haulage—and as our combined loot's weight now exceeded the Unguent's lift, we must fly twice to the coast and back, leaving it in unguarded halves at either end of the transit. More than this, should we once be seen in flight, the report of it must fly as well. We could not thereafter come to ground with the anonymity we now enjoyed, and in this anonymity lay our best security.

The day declined. Big, black-winged krawks circled in the perfect blue, above canyons brimming with purple shadow. The sun's all-gilding, all-ennobling eye, for which great 'Omphalodon lies bound in stone, blazed gloriously, though I had scant attention for it now. Potential ambushes loomed everywhere along a highway that wound through so many ravines and defiles. I rode so tensed for action that I was slow to wonder at the highway's emptiness, but our Dry Holers were less so.

"Not one soul all afternoon!" cried Klaskat. "This is rare indeed, Honor Nifft."

"And do you know," Klopp added, "it's been a few days since we saw anyone passing up at the mine. The boys at the Lucky Gasket remarked on it too, I think."

We retired up a sandy wash to pass the night. I sat my watch under the stars, savoring the sight of them now and then, but more and more wondering at the unbroken emptiness of this broad, smooth, moonlit highway. If we once attained Dry Hole, we would be within a day and a half's dash of the coast, where four hundred lictors could buy us a slender carrack of Minuskulon make. But why came there no trafic *from* Dry Hole? That city thronged with mountain trade. The vacant highway grew ever more ominous.

Our wagon was rolling at first light, and before dawn we met, at last, another vehicle—a freight wagon of sap-barrels, returning with its load undelivered. We were sure now of trouble, even before speaking with the driver, a red-bearded lout in ill humor. "The causeway's collapsed! A league and more above the city! The span across Dead Plod Arroyo is fallen, and as far as I could see beyond it, all the stretches on pilings are fallen to rubble in the canyon-bottoms! They don't pay me enough to haul these barrels into town on my back, thank you!"

The incurious fellow had only a shrug for our anxious questions. Who knew the why of it? Not he. Full of his choler and his refusal of further responsibility, he geed up and sped on, rehearsing some choice things to say when his barrel-boss reproached him for his undelivered load.

❖   ❖   ❖

Hurrying now to know the worst, we pushed on. A panicky notion took root in my mind that our huge wealth cried aloud through its canvas shrouds. The sheer mass of it called danger down upon us, summoned perils of commensurate size. Some grave disaster lay ahead and it seemed fitting, even inevitable that a prize such as ours must challenge Misfortune's mightiest manifestations. I almost cringed from this silent outcry I felt emanating from those canvas bundles, as though it would call something out of the sky any moment now.

Further enlightenment came just after sunrise, when there approached us a creaky wain of the high-gated style that hauls hay. This one was heaped with furniture, and textiles, and caged fowls squawking. There were even suckling pigs, in makeshift cages of house shutters, befouling one corner of the van. In hammocks strung between the heavier pieces of furniture, three tousled and haggard children snored the throaty sleep of infantile exhaustion. A compact little bald man with sinewy hands was driving. A mound of blankets in the box beside him was probably an exhausted wife. Hanging from the box at his right hand, a belt of joiner's tools had equal place with an old shortsword that looked long out of use.

Klaskat hailed him excitedly. "You're the Wainwright Brattle, down on Cloven Lane, are you not?"

"Aye, I was he!" So loud and brassy did the man shout, we wondered that none of his family was wakened. His face looked drained and fatigued, but his body was taut and trembly, and a kind of madness simmered in his eyes.

"What news of 'Hole, sir?" Klaskat urged him. "We've met a drayman says the highway down into 'Hole is all collapsed."

"Collapsed it is. Oh, yes indeedy! Not a span or a piling but is all collapsed!" Brattle smiled, his mad eyes almost merry. "It's in ruins full three miles up into the mountains from 'Hole. It was wiped out in the first great stampede, a week ago now! We left the next day. I've been five days dragging what's left of our livelihood up dry gulches and down narrow old prospector's trails. I just reached the highway last night! I mean to make time, now that I can, and put god-cursed Dry Hole, befouled past remedy, far far behind us! Somewhere a new life awaits me and my family, and by the Crack and all that crawls from it, we'll find it! Stand away!" He'd talked himself into a bellowing wrath. He stood up and made his whip crack like lightning; his quartet of plods, weary but strong, surged ahead—Barnar had to pull our wagon smartly aside.

We let Klaskat and Klopp ride foremost, more schooled in the roadway. They set a quick pace, fearing now for kinfolk and family property. I tried to imagine what disaster might produce a "god-cursed Dry Hole, befouled past remedy."

I became aware of a buzzing noise and a wafting stench; a moment after, we reached Dead Plod Arroyo. The bridge that had spanned it was now two stumps of stonework; the dry ravine yawning between them a hundred feet deep.

"What is that smell! Is it manure? Are those flies I hear?"

"He spoke of a stampede. . . ."

"What can we do as a packtrain through these last few miles?" Barnar asked Klaskat.

"We could do it. The terrain can be managed."

"We will pack the beasts," I told him. "You two scout our trail through this ravine and see what you can beyond it."

When they were well down into the arroyo we remade our bundles. Our string of nine beasts bore less than four hundredweight each, a heavy load, but not cruelly so. In the re-packing, our subworld loot flashed luridly; in sunlight it had a corrupt and somehow shameful brilliance. From the unseen terrain beyond the arroyo wafted the scent of shite and the noise of myriad flies, sensations mundane enough, yet sinister, that teased us as we worked. Just as we finished we heard the amazed cries of Klaskat and Klopp, who had ascended the arroyo's far wall, and now viewed beyond it.

"Key, Cauldron and Calipers!" Klopp distantly bellowed. "It's . . . it's a hornbow! It's as big as a whale!"

They came back and met us down in the arroyo to help us lead the packtrain across. They prepared us for what we would see, but this did not lessen the impact of it when we saw it for ourselves. Down in the next gulch, amid the tumbled arches of the viaduct, the stupendous ruminant lay rotting. Farther down the ravine another bovine colossus putrefied. Not this alone set the fog of flies dancing (thicker than the bees in the flower-fields of Dolmen!) but also little hills of bovine ordure beckoned them to their buzzing bacchanal.

More of these giant cattle littered the canyons filled by the toppled highway's rubble. They were hornbow, crucicorn, palomanes—every common breed lay in the gulches and gullies amid the shattered stonework, whose ruin their combined weight had clearly caused. Their corpses looked hale enough, if a bit obese, even discounting for their ripeness. Their nostrils, big as doorways, had spewed white froth in death. Twice, where the vast carcasses spanned difficult ground, we used them for bridges, though our skinnies were uneasy at such footing. Barnar and I exchanged just one look that said all. Costard's little venture with his share of the giants' pap was now revealed to us. We did not share our insight with our employees.

At length, a last ravine opened out ahead, and Dry Hole was revealed, spread below us.

XXV

Oh lead thy kine to Cattle Town,
But feed them not too full!
Lest Cattle Town should rattle down
And break upon thy skull.

I REMEMBERED this vista as it had appeared not many weeks before, all Dry Hole's handsomely carpentered homes sweeping downslope to the distant river, their rooftiles burnished by the setting sun. Upon this lovely panorama blight and ruin had fallen. A blanket of flies buzzed and boiled above it; the quiltwork of its rooftops was cratered with shattered structures and strewn debris, and heaped with dung in mounds so copious as to bury entire buildings. Klaskat and Klopp groaned aloud.

"Out on the plain beyond the river—what are those heaps, and those black clouds of things above them?" Barnar asked. "They're thick as flies, but at this distance must be something much bigger—carrion birds, perhaps? Feeding on more carcasses?" But Klaskat and Klopp had eyes only for their own sectors of the city. To prevent their outright defection from our employ, we had to agree to seek out their families and learn their state. They agreed they would continue in our service if they possibly could. In truth their company was dangerous, for they could link us with Costard whose name, if known, must be purest poison here; at the same time, two natives could best steer us through this stricken city.

Bound kerchiefs excluded the flies from our mouths and nostrils, but they bombarded every other inch of our bodies, bumping into us like carnival revelers reeling with surfeit. We followed a maze of undamaged streets where the only hindrances were the flies and the crush of traffic. Dray wagons hauling dung and broken buildings slowed our progress to a crawl, and had we not been able to thread our beasts single file, we might have been stopped altogether. At one pause to let debris wagons pass, Klopp hailed a man, an unhoused grocer by the look of the barrels and sacks and crated foodstuffs in his buckboard. "Ho, Roddle! What happened? Is your shop destroyed?"

"The ground floor's intact! But my top floor was bitten off! The accursed brutes *grazed* all through the town before they went mad! They crunched up thatched roofs and shingles and stone slates alike, munched wooden walls like jackstraw!"

"But what happened? Where did they come from?"

"Some pestiferous square-head, some outlander, some sap miner came down and leased the pasturage in Sparse Meadow Vale just out of town. He bought a few head here and there—bought some of your uncle's hornbow I think, said he wanted to experiment with a small herd of mixed breeds. The fool had some boughten wizardry it seems. His cattle came wandering out of the valley a week ago, and stayed near the river at first, drinking and drinking. How we all went and gawked! You could almost see them growing, one hour to the next! I must be off— your uncle's stables survived; talk to him!"

The pulse of civic energy was strong in Dry Hole. All

was clearance and repair, improvisation, shared resources. It took two hours to reach Klopp's Uncle Hebneb's stables, a place still well up in the foothills, and whence, through the clouds of flies, the seethe of activity down on the plain was not much more visible, save that the huge mounds around which the activity boiled became unmistakably identifiable as more of the giant cattle carcasses.

Bald, bulky Hebneb and three of his sons were unharnessing a dung-wagon's sweating team, and mustering fresh plods to the traces. He greeted his nephew with a sharp look, and came out to us.

"Your employer, Klopp! Bragg came down from the Lucky Gasket and told us you'd hired out to that fool, that Costard, that's just managed the Superior Mine to ruin! Guarding the mine for him, was it? So the idiot could come down and do this!"

"Yes, but Uncle, I . . . how could we . . . I never had any idea that . . . I mean we just guarded his mine, Uncle Hebneb! We work for these men here, now, Uncle—they work for Costard too!"

"We did indeed," I affably affirmed, "work for young Costard. We tapped for him, and when he proved—most infuriatingly, I assure you—unable to pay us, we agreed to take payment in larval aromatics. We've only now come above-ground. I promise you we never dreamed he had anything to do with cattle-raising. We thought him a respectable sap miner, at least till we tried to get paid."

"Oh that pompous little milksop!" The stabler's thick neck corded with anger. "I actually sold him twenty head of hornbow from our own pasture down-river! Our own kine, raised by our own hands, to have them come crush our houses and befoul our streets! Your father sold him some too, Klaskat—you'll find him down by Third Bridge where they're curing the meat. The fool went to see everyone and bought a few head from a dozen different cattlemen, making a big display of secrecy about marvels he was working! The callow dolt! How could we have guessed he had real power of any kind? Oh, we had a good laugh about him down at the Dusty Hoof. 'I'm dabbling in carniculture,' he tells me! Carniculture! 'I wish to assess the, ah, responsiveness and potentialities of all the common breeds,' he tells me! Who could have guessed the ninny's power to harm? He came down to the taverns to sup through the first week or so, fairly swollen with mysterious importance, hinting wonders. Why weren't we more curious? If only someone had gone up to Sparse Meadow for a look early on! But no, we must wait till ten days ago, when a crucicorn the size of a rich man's house walks out of the hills! We went up to him then, quick enough, but what could be done with him? He threw a hay wagon at us!"

"What!?" Barnar cried.

"He—hold there! Harv! Give them the dapples! The debris wagons need the heavies!"

Hebneb rushed back to work, as two more dray-wagons pulled into his yard, one still heaped with its load of dung and bringing a veritable blizzard of flies with it. We huddled in their battering onslaught while Klopp secured his uncle's assurance that he could be spared to serve us, as his wage would be useful in the hard times ahead.

The hardy, stoic Dry Holers, working furiously, gave questions short shrift, but we pieced together most of the tale as we wound our way down to the river. By the time the crowd of citizens roused by advent of the giant crucicorn had gone halfway up to Sparse Meadow Valley, full three or four score more cattle of equal size had come ambling down the hills, grazing on trees, which they munched down to stumps, and on various cottages and ranchers' domiciles, whose wooden walls and shingles they seemed to find acceptable as fodder. Men who had set out as a confused committee of inquiry arrived at Sparse Meadow as an outraged mob.

"We were ready to hang that pipe-neck shorthorn," a saddler told us. "We found his whole range a sea of flops raging with flies, the forest clean gone—just stumps—halfway up the hills all around. The ranch house was burst open like an egg, and that Costard, as *big* as a house, had his arms round the barn and was struggling to sit himself up. The sight fair paralyzed us where we stood! 'Help!' he blubbers. He looks like a giant baby, all fat and hideous naked, for he's split his clothes long past. 'Help me! I ate some by accident! I didn't wash my hands!' His very words, if you can find sense in them. The madness of it! Some men who'd lost property began to shout at him and shake their fists and threaten him—to what end, I ask you? But we were all in shock. His eyes went mad then— we were to see it in his cattle later. He frothed and bellowed and flung a hay wagon clear up the hill at us!"

No more was to be learned of Costard. Dry Hole's defense immediately absorbed her citizens. The giants were drawn first to the river, where they lingered a day or so, drinking prodigiously. They were vague and torpid—even for cattle—and utterly indifferent to what they trod upon, and they continued to grow, almost visibly. While they hugged the river, crossbows and torches and catapults were tried on them; it was learned that assault elicited most unbovine behavior—they seized attackers in their jaws and chewed them. Then the giants began slowly dispersing to graze—most out on the plain, destroying corrals and feedlots and scattering herds—and a hundred or so up into the city, eating buildings. The salvation of property was now the city's sole labor. "There were some wild rescues of moveable goods," the saddler told us, "for the brutes would only step on you by accident. Remember Klaagi, the smith? He'd got a whole wagon of his gear, even loaded his littler forge, and made his break up Cedril Street, flogging the team. He got almost clear, and *flop*—poor Klaagi, his wagon, his team, were buried alive by a patty—and his smithy was spared in the end, unscathed!"

Then came the morning when a madness struck the giants, all of them almost simultaneously, it seemed. Bellowing, frothing, glassy-eyed, they ran in ponderous stampede—scattering, re-converging, trying to escape some inner agony. Some fled up the highway into the mountains; its great supports sustained them for a while until the massed vibrations of their tread shattered several miles of it at once. If the fall killed these, it took but little life from them, for all the other giants out on the plain had dropped dead by that day's close.

The grit and resolution of Dry Hole's citizens were not fully known to us till we reached the highway by the river and saw how the townsfolk had turned the huge carcasses that littered the plain into a meat quarry. Kites and krawks and guzzlars thronged the sky, indignant at this human thievery of their alloted feast. Men with every butcher's tool, with saws and swords to boot, swarmed scaffolding upon the giant dead. Hide was being stripped and tanned in sections big as mainsails. Vast shavings from the marbled walls of meat were being smoked above beds of coals on frames improvised from broken corral posts. The highway thronged with wagons from the south bearing barrels, and salt, and pickling brine, and charcoal for the curing fires. And equal traffic ran the other way, bearing smoked meat and hides back to KairnGate Harbor, whence it would be shipped south to help recoup Dry Hole's civic losses.

Klaskat found his father receiving these shipments in one of his stockyards, collecting bills of lading, sending his assistants off with the teamsters to guide them to their points of delivery out on the swarming plain. This Clyster was a big, peremptory man with an aura of status and property, and a probing, glittery eye.

"Worked for Costard, did you? Well, I can't well blame

you when my son's made the same mistake. Yes, I'll rent you a wagon—he can bring us back barrels and salt. You say Costard paid you in 'aromatic scrapings'? I've never heard of these."

"Nor had we, though of course we were novices at tapping. He assured us the waxen scrapings from larval hides are quite valuable to perfumers of the Ephesion Isles." My heart hammering, I strove to look simple, a man imposed on, now touched by doubt. "Surely he would not have told us . . . an untruth?"

Clyster shrugged; it suited him to send a wagon south with us for his son to bring back laden, and earn a wage as well. "No doubt he knew more about sap mines than cattle. Mayhap you'll meet him—it's said he's dragging himself south through the hills. If so, you can tell him we intend to teach him, by demonstration upon his person, some of the fundamentals of cattle-raising, to wit, notching, branding, castrating, flaying, and butchering— not necessarily in that order. Inform him his instruction commences the instant we can find the time for it."

The highway snaked silvery across the tawny grass, rolling into and out of gentle valleys. Soon it would reach the steep cliffs of the coast, and turn to run along them where they sloped down to KairnGate Harbor. Before nightfall we would have our wealth in a trim little carrack, and anchored safe offshore.

At last there ahead lay the sweeping turn the highway made to follow the coastal cliffs. But just at this turning, we beheld a crowd of travellers and their vehicles clustered at the roadside. They were looking down into a narrow valley whose farther slope levelled to clifftop, with the empty air and the shining sea beyond.

"What are they looking at?" I foreknew, with dread, the question's answer even as I asked it.

Costard, almost as big as a whale, his ghastly nudity besmeared with earth and crushed foliage, had crawled halfway up the valley's seaward slope. It seemed, by the quiverings of his blubbery limbs, that he still struggled to reach the clifftop, but could muster no further propulsion. Barnar reined up and the rest of us dismounted. We stood and stared—how could we do otherwise?

Then Costard's glassy gaze, roving desperately between earth and sky, lit on the crowd above him, and grew sharper. "Uncle Barnar! Nifft!" he boomed. "Help me!" How huge his voice was! The crowd looked at us oddly. Never have I known such mortification!

"But how *can* we help you!?" Barnar despairingly bellowed back.

"I can make it up with just the slightest pull, and then I can roll the rest of the way! Oh hurry, before I grow bigger! I must reach the sea! I can't breathe! I must float! I'm crushing myself!"

A freight hauler, his load of rock salt and charcoal bespeaking his Dry Hole destination, geed his heavy team and drew his wagon next to ours. "He seems to be kin of yours. I'll be glad to assist you, no charge, if you'd kindly help him drown himself, like he wants." And he held up several coils of heavy hauling cable.

We eased our wagons off the highway, and out along the grassy rim of the cliff. Twenty strides to our right, white-bearded ocean grumbled at the precipice four hundred feet straight down. And here now was the great pallid face of Costard directly below us, a moon of dirt-daubed anguish, sweating to rise. His vast legs churned sluggishly; he rose fractionally up the slope, then slithered back again. "By all the powers," groaned Barnar, "you headlong young idiot, what have you done?"

"It was an accident, Uncle! I failed to wash my hands of the ichor, and it impregnated some bread and pickled quiffles that I ate . . . Oh hurry, please hurry, if I get heavier I'll never reach the sea."

Costard's gross, ballooning nudity was a powerful

added inducement of an aesthetic kind to dump him into
the sea as soon as possible, and hide him from sight. The
hauler, a red-haired man who did not mask his bitter
amusement as he worked, rigged his cables in a "Y"
whose branches he anchored to the axle trees of our
wagons.

"Your mother, my sister Anhyldia," Barnar told the
youth mournfully, "will kill me for this. I mean that quite
literally. I dare not face her again in this life!"

"Now look you, Costard," I told him quite urgently
as we prepared to give him his end of the cable. "You
must release this cable before you tilt over the cliff—
you *must*." He nodded, but his mooncalf eyes looked
blank of comprehension. He gripped the cable and
wrapped several bights around his wrist. Klaskat and
Klopp, with rope from their pommels to the yoke-tree,
prepared to add their pull to our team's efforts, but I
rode free. I drew Ready Jack, and tested his edge. We
turned the wagons to run along the clifftop, and geed
up, giving Costard a diagonal pull slantwise up the last
bit of slope to the cliff.

Our beasts strained, every thew etched. Costard's
frantic feet and fingers churned the grassy loam of the
hillside. Perhaps our jot of help made the difference, or
perhaps it merely woke some last reserve of the bloated
young wretch's will, but up he heaved, floundering and
quivering, his free hand gaining the level clifftop. He
heaved again, and he slithered his middle up.

"Let go of the cable!" I bellowed. He heard me not,
or cared not. He thrust both hands towards the brink
of the precipice, and his effort jerked the wagons after,
the teams screeching and stumbling.

My whole career of thieving rose before my eyes in
that instant, when I saw our wagon dancing backward
toward the cliff. Every great prize in a long career, every
failure, whipped past my eyes like wind-driven phantoms,
and all were as nothing to the colossal fortune in that

lurching buckboard with Barnar reeling helpless at the reins.

I spurred my mount forward. Costard reached again, and this time got a grip on the brink, wrenching the wagons yet nearer the abyss. I charged the cable, which was taut as bowstring, and I sheared through it with one mighty sweep of Ready Jack. In the same instant Costard heaved himself outwards, off the precipice.

It seemed he hung forever in the air, slowly, slowly falling with an indescribable fatty shimmy all over his hugeness, fleetingly putting me in mind of Behemoth larvae wriggling in the brood-mass.

"Will he float, do you think?" Klaskat awedly asked, just before Costard smote the ocean with a burst of foam and sank like a stone, his wobbly pallor dwindling to a glimmer in the blue-black deeps, and vanishing.

XXVI

Oh, let me and my fortune ride the sea,
On Ocean's bosom know—at last!—repose!
There nor flame nor thief need dreaded be,
And lapping swells lull weary lids to close . . . .

KAIRNGATE HARBOR will forever wear the friendly luster of a safe haven to my eyes, for the way it looked at that day's end. The water wore the setting sun, and the little bay was a single coin of gold. At a shipyard, whose master we caught just locking his gate to leave, we found a yare little caravel he'd just refitted, with a stout four-oar skiff aboard her. We let him wangle a fiveweight for her in our craving for the peace it would give us to have our treasure shipped and safe offshore at last.

Klaskat and Klopp we sent off with two hundred lictors each. We might not have spared so much, but in our impatience to be loaded we let them help us lay our bales aboard, and they, as they worked, allowed their looks to display their doubt that what we shipped was truly larval scrapings. They handled the bundles roughly enough to make them chink metallically. Hence the handsomeness of our stipend. Even so they drove off laggingly, with wistful backward gazes.[4]

We named our caravel *Bounty*, and by the rising of the gibbous moon, we had sailed her out and anchored her in an untrafficked reach of the harbor. She rode in plain sight of the balconied dockside refectory where we proposed to sup. With our Unguent strapped to our middles beneath our jerkins, and our beloved *Bounty* never out of our gaze, we could be aboard her in mere seconds at the first sign of threat.

We rowed ashore in silence, in silence took our table on the crowded balcony, bespoke our meal, awaited it and ate it in silence. Our treasure was won, and was shipped. Now came the having, the spending. Now, whenever Barnar and I faced each other, we faced the gulf that yawned between us. And so we avoided one another's eyes.

Down in our little *Bounty* there, sitting on moonlit water as still as hammered pewter, lay a cargo of wonders. And contained within that wealth, as the progeny lies in the womb, were deeds to make our names ring down through the ages in the annals of thievery.

And these yet unborn marvels tormented me. I saw my hands, in Pelfer's gantlets, touch the iron gates of

---

4. In fairness to the reader unfamiliar with coinages predominant along the trade axis that joins my native Ephesions, the Kairnish Continent, and the Minuskulon Chain lying between, as well as to the reader who is unprepared to form some reckoning of the value of Nifft's booty, I feel required to speak here. Of the demon artefacts and art in their booty I can make no valuation, but extrapolating from the worth of demon gemstone alone, I can assure the reader that the swag shipped on the *Bounty* was worth ten million lictors at the very least, and was most likely worth many multiples of that sum. Fairness to Nifft and Barnar in turn, of course, requires me to note that at current Kairnish day-labor rates, Klaskat and Klopp were receiving almost twice what they might have expected on a per diem, per distance basis.　　　　　　—Shag Margold

Mhurdaal's Manse (all hung with corpses of unsuc-
cessful thieves, still fresh and bleeding though long
centuries slain); I heard the gates groan, and gape
asunder. I saw Mhurdaal's Library, labyrinth of lore, saw
plague-touched cities full of folk a-sweating out pure
gold. . . .

And here sat Barnar, also gazing on the *Bounty*, and
seeing forests of skorse, stubbornly dreaming of stands
of timber, himself as thick and rooted as a tree in his
infuriating willfulness. It did not matter what our halves
of this fortune might do. Entire, our fortune was a bridge
to glory, to immortal exploit. Half a bridge leads but to
an abyss. Barnar had sworn to the exploit, and I could
not, would not let it go. So we sat there, the silence
between us like a spectral Third at the table.

Until Barnar said, "That woman at the railing . . . do
we know her?"

"Is that not Niasynth?"

"Yes, I think it is!" The young-ancient woman looked
travel-ready in a shortcape, tunic, boots and shortsword.
She sat gazing at the moon and sea. A rapture, a zone
of privacy long centuries deep, enveloped her, and we
made no move to rupture it. We watched her, and our
own memories of the subworld's eternity seemed to
enfold us, so that we jumped when a woman's voice
greeted us from close at hand.

"This is well-met, good thieves!" Sha'Urley stood at
our table. "Let's have a hug and a kiss, oh thou miserly,
greedy, tight-bungholed Nifft!" I embraced her, though
I could have wished her ebullience more seemly-spoken.
She sat, and took wine with us. Her accoutrement was
like Niasynth's, towards whom her smiling eyes continually
slanted as she spoke with us.

"What a delight to meet you like this!" I told her.
"Perhaps we can settle that fiftyweight of gold still owed
us here and now. Then we need make no stop in Dolmen
Harbor."

"Alas, there you must stop, I'm afraid, and deal with Ha'Awley. I've ceded to my brother all my interest in his enterprise of the giants' pap. He is the repository of any and all revenues it may have drawn. The only coin I bear is needed for our travels, Niasynth's and mine."

"Travelling?" I asked, but we understood, I think, even before she explained.

"She has a new world to learn," Sha'Urley said. "And as I tried to tell her about this world, I discovered how little I knew it myself. I found that I have the same world to learn as she does. The pair of you too had a part in rousing me. The places you will *go* on a venture! You are both no less than inspirational!"

"There's no finer thing than setting out to see what you can see!" I told her. I was envying her a bit for some reason, as if I weren't as footloose as she. "We congratulate you. But, dearest Sha'Urley, forgive our closer inquiry into your brother's affairs. He does indeed have our fiftyweight of specie, does he not?"

Sha'Urley laughed. "Whatever his other difficulties, lack of specie is not one of them. Bunt Hivery remains one of the foremost in the Angalheim chain."

"I beg your leave to press a bit," Barnar told her. "How *does* his enterprise with the ichor fare?"

"To be honest, good Barnar, that is precisely what I am studiously trying not to know. This is as far south as we came with him, and we have not seen him for near a month. We have toured southern Kairnheim while Niasynth regained her strength. We are here only to set sail with the morning tide for the Minuskulons. I have avoided even news of Dolmen, lest it ensnare me. 'Who means to fly, takes wing at once.'"

"Dearest Sha'Urley," I put in. "Believe me, I appreciate the perilous poise of spirit you have come to, and we do not wish to jar you, but—"

Smiling, she raised a preventing palm. "Peace, sweet

thief. I know why you have grounds for fear. Costard's doings, and his fate, have reached us here."

"Even his final attainment of the sea?"

"No. We knew he crawled coastward, no more."

When she had heard from us the details of Costard's recent plunge into the deep, which we strove to render vividly, she covered her face a moment, concealing some emotion which caused a slight tremor of her shoulders.

"Well," she said at length, with a solemn face, "I can tell you only that poor Costard's . . . abandon is not a flaw my brother shares. If profit can be had from this ichor outside its ordained sphere, Ha'Awley will extract it, both methodically and cautiously." A shadow touched her eyes here. "It has been impossible not to gather that some kind of unrest lies on Dolmen in recent days. And looking across the channel this morning, I noticed in the oblique light of sunrise some shadowy suggestion of airborne turmoil above my homeland's heights. More I cannot say, and *will* not know. Indeed, we're going to board our ship within the hour, and lie safe from hearing further news before we sail."

I could not help but sigh. "Well, it is a nuisance to have to put in at a troubled port! Still, a fiftyweight of specie is no trifling sum."

"Forgive me if I smile," Sha'Urley said. "Forgive me if I'm wrong in thinking you have ten thousand times that value even now in hand, perhaps down in that caravel anchored there, that your eyes seldom leave for long."

"Even as yours seldom leave Niasynth for long?"

She grinned at this. "Yes. Even so. And I hope your obsession will make your hearts soar as high as mine does, every time I look at my dear Niasynth. But just consider, friends: why don't you let that fiftyweight go? Not for my brother's sake, but in a spirit of libation, of a little thanks-offering to Luck? The way you've been squeezing and grabbing pelf down in the underworlds, madly fanatic as demons yourselves . . . I'm saying you need to unclench, to ease out of avarice's frenzy. Forget the fifty as a purely moral exercise."

Plainly, Sha'Urley's heart being light, her reason too had slipped its tether. I forgave this grotesque suggestion as the mere ebullition of a fevered fancy.

We lingered drinking with her a while, and then parted with great affection—and before Niasynth had yet come away from her revery at the railing. She seemed to sit in a space still too far from this world for our voices to reach her. Surely a speech that was more than words was all her mind could really hear as yet, a speech such as Sha'Urley must use with her.

XXVII

Come golden sweetness! Overbrim each cell
Of Fortune's labyrinthine honeycomb.
Swell! Gather to one shining drop, and fall,
Delicious sphere, upon my tongue, thy tomb!

THE SUMMER NORTHERLIES were done. A southwest
breeze with a nip of autumn in it arose some hours
before dawn, and we hoisted sail and tacked for Dolmen.
Sunrise found us scudding smartly, keel kicking spray
from the chop. Our little *Bounty*'s friskiness seemed to
coax me to sail straight out for the open sea. *Forget
Dolmen, forget further complication. Drive straight to the
open Agon; make landfall in the Minuskulons in a twenty-
night, make Pardash and Karkmahn-Ra in the same again.*
Perhaps the morning wind whispered the same to Barnar.

But then I asked myself: What sane man could leave
a fiftyweight of gold lying by when he might have it for
three or four steps out of his path? Was it not blind
foolishness not to take one's own? And no doubt Barnar
asked himself the same.

The wind dropped as Dolmen's peaks loomed bigger,

221

but the channel current pulled us steadily along. Dolmen was mantled in some thin cloud and haze, and we had drawn quite near when the noon sun thawed the sky and raised the winds again, and blew the island jewel clear. There was indeed a fretful turmoil in the air above the highlands; bursts of smoke roiled up into the winds, and were snatched to tatters. There was a scent, too, on the breeze, a taunting whiff that was and yet was not like burning flesh. . . . And was there not a fierce music as well, that came to us fitfully on the wind? A humming, buzzing ground-note, and the shrill voices of men, as at war?

"Smoke. What next?" I said bitterly. "Will we never have done with obstacles and complications?"

"Look how the harbor swarms!"

Taking in canvas, we slipped round the harbor's northern spur. We peered a long tense moment at the bustle of ships, the throngs on the quays, the laden wagons jostling on the upland highways, before determining, with relief, that this was a swarming more of business than disaster.

Nonetheless we anchored our *Bounty* well outside the thick of the traffic, then lowered our skiff and oared in toward the docks. "Shall we make for that wine shop?" Barnar suggested. "The outside tables should give a good view of her."

All the moored ships loomed big above us, and not a few of them were Bunt Hivery's freighters, big but graceful vessels, castled fore and aft, with Bunt's escutcheon on the foresail, and more of these appeared to be offloading than taking cargo on. Teamsters held their dray wagons steady to take on packets of heavy lumber, kegs of pitch and bales of torches, stacks of hinged, folded timbers that might be collapsible derricks or siege weapons, and packets I could not at first identify, but which proved with closer looking to be bundled darts for a large ballista, each missile near big as a man.

"Seems we have a distinctly military kind of commerce

here," Barnar mused. "And at the same time not a few of the locals look to be taking up travelling." For mixed with the freighters were not a few other craft taking on passengers, while everywhere on the docks the dray wagons were interspersed with little knots of folk waiting to take ship, most of them caped for open sea breezes and hovering protectively round their little cargoes of baggage.

"Yes. Things are definitely a-boil," I answered. "*Bounty*'s well anchored outside this mess. If Bunt's in a pickle I'd best have the coin straight out of him, in case he's a-sinking. I'll try his manse first."

Barnar climbed up to the quay and took an outside table at the wineshop, beginning his watch on *Bounty*. With his Unguent strapped to his middle beneath his jerkin, he would not need the skiff, which I rowed cross-harbor, weaving easily amid the larger craft, and making better time than I would afoot through the crowds on the quay.

I tried to read Dolmen's situation as I oared my way. Whatever was going on up in the highlands, there was much of war and siege about it. An unbroken snake of traffic rippled up the switchbacks of both the main upland highways. The downcoming wagons were mostly empty, and those climbing bore baled torches and barrels of pitch and the like.

"Ho, lanky Karkmahnite! Sweet Nifft! Withstay thy sinewy arm a moment from thy toils, my lizardly darling!" This merry salutation, brazen as trumpets, blared down upon me. Looking up, I saw perched in the forecastle of one of Bunt's freighters, lissom Higaia—in arms, and looking quite dazzling so. She wore a snug pectoral plate of brass, molded to the ripe economy of her breasts, which it enshrined in lovely sculptures of themselves. She had a stout gaffing hook for cargo handling which she gripped two-handed, its shaft across the back of her neck—the way a resting trooper will wear his javelin like a yoke—but in the next instant her vessel's creaking cargo boom caught her attention. She whirled and brandished the gaff like a baton of office then: "Ease it there! *Slow* on that windlass! Easy down, Hoofa! Easy down!" Her freighter was one of the few taking on rather than discharging goods.

I tied up to the ladder she dropped me, and climbed it. We hugged each other with a will, Higaia and I, while over the crown of her raven-black head I saw a big flat packet of canvas lowered into her freighter's hold.

And her freighter it was, or half hers. She was cargo-master—boss of the freight and its handling, co-equal, in Bunt's commercial fleet, to the vessel's captain. This was Radula, a nervous, friendly man with an unusually fair skin that ran heavily to freckles and sunburn, unfortunate skin for a sea-captain. He greeted me very civilly and then told Higaia, an odd quaver to his voice, "I'd like to be standing well away within the hour, my dear. Can you manage it?"

"With ease, Raddy, with ease. I'm going down now to see the comb secured. Come on, Nifft. Are you heading south? We're bound for the Minuskulons."

"As are we, and beyond them to the Ephesions. There rides our little carrack *Bounty*, yonder. We're just putting in to collect a fiftyweight Ha'Awley owes us."

Higaia paused at the hatchway, looked at *Bounty*, and then looked at me rather sharply, before she led me down the ladder into the hold. Its gloom was fragrant; aromas of brine and sweetness warred. Her voice echoed below me, "A fiftyweight's no trifle, I suppose . . . but you'll have to go up to the meadows for it."

"Do you imply that this is difficult, or dangerous?"

"Let me show you something."

Leading me over to the canvas balke that had just been laid upon a dozen like it—and the whole hold was stowed full of the same—she plucked from her belt a dagger honed sharp as a razor, and, crosswise down one corner of the packet, she slashed out a narrow flap perhaps a cubit long. Within it was honeycomb, half a cubit thick. Each cell could have coffered the head of a man. In the shadowy hold, the sheen of the wax dimly glimmered, and the liquid gold within it looked dark as amber. It made the scalp prickle with that flush of danger riches give you.

"It was for harvesting this," Higaia told me, "that I got my promotion from the bath-house. For you see, when they were producing comb on this scale, though huge, the bees could still fly, at least for short stretches, and they had begun attacking men and women. Bunt suddenly needed men-at-arms. For thrice the pay of the baths you may be sure I made my skills known to him."

"I knew you were a dancer. I don't wonder you're mistress of the dance of arms," I answered, distracted. I was picturing this monstrosity that had come to pass in Bunt's flower fields. "These giant bees," I prompted, "defended their comb, then, from the harvesting?"

"No. Their attacking seemed spontaneous, a kind of hunting. They had a week before devoured the last of the flowers right down to the roots—all the meadows are bald dirt now. The bees were evidently trying to eat their victims, but naturally their mouthparts were wrong for the work. It is of course as fatal to suffer an attempted eating, by an insect of that size, as it is to be eaten."

"You distinguished yourself, plainly, to be given this command."

"I did indeed, my dear. I'm quite an adept of both axe and cudgel, and though this was shield-and-torch work, I distinguished myself in many a battle. It has been Bunt's salvation that, with a bit of pitch flung on them, these monstrosities will burn so readily. When the pressure of battle declined, he was quick to redeploy us for shipping the harvest out—he needs to recoup the hemorrhage of gold he has suffered from this nightmarish metamorphosis."

"The battle has slackened off, then?"

"Not exactly. Rather, the defense needs somewhat fewer troops, for when the newer, bigger generation emerged from the hives—which are now great dug caverns in the earth, under where the hive houses stood before—when this flightless generation emerged from the earth, we found they could be barricaded; dammed up in their sluggish, lurching onslaught, and burnt by the score. Still, they come out of the earth in numbers that our decimations barely match."

"To what dimensions have they now attained?" I asked, a touch of frost upon my spine.

"Big as titanoplods, or near. Their legs do them little good anymore, but they have a slow, blundering power, lurching like grubs. At favorable points of terrain, our troops have grown adept at throwing up collapsible barricades across the bees' line of progress, and while the brutes are baffled, pitch and torch them."

"Do you tell me, then, that Bunt holds disaster at bay?"

"Seemingly. There are some grounds for anxiety. As I've said, the hives expanded, and the bees dug them underground as they grew. I have been down here this last two days but people have been telling me the earth in the uplands is unquiet. And more than one person has also said that the ground around the hives is swelling, rising, doming up, as at huge movement underneath. My dear—may I presume a bit?" Here Higaia reached up and affectionately touched my cheek. She had an air of soothing me as she spoke, as if I suffered from some fever. "You have a nice little carrack, sweet Nifft, and your moneybelt feels quite hefty when I hug you. Let go of this fiftyweight. For one thing, Bunt must be nigh paupered. His bees devoured *all* the flower fields, including those of the other Dolmen hiveries, and Bunt stands liable to enormous indemnities. And for another thing, I feel to my bones that the worst hasn't happened yet, and I'm glad to be gone from here myself inside the half hour. Quit this place when I do, Nifft! Run with us down across the Agon, and in a fortnight we'll be having some fine mulled tartle together at an inn I know in Quincipolis!"

Leave fiftyweight lying, and walk away? What was this madness that seemed to run like plague among my woman friends? There was something almost ominous about it, and I frankly gaped at her. There was a commotion of voices topside. Higaia sprang up the ladder, and I followed her.

A shouted conversation was in progress between a group of cargo handlers at the port rail, and some mercenaries on the dock below. These men-at-arms—the loudest their seeming captain, a gnarled man with a scarred face—seemed to be demanding something the handlers denied. Higaia came to the rail, silencing her crew, and greeted the captain, "Good morrow, Hob. What are you after?"

"We need half a dozen of your longshoremen, Higaia. We're short troops round the South Dandinnia."

"Come up and talk to me, Hob."

As the gnarled veteran came up the gangplank, Higaia explained, "The South Dandinnia is one of Bunt's hives. It's the one lying nearest the highway, just beyond that crest up there."

We led Hob to the forecastle for privacy after Higaia set her crew back to shipping the last bundles of giant comb. "Is it Bunt sends you?" she asked Hob. "When last he was down here he was most urgent this cargo should be shipped and away—he needs the capital."

"He needs a hundred more men round South Dandinnia, Higaia, whatever else he thinks he needs. I haven't seen him and there was no time to go asking. The ground is shaking and around the hive it's swollen into a hill! If a wave of even bigger bees comes out we'll need a big wall ready for them and torchmen enough to man it! Bunt's over in the central fields, on the barricades round the oldest hives. I'd be longer getting there and back than coming down here."

"Well, take them, if they'll go, though if any want to set sail with me I won't deny them passage." She and Hob locked eyes here a moment. The veteran's flinty gaze conceded something. "I might go with you myself," he said, "but I don't like leaving conflicts unresolved."

I had been listening with a sinking heart, as it grew plainer that Bunt, encircled by disaster, would probably be powerless to pay us our fiftyweight out of pocket. But then I was inspired with a solution. "Good Hob, might I follow you back up to the highlands, and be directed thence to where Bunt is?"

"How not? But let's make haste."

"One minute more I beg! Dear Higaia, if I came back with a fiftyweight draft signed by Bunt, could I not draw it in shares from the sale of your comb?"

"With a properly drawn instrument, my dear, greedy Nifft, how not?"

Hob took some little further time to recruit more men from another of Bunt's ships, and Higaia's freighter was already getting under way as we trotted single file up the first few switchbacks of the highway. As our line threaded its way up between wagons heaped with bales of torches and kegs of pitch, I could see tiny Higaia standing with Radula on the foredeck, conferring over something, their little features so plain in the limpid air I could make out the bright red of Radula's sunburned nose. Another ship—not one of Bunt's—was standing out across the harbor at about the same time. A knot of emigrants crowded amidships at the port rail, their heads turned in troubled unison toward the home they were leaving, some of them gazing upwards past us at the heights, whence ragged scarves and banners of smoke still blew, and the gusted noise of strenuous multitudes at work, or war, or both.

Hob had a good threescore men in tow. I'd noted at once that, however mixed their gear, these men had heavy leathers in common—jerkins or doublets above, trousers or chaps below. Each, moreover, had some kind of stout headpiece about his person, be it a half-casque, or just a skullcap with metal plates sewn on, and that all this varied head gear had in common a heavy leathern back flap to protect the neck—clearly standard issue provided by Bunt for hirelings he had drawn from varied sources over the recent weeks of his accelerating disaster.

At first I hung back in the line to hear scuttlebutt, though most of these fellows were short-spoken, seeming winded by the climb; between working on the "lines" up top, and as cargo handlers down on the docks, most of them had already pulled long shifts over the last few days. Only a worried-looking youth made me much answer to my sociable probings. "Master Bunt must be quick with a lictor to get such work from you fellows, eh?" I asked him.

"Why, I should think so! If it wasn't for payout every second sunset, and regular gold in my belt, I'd have shipped out a week ago! I mean didn't I see Tark get his head pulled off? See it with my own eyes. Tell me if I didn't see it, Weppel! Eh?" This last was addressed to the man jogging ahead of him, and punctuated with a poke of a finger.

Weppel shrugged off the touch, and snapped without turning, "So you saw it! We all did! Have done! That risk's past in any case. The monsters can't get airborne any more and pounce on us like that. Have done!"

"All I mean is," the youth nagged, "was having his head pulled off worth five lictors a shift and kip-and-commons? You think poor Tark thought it was worth it as that damned bee tugged his head off so . . . so *clumsily?*"

"Get off the road, then, you nanny's brat, if you don't like the wage!"

This riposte came not from Weppel but a teamster

we jogged past, sweating his team up through a turn, his wagon overloaded with pyramided casks of pitch.

"Stow the jabber!" Hob barked from above. I would learn most from him in the end, so I worked my way toward the head of the line. We were now a quarter mile up the heights, and the swarming harbor looked small below. The perspective allowed me to notice anew how deep the little bay was, with a brief, grey ring of shallows round the dockside rim, then plunging steeply to blue-black, thousand-fathom depths. There was little *Bounty* riding on the deep water's edge.

"I gather then, Captain Hob," I ventured cheerily, coming up with him, "that Bunt keeps ample specie on hand, and pays his troops every two days."

He gave me little more than his dour, scarred profile in answering. "True. But how much he has left, and how much he'll pay you, are other questions."

"No doubt. His draft-in-hand will do if cash be short. What do you make of his chances of saving his enterprise—speaking soldier to soldier you understand, just between us."

I got Hob's whole face for a moment at that, and a glare of surprise. "You look a man of the world, sir," he growled, facing crestward again and redoubling his pace. "What do you think?" We were near the top now, and with the gusts of smoke, the scents of pitch and strange meat burning came wafting down more thickly, and the hubbub of men's voices had a shrill and desperate note.

And here, in further answer, came an empty wagon clattering down from the crest, the driver wild-eyed, flogging his team and bellowing. He came at once in collision with an up-bound wain of field-rations, pulled by heavy plods among which his team entangled themselves.

Hob, with a roar, led us pelting up the highway. He grabbed the panicked teamster from his seat before the man's wild shouts had grown coherent and, masking the

movement skilfully, clubbed him senseless as he brought
him to the ground. Hob then smartly set his men to
disengaging the tangled teams, and bringing the vehicle
out of the highway, and once the way was clear he roared
them to press on double-time up to the crest. Traffic,
after a ripple of hesitation, flowed smoothly again. A pulse
of panic had been masterfully damped out by the canny
old veteran captain. Now we topped the first tier of the
heights, and a broad reach of the bee-pastures stretched
before us.

I was the more appalled by what I saw because my
last view of this prospect, some months earlier in
Ha'Awley Bunt's phaeton, had so smitten me with its
polychromatic glory. A rainbow blaze of blossoms, like
the wing of some impossible, gigantic blutterfly, had lain
draped across the hills. These rolling meadows had
glowed crimson, saffron, sapphire, rose and violet, all
drenched in wind-cleansed sunlight purely gold as
honey! Now stenchful smokes tumbled across torn,
naked dirt, and wherever the wind briefly jerked aside
the black and smutty curtains, it was to display the litter
and wreckage of war: Huge, charred carcasses smould-
ered amidst the wreckage of barricades; smudged,
scorched troops limped to or from new battlements
which scores of wagons served with casks of pitch and
torches. At one place the smoke parted and, for an
instant, framed a huge ballista which launched a blazing
dart, before the fumes re-engulfed it from my view.

Into this confusion Hob plunged with his men at a
gallop, and I must needs follow, or lose his directions
to Ha'Awley Bunt. But at the crest of a hilltop I paused,
instinctively, for a last view down upon the harbor, and
saw something that froze me where I stood.

Out in the open channel, just a bowshot outside the
mouth of the harbor, a huge pallid shape slid up from
the blue-black deeps. It was Costard.

In the brief interval since we'd parted he had grown

in bulk, and in deformity. His limbs, sunk in his sleek
obesity, had shortened, broadened. His jaw jutted hugely,
and if humanity remained in his contorted eyes, it was
the fleeting, fitful consciousness of the lunatic that
flickered there. And then I saw that he was pursued.
Huge black haggards, a whole hunting pack of them,
dogged his suety flanks, and one nipped a little red bite
from his buttock. Costard's blood clouded the water and
inflamed the pack with hunger.

But the wound galvanized the bloated metamorph as
well; he blew a wrathful geyser of spray, and wheeled
in the water, and plied his haggletooth jaws, biting the
haggards in twain. Their blood in the water woke him
to a hunger that eclipsed his initial wrath, and he fell
to devouring his fragmented attackers.

The whole spectacle transpired in moments. Costard
searched fretfully for further victuals, and then seemed
to grow aware of the harbor before him and its swarm
of ships.

It was at this precise juncture that a mighty cry went
up from the fields behind me, and a great, dense wall
of smoke whelmed against my back, engulfed me,
swallowed breath and sight at once, even as the earth
shook under me, and I heard, above a thousand fright-
ened cries, an earthquake noise, the sodden groan of a
hillside breaking open.

Thus benighted, I experienced the tearing of an inner
veil from my greed-ensorcelled understanding. We should
not be in this place, convulsed with dangers as it was.
We should never have brought our precious *Bounty*
within a league of it!

I plunged, blind and choking, back the way I had
come, praying to feel the highway underfoot, finding it,
and pelting down it.

I dodged between the wagons. The draybeasts screamed
as the teamsters fought to turn them. I vaulted the backs
of beast and man, overleapt tilting vehicles caught up

and toppling in the turmoil of retreat. Below me, the pale leviathan that had been Costard—red gobbets of haggard eddying about him—nosed zig and zag, tentatively into the harbor-mouth, the traffic of ships still unaware of him, most eyes bent dockwards, though I thought in the tiny multitudes I saw faces turning up towards me, tiny arms pointing. Above and behind me the hilltop thundered with a heaving hugeness whose tremors I felt through my footsoles. Though I fought my way down, down through the switchbacks, still these concussions drew closer, while screaming voices came avalanching down behind me, fleeing troops in whose shrill outcry recurred the word *queen* like a refrain.

Will my folly be believed? Can such utter abdication of my faculties be credited? I, veteran of a thousand near collisions with calamity, to prove so fuddled with the jostle and uproar. I leapt most acrobatically—twice, straight down across the switchback at a leap, landing once most catlike on the hub of a toppled wagon's wheel after a vault of full two rods and more! My eye danced bayward, gauging monstrous Costard's quickening advance into the harbor, then shot crestward, seeing a great wall of smoke billow out from the meadow, as if the approach of something huge were thrusting the fumes ahead of it. I actually tried to judge the distance I might run before either impending disaster fell, and if I would be in earshot of Barnar (who surely must be looking crestwards soon, as the tiny multitude were beginning to do) in time for him to anoint his hands and feet, fly out to *Bounty*, cut her hawsers and drag her out to open sea . . .

And then, of course, it smote me—what I should have done the *instant* I knew of Doom's advance. I thrust my hand within my jerkin, and anointed my *own* hands and feet, and leapt into the air!

And as I did so, the smoke bulged again from the crest, and the wind plucked it away in streamers, and a Queen Bee rolled out onto the very brink of the highlands.

By the Crack, and by all that crawls out of it! Ten times as big as a Forager she was! Though of a tiny race, it seemed Her Royalty had taken disproportionate impetus from an ichor brewed by a not wholly alien species.

But Her Royalty was defaced in her deformity. The amber fur that ermined her black, armored head and thorax, blazed glorious gold in the sun, it is true, but her stumplike wings and spindly legs were nigh powerless to move her swollen hugeness. On her abdomen's ballooned distension the black-and-gold armor that sheathed it had separated, the sclerae stretched apart, like polished warshields on a white wall. Her inexorable advance was achieved by a convulsive larval wriggle. I could not turn my face away from her poised immensity. I swam backwards down the air, as one who tilted back and fell. Thus my bellow was aimed at the sky:

"Barnar! Cast off the *Bounty*, Barnaaaar!"

I was still too high to be heard in any case, yet there he was when I craned back to see, swimming through the lower air from the dockside toward our *Bounty*, and there was the crowd in two waves rolling back along the docks and quays, recoiling from the path of the Queen, should she fall.

She towered and teetered there, as the shifting winds scoured her bright in the blaze of noon, as the sun struck a royal largesse of gold from her fur, and painted splashes of rainbow across her great faceted eyes.

I heard it an instant before my eye could tell: "Here she comes!" someone bellowed above me. But already I swam furiously down toward the bay. Tilting immensely forward, the Queen Bee fell, tumbling across the sun, flinging down shadow where I flew.

I plunged toward the *Bounty*, where even now Barnar, Old Biter high, swept at the hawser of her stern anchor. The Queen tumbled majestically through the brilliant air, her stunted wings buzzing futilely, flashing like a thousand swords. Halfway down she smote the mountain flank, thundering, vaulting out again adown the air.

I swooped down to Barnar as he cut the hawser with one mighty axe-stroke—and as Costard's dripping hugeness surged up from the water at *Bounty's* stern.

The hapless leviathan meant, I think, a greeting, a familial embrace. Costard's huge, addled eye noting Barnar aloft at his axe work, and recognizing him. But so close he came up that Barnar leapt aloft, and I with him, recoiling wildly, as Costard's eye saw something else above him, and blinked with awe, and Barnar and I swam wildly upwards as darkness leapt down at us and struck the sea.

Our terror put us well aloft, and we looked down from high on that awful sinking. In a towering explosion of foam the Queen snatched under a dozen vessels, our dear, doomed little *Bounty* dead smack in their midst. She snatched them down brusquely, in the way a gambler's hand might sweep his take off of the board. In a great cloudy fist of bubbles those ships, and Costard with them, were snatched below, sliding down the steep flank of the drowned peak, a seething whiteness dwindling, dwindling, dwindling in the blue-black deeps, then swallowed by the thousand-fathom dark.

We hung there seeing that descent long after it had ceased to be visible. We imagined her down there, the Queen, furrowing the steep mud slope like a great ploughshare, and planting in that furrow our poor beloved *Bounty*. All of our immense treasure was dwindled to a little golden seed entombed where sunlight would never touch it in a million years.

XXVIII

Where wild winds shepherd their cloudy kine,
Where lightnings unborn sleep sheathed in the
   blue,
That's the bright country that I would call
   mine,
And there would I do what the winged ones do!

ALL BUNT'S QUEENS had imbibed his fateful potation. Their eruption from the earth, almost simultaneously throughout the fields, was a final frenzy heralding death, much as with Costard's cattle. The drowned Queen's demise preceeded her sisters' by less than an hour.

Dolmen's highlands now lay utterly desolate of apian life, a vast scab of scorched dirt. Dazed-looking troops came down, and helped at harborside, where dazed Dolmen Harbor worked to mend the hole torn through its body.

A big section of dockside, and an inn or two, had been snatched down to the deeps by the sinking Queen. Her hesitation up on the precipice had been just long enough to warn the multitudes below. The Royal Death had plucked but a few score human lives down with it. Barnar and I joined the general reconstruction. From barges and wherries we gaffed in debris from the harbor, retrieved the dead (where we could), set new pilings and planking, looked after the bereaved and the ruined.

To Ha'Awley Bunt's credit, he came down and worked with the rest, perhaps more dazed than anyone, save Barnar and myself. A curious zone of respect enveloped the hive-master in the midst of his townfellows, that little bubble of silence and averted eyes that surrounds the sacrifice, Disaster's Chosen One.

I do not think his precise agency in this disaster was widely understood, but this was not from any secrecy of his own in the matter, at least not now that all was destroyed. On that first eve of the tragedy we found ourselves sitting at table with him in the same mead hall where we had met. Scores of men did as we did that night, sat numbly drinking, till we laid our heads upon our arms and slept thus through the night.

How vividly I see Bunt still as he was that evening, his tired head drooping as low as his flagon, his faint, far-off voice marvelling, as if he spoke his protests to some invisible tribunal in the air beyond us: "I put so little in their little jaws! I wet a pinhead in the pap, and touched *lightly*! *Lightly* I touched it to their tiny mouths! That one time only! Weeks ago! I still have practically the whole jar of the treacherous, insidious ichor!"

"Perhaps in itself, in its own sphere," I dully chided, "it is neither insidious nor treacherous, but needs active cupidity to make it so."

He looked at me, his eyes bleak beyond riposte. Still, his amazement was strongest in him. "So little, Nifft! As if but the *scent* of Behemoth's Queen breathed on them, as if she but whispered to then, and on that hint, that rumor only, they grew gigantic and devoured me whole! Such potency! At least, with the pap, I shall recoup some capital. No power so dangerous that someone will not crave it."

Even numbed Barnar shuddered at that. "Where will you sell it then, oh honest merchant? We would know where to stand clear of."

"As yet I do not know. Do you reproach me, gentlemen? I am a man of business—what would you have? You may be sure that when my fortune is but part-repaired, I'll pay indemnities aplenty here, and mend what can be mended of what's marred. . . ."

I did not doubt him then, and do not now. I did not care. All light had left my life, all hope my heart. I stolidly drank my head heavy enough to sink, and sink, and sink until I slept.

We rose in the early morning. I have never felt graver or grimmer, and yet at the same time I felt unaccountably refreshed, freed of some chronic weariness I had not known I suffered. We had already determined how we would proceed. At a ship chandler's we bought two of the votive wreaths which sailors cast out in open-ocean burials.

We set out walking along the southern rim of the harbor. On the south it narrowed to a sharp little spit of rock with the sea on both sides of it; we had come round this spit on foot when we first arrived here, still wet from the maw of the glabrous, and we remembered the solitude of the place. When we reached it we found that the wind of the open channel there erased the noise of the distant docks, still swarming with repair.

We stripped down to bathe in the sea. As I laid my arms on the rock, and then my gear and my garb, I greeted each article as a part of myself, comprising, in the aggregate, my All, my Fortune. Videlicet: old, battered, handy Ready Jack with his chipped pommel-stone, and the ghul-skin sheath I bought in Cuneate Bay; my stout jerkin that keeps me so warm in keen mountain winds and is tough enough to turn a knife blade too, with a little luck; my old moneybelt here, provisioned heftily enough now (save when I thought what had been lost!); my buskins stout and supple; tough, trusty leg armor that yet lets me sprint, withal; and my leathern amphora of the Unguent of Flight.

I laid it all out on the rocks, and dove into the sea. We swam a furlong or two. I realized I had not until this very moment really emerged from the underworlds— that one never can until he has taken a plunge in the sea, snorted the brine. This alone can cleanse the last whiffs of subworld air from the nostrils! The morning sun touched our skins through the waters' chilly velvet, and we were home again under the sky.

At length we swam back and re-dressed, and performed the simple, homely ceremony we had conceived. The pair of us stood ourselves side by side, facing out over the harbor deeps, our little *Bounty's* drowning place. Barnar, in his beautiful, surprising baritone, sang Passarolle's *Hymn to Having Had:*

> *How you gleamed! How you dazzled me,*
> * shone in my arms*
> *When I hugged you, and held you, and*
> * had you for mine!*
> *But all things that live must at length*
> * come to harm,*
> *If it's only the harm of their ceasing to*
> * shine.*
>
> *You blazed when we loved! You were both*
> *flame and wick.*
> *How meltingly glowed you your body*
> * away!*
> *And all our sweet nearness, we lived it up*
> * quick!*
> *Now, somewhere, the still-fleeing light of*
> * our days*

*Wings shining along with the lie we still
    love,
Though long have our hands and our
    hearts ceased to move.*

We cast out the wreaths, and watched them till they grew sodden, and sank. Only at that moment, I think, did my soul finally and fully let go of my lost fortune. It seemed to me that a transparent empire of phantom wonders flickered in the sky above me, and melted away forever—castles and splendors, steeples and towers of Exploit standing tall on history's horizons . . . all of it a thousand fathoms down now. Dark.

And in that moment the wreaths went down, something heavy seemed to sink out of my heart as well. How much less I had now than before! But I seemed to know myself again.

"A good fortyweight each of specie in our moneybelts," said Barnar. "Our weapons, our gear . . . . And tenweight each of the Unguent of Flight . . . ."

How good it was that our eyes could meet again, Barnar and I, and we could laugh!

"Well, old Ox-Back," I suggested, "let's fly on down to the Minuskulons."

"What a splendid idea!"

We anointed our hands and our feet with the Unguent of Flight, and we climbed into the air.

Back down in the subworld, when we had followed the New Queen's ravening army for some days, but had not yet grown greatly laden with our plunder, Barnar and I found ourselves almost directly under the polestar and murky sun of that region: the red-weeping Eye of Heliomphalodon Incarnadine.

And the whim took us to fly up near that monstrous orb and see what could be seen within it.

The demon's pupil yawned above us, a sawtoothed wheel of black. Its simple hugeness made us hang in terror, halted still some quarter mile below it, and from even this remove its dark sentience sucked with a whirlpool's force at us, irresistibly pulling our buoyancy up into itself.

And we saw that red shadows thronged that abyss at every depth, they bloomed and melted, making those deeps as populous as a night sky is with stars. And I believe—though it stirs the hairs along my nape even to think it now—I believe the Demon noted us, and knew us for humankind. Knew us for possessors of the sun he craved, the sun he had destroyed himself to reach, his blazing Grail of exploit.

And I will always think that I saw more, that I saw the sun 'Omphalodon dreamed of, saw it there in the gulf of his gaze: a furious contorted coal of ruby light, poisonously hot and murky, but burning colossally, a titan in its sea of blood-red worlds. I directly beheld 'Omphalodon's dream, and I pitied him. This blood-hued, scalding pustule of a sun, its rage all heat and little light—thus high was all the demon's imagining could achieve, origined as he was so deep in hell.

Now Barnar and I, from the south lip of half-ruined Dolmen Harbor, took to the air, and climbed straight up toward the sun itself. Its inexhaustible gold bathed us in the ultimate, the only wealth—sweet Light! Where is the joy of anything else without it?

Now in this cloudless windy noon, this scoured blue sky, we flew. And despite all the leagues we had swum the vaulted skies of the subworld, we flew now for the first time, except, perhaps for those first moments of wild discovery flying up the wall of 'Omphalodon's buried flesh.

We felt snug and free as fish in the wind's liquidity; we soared, grabbing handfuls of the atmosphere. Dolmen's blackened crown, still leaking smoke from smouldering carcasses, dropped away beneath us.

We spurned them, and climbed higher, and the island dwindled to let us see others of the Angalheims, strung out to the south, a great flotilla of islands cruising in to dock at Kairnheim's shore, the green scrub on their flanks all polished and glossy like new armor scoured by the wind's whetstone. Here and there other, more peaceful flower fields showed, shards of rainbow in the uplands.

We gaped astonished on the earth, on one another. We had life, and flight, and some time left under the sun of this wide mad wealth, this World of Light.

"We're rich!" I howled.

"Away!" Barnar bellowed, and we pulled up into a sharp climb toward the zenith.

Paksenarrion, a simple sheepfarmer's daughter, yearns for a life of adventure and glory, such as the heroes in songs and story. At age seventeen she runs away from home to join a mercenary company, and begins her epic life . . .

ELIZABETH MOON

THE DEED OF PAKSENARRION

"This is the first work of high heroic fantasy I've seen, that has taken the work of Tolkien, assimilated it totally and deeply and absolutely, and produced something altogether new and yet incontestably based on the master. . . . This is the real thing. Worldbuilding in the grand tradition, background thought out to the last detail, by someone who knows absolutely whereof she speaks. . . . Her military knowledge is impressive, her picture of life in a mercenary company most convincing."—**Judith Tarr**

About the author: Elizabeth Moon joined the U.S. Marine Corps in 1968 and completed both Officers Candidate School and Basic School, reaching the rank of 1st Lieutenant during active duty. Her background in military training and discipline imbue The Deed of Paksenarrion with a gritty realism that is all too rare in most current fantasy.

"I thoroughly enjoyed *Deed of Paksenarrion*. A most engrossing, highly readable work."
—**Anne McCaffrey**

"For once the promises are borne out. *Sheepfarmer's Daughter* is an advance in realism. . . . I can only say that I eagerly await whatever Elizabeth Moon chooses to write next."
—Taras Wolansky, *Lan's Lantern*